# The Chemistry of Tears

## Peter Carey

W F HOWES LTD

This large print edition published in 2012 by
W F Howes Ltd
Unit 4, Rearsby Business Park, Gaddesby Lane,
Rearsby, Leicester LE7 4YH

1  3  5  7  9  10  8  6  4  2

First published in the United Kingdom in 2012
by Faber and Faber Limited

A CIP catalogue record for this book is available
from the British Library

ISBN 978 1 47120 432 6

Typeset by Palimpsest Book Production Limited,
Falkirk, Stirlingshire
Printed and bound in Great Britain
by MPG Books Ltd, Bodmin, Cornwall

For Frances Coady

# CATHERINE

Dead, and no one told me. I walked past his office and his assistant was bawling. 'What is it Felicia?'

'Oh haven't you heard? Mr Tindall's dead.'

What I heard was: 'Mr Tindall hurt his head.' I thought, for God's sake, pull yourself together.

'Where is he, Felicia?' That was a reckless thing to ask. Matthew Tindall and I had been lovers for thirteen years, but he was my secret and I was his. In real life I avoided his assistant.

Now her lipstick was smeared and her mouth folded like an ugly sock. 'Where is he?' she sobbed. 'What an awful, *awful* question.'

I did not understand. I asked again.

'Catherine, he is dead,' and thus set herself off into a second fit of bawling.

I marched into his office, as if to prove her wrong. This was not the sort of thing one did. My secret darling was a big deal – the Head Curator of Metals. There was the photo of his two sons on the desk. His silly soft tweed hat was lying on the shelf. I snatched it. I don't know why.

Of course she saw me steal it. I no longer cared.

I fled down the Philips stairs into the main floor. On that April afternoon in the Georgian halls of the Swinburne Museum, amongst the thousand daily visitors, the eighty employees, there was not one single soul who had any idea of what had just happened.

Everything looked the same as usual. It was impossible Matthew was not there, waiting to surprise me. He was very distinctive, my lovely. There was a vertical frown mark just to the left of his big high nose. His hair was thick. His mouth was large, soft and always tender. Of course he was married. Of course. Of course. He was forty when I first noticed him, and it was seven years before we became lovers. I was by then just under thirty and still something of a freak, that is, the first female horologist the museum had ever seen.

Thirteen years. My whole life. It was a beautiful world we lived in all that time, SW1, the Swinburne Museum, one of London's almost-secret treasure houses. It had a considerable horological department, a world-famous collection of clocks and watches, automata and other wind-up engines. If you had been there on 21 April 2010, you may have seen me, the oddly elegant tall woman with the tweed hat scrunched up in her hand. I may have looked mad, but perhaps I was not so different from my colleagues – the various curators and conservators – pounding through the public galleries on their way to a meeting or a studio or a store room where they would soon

2

*interrogate* an ancient object, a sword, a quilt, or perhaps an Islamic water clock. We were museum people, scholars, priests, repairers, sand-paperers, scientists, plumbers, mechanics – train-spotters really – with narrow specialities in metals and glass and textiles and ceramics. We were of all sorts, we insisted, even while we were secretly confident that the stereotypes held true. A horologist, for instance, could never be a young woman with good legs, but a slightly nerdy man of less than five foot six – cautious, a little strange, with fine blond hair and some difficulty in looking you in the eye. You might see him scurrying like a mouse through the ground-floor galleries, with his ever-present jangling keys, looking as if he was the keeper of the mysteries. In fact no one in the Swinburne knew any more than a part of the labyrinth. We had reduced our territories to rat runs – the routes we knew would always take us where we wanted to go. This made it an extraordinarily easy place to live a secret life, and to enjoy the perverse pleasure that such a life can give.

In death it was a total horror. That is, the same, but brighter, more in focus. Everything was both crisper and further away. How had he died? How *could* he die?

I rushed back to my studio and Googled 'Matthew Tindall', but there was no news of any accident. However my inbox had an email which lifted my heart until I realized he had sent it at

4 p.m the day before. 'I kiss your toes.' I marked it unread.

There was no one I dared turn to. I thought, I will work. It was what I had always done in crisis. It is what clocks were good for, their intricacy, their peculiar puzzles. I sat at the bench in the workroom trying to resolve an exceedingly whimsical eighteenth-century French 'clock'. My tools lay on a soft grey chamois. Twenty minutes previously I had liked this French clock but now it seemed vain and preening. I buried my nose inside Matthew's hat. 'Snuffle' we would have said. 'I snuffle you.' 'I snuffle your neck.'

I could have gone to Sandra, the line manager. She was always a very kind woman but I could not bear anyone, not even Sandra, handling my private business, putting it out on the table and pushing it around like so many broken necklace beads.

Hello Sandra, what happened to Mr Tindall, do you know?

My German grandfather and my very English father were clockmakers, nothing too spectacular – first Clerkenwell, then the city, then Clerkenwell again – mostly good solid English five-wheel clocks – but it was an item of faith for me, even as a little girl, that this was a very soothing, satisfying occupation. For years I thought clockmaking must still any turmoil in one's breast. I was so confident of my opinion, so completely wrong.

The tea lady provided her depressive offering. I

4

observed the anticlockwise motion of the slightly curdled milk, just waiting for him, I suppose. So when a hand did touch me, my whole body came unstitched. It felt like Matthew, but Matthew was dead, and in his place was Eric Croft, the Head Curator of Horology. I began to howl and could not stop.

He was the worst possible witness in the world.

Crafty Crofty was, to put it very crudely, the master of all that ticked and tocked. He was a scholar, a historian, a connoisseur. I, in comparison, was a well-educated mechanic. Crofty was famous for his scholarly work on 'Sing-songs' by which is meant those perfect imperial misunderstandings of oriental culture we so successfully exported to China in the eighteenth century, highly elaborate music boxes encased in the most fanciful compositions of exotic beasts and buildings, often placed on elaborate stands. That was what it was like for members of our caste. We built our teetering lives on this sort of thing. The beasts moved their eyes, ears and tails. Pagodas rose and fell. Jewelled stars spun and revolving glass rods provided a very credible impression of water.

I bawled and bawled and now I was the one whose mouth became a sock puppet.

Like a large chairman of a rugger club who has a chihuahua as a pet, Eric did not at all resemble his Sing-songs, which one might expect to be the passion of a slim fastidious homosexual. He had

5

a sort of hetero gung-ho quality 'metals' people are expected to have.

'No, no,' he cried. 'Hush.'

Hush? He was not rough with me but he got his big hard arm around my shoulder and compelled me into a fume cupboard and then turned on the extractor fan which roared like twenty hairdryers all at once. I thought, I have let the cat out of the bag.

'No,' he said. 'Don't.'

The cupboard was awfully small, built solely so that one conservator might clean an ancient object with toxic solvent. He was stroking my shoulder as if I were a horse.

'We will look after you,' he said.

In the midst of bawling, I finally understood that Crofty knew my secret.

'Go home for now,' he said quietly.

I thought, I've betrayed us. I thought, Matthew will be pissed off.

'Meet me at the greasy spoon,' he said. 'Ten o'clock tomorrow? Across the road from the Annexe. Do you think you can manage that? Do you mind?'

'Yes,' I said, thinking, so that's it – they are going to kick me out of the main museum. They are going to lock me in the Annexe. I had spilled the beans.

'Good,' he beamed and the creases around his mouth gave him a rather catlike appearance. He turned off the extractor fan and suddenly I could

6

smell his aftershave. 'First we'll get you sick leave. We'll get through this together – I've got something for you to sort out,' he said. 'A really lovely object.' That's how people talk at the Swinburne. They say object instead of clock.

I thought, he is exiling me, burying me. The Annexe was situated behind Olympia where my grief might be as private as my love.

So he was being kind to me, strange macho Crofty. I kissed him on his rough sandalwood-smelling cheek. We both looked at each other with astonishment, and then I fled, out onto the humid street, pounding down towards the Albert Hall with Matthew's lovely silly hat crushed inside my hand.

## 2

I arrived home still not knowing how my darling died. I imagined he had fallen. He had hit his head. I hated how he always tipped back on his chair.

Now there would be a funeral. I tore my shirt in half, and ripped the sleeves away. All night I imagined how he had died, been run over, squashed, knifed, pushed onto the tracks. Each vision was a shock, a rip, a cry. I was in this same condition fourteen hours later when I arrived at Olympia to meet with Eric.

No one loves Olympia. It is a hateful place. But this was where the Swinburne Annexe was, so this was where I would be sent, as if I was a widow and must be burned alive. Well, light the leaves and pyre wood, I thought, because nothing could hurt more than this.

The footpaths behind the exhibition centre were unnaturally hot and narrow. The lanes were looped and dog-legged. Lethal high-speed vans lifted the dust and distributed the fag ends up and down the street where the Annexe awaited. It was not a prison – a prison would have had a sign – but its high front gates were festooned with razor wire.

Many of the Swinburne's conservators had spent a season in the Annexe, working on an object whose restoration could not be properly under-taken at the main museum. Some claimed to have enjoyed their stay, but how could I be severed from my Swinburne, my museum, my life where every stairway and lowly hallway, every flake of plaster, every molecule of acetone contained my love for Matthew and my evacuated heart?

Opposite the Annexe I found George's Café with its doors wide open to the freakish heat.

You would think the author of *Balance of Payments: The Sing-song Trade with China in the Eighteenth Century* would be clearly distinguishable from the four sweaty policemen at the back booth, the drivers from Olympia, the postal workers from the West Kensington Delivery Office who, it seems, had been given permission to wear shorts. Not a good idea, but never mind. If the distinguished curator had not risen (awkwardly, for the plywood booths did not encourage large men to make this sort of motion) I might not have picked him out at all.

Crofty liked to say that he was a *perfect no one.* Yet although he was so opaquely estuary and his bone-crushing handshake had roots somewhere in the years of his birth, in the manly 1950s, he might turn up to drinks for the Minister for Arts where you, if you were lucky enough to be invited, might learn that he had been in Scotland hunting with Ellsworth (Sir Ellis Crispin to you) on the previous weekend. It appeared that I was now to be protected by this powerful man.

I saw his eyes – all the frightening sympathy. I fussed with my umbrella and placed a notebook on the table, but he covered my hand with his own – it was large and dry and warm like something you would hatch eggs in.

'What a horror it all is,' he said.

'Tell me. Please, Eric. What happened?'

'Oh Christ,' he said. 'Of course you do not know.'

I could not look at him. I rescued my hand and hid it in my lap.

'Heart attack, big one. So sorry. On the tube.'

The tube. I had seen the tube all night, the dark hot violence of it. I snatched the menu and ordered baked beans and two poached eggs. I could feel Eric watching me with his soft wet eyes. They were no help, no help at all. I rearranged my cutlery violently.

'They got him off at Notting Hill.'

I thought he was going to say that this was good, to die so close to home. He didn't. But I could not bear the thought that they had taken him back to her.

And she, that great designer of marital 'understanding', would play the grieving widow. 'I suppose it is Kensal Green, the funeral?' Just up the Harrow Road, I thought, so handy.

'Tomorrow actually.'

'No, Eric. That is totally impossible.'

'Tomorrow at three.' Now he could not look at me. 'I don't know what you wish to do.'

Of course, of course. They would all be there, his wife, his sons, his colleagues. I would be expected to go, but I could not. I would give everything away.

'No one gets buried that quickly,' I said. 'She's trying to hide something.' I thought, she wants him in the ground away from me.

'No, no, old love, nothing like that. Not even the awful Margaret is capable of that.'

'Have you ever tried to book a funeral? It took me two weeks to get my father buried.'

'In this case, they had a cancellation.'

'They what?'

'Had a cancellation.'

I don't know who laughed first, maybe it was me because once I started it took a while to stop. 'They had a cancellation? Someone decided not to die.'

'I don't know, Catherine, perhaps they got a

lower price from a different cemetery, but it is tomorrow at three o'clock.' He pushed a folded piece of paper across the table.

'What's this?'

'A prescription for sleeping pills. We'll look after you,' he said again.

'We?'

'No one will know.'

We sat quietly then, and a suffocating mass of food was placed in front of me. Eric had wisely ordered a single hardboiled egg.

I watched him crack its shell, peeling it away to reveal a soft and shiny membrane.

'What happens to his emails?' I asked, because I had been thinking about that all night as well. Our personal life was preserved on the Swinburne server in a windowless building in Shepherd's Bush.

'It's down,' he said.

'You mean down, or you mean deleted?'

'No, no, the whole museum system is down. Heat wave. Air conditioning failed, I'm told.'

'So it's not deleted at all.'

'Listen to me Cat.'

I thought, Cat is not a word that can live in public air. It is a frail naked little thing, all raw and hurting. Please do not call me Cat.

'Tell me you didn't write to each other on office email.'

'Yes we did, and I won't have strangers reading them.'

'It will have been taken care of,' he said.

'How can you know that?'

This question seemed to offend him and his tone became more managerial. 'Do you remember the scandal with Derek Peabody and the papers he tried to sell to Yale? He came back to clear out his office and his email was already gone. Over.'

I never knew there was a scandal with Peabody. 'So his email was deleted forever?'

'Of course,' he said. He did not blink.

'Eric, I don't want anyone to access those emails, not IT, not you, not his wife, not anyone.'

'Very well, Catherine, then I assure you that your wish has already been granted.'

I thought he was a liar. He thought I was a bitch.

'I'm sorry,' I said. 'Who else knows?'

'About you and Matthew?' He paused, as if there were all sorts of different answers he might give. 'No one.'

'I'm rather shocked *anyone* knows.' And then I saw I had hurt his feelings. 'I'm sorry if that sounds offensive.'

'That's all right. I've arranged for a little sick leave. You have been diagnosed with bronchitis if anybody asks. But I thought you might like to know that there is a future. Perhaps you should peek at the object that will be waiting for you when you finally come back to work.'

So he was *not* going to insist I go to the funeral. He should have, but he didn't. His eyes had changed now and I was witness to some quite different emotion triggered by the 'object', which I assumed would be some ghastly Sing-song mechanism. Connoisseurs can be like that. Not even a colleague's death could completely obliterate the pleasure of his 'find'.

I was not particularly offended. If I was raging it was because I was excluded from the funeral, but of course I was far too unhinged to be at Kensal Rise. Why would I lower myself to stand with them? They didn't know him. They didn't know the first thing.

'Might we talk about it just a little later?' I said, and knew I had been rude. I was so sorry. I did not want to hurt him. I watched him unscrew the top of the clogged shaker and make a little pile of salt. In this he dipped his naked egg. 'Of course,' he said, but he was slighted.

'It "surfaced" somewhere?' I suggested.

In return for this tiny show of interest, he bestowed upon me a rather feline smile. So I was forgiven, but I was not nice.

I thought, while Matthew's heart attack was crawling up his legs, Eric had been trawling in the museum's old catalogues. He had found a treasure that none of the present curators knew about, something weird and ugly he could now make the subject of a book.

I wondered if the object catered to the obsession of some posh person, the hobby horse of a minister, a board member. I could have politely questioned him about it, but I really didn't want to know. A clock is a clock, but a Sing-song can be a nightmare, involving glass, or ceramics or metal, or textiles. If that was so I would be forced to work with conservators from all those disciplines. I would not, could not, work with anyone. I would howl and weep and give myself away.

'I'm sorry,' I said, hoping to cover all my offences. And they were offences, for he was being so extraordinarily kind.

We left the greasy spoon. There was a pristine red Mini Minor parked in front. It was not the Mini that I knew, but it looked just the same and I could feel Eric wished to talk of the coincidence. But I could not, I would not. I fled across the road, and entered the most secure museum facility in London.

Of course the chaps in Security had no interest in horology. They would rather be on their Harleys, screaming like mad bees around the North Circular. To my astonishment they knew who I was and displayed towards me an unexpected tenderness which made me mad with suspicion.

'Here you are darling, let me swipe that for you.'

As we moved through the first secure door I was still very shaken by the Mini. I could feel Eric's meaty hand hovering about an inch behind my back. He meant only to comfort me, but I was a mad woman. The hand's proximity was oppressive, worse than actual contact. I *swatted* at it, but there was no hand at all.

On the fourth floor I was permitted to swipe my own card. We entered the rather too cold window-less corridor, strip lights above, tiled walls, mostly white. I felt the hair of my neck lifting.

I had half a 0.5 mg Lorazepam in my purse but I could not find it – it had clearly become lodged with fluff along the seam.

Eric swung open a door and we frightened a very small bespectacled woman at a sewing machine.

The next door, the correct door, remained jammed shut until it swung back on its hinges and crashed against the wall. I was immobile, as was the whole brutal concrete structure of the Annexe. Horologists do not like alien vibrations, so it would be thought that this was a 'good' place for me to be. I felt intensely claustrophobic.

There were three high studio windows suffused with morning light. I knew too much to raise the blinds.

There were eight tea chests and four long narrow wooden boxes stacked against the wall below the blinds.

Was I the first conservator on earth who did not wish to open up a box?

Instead I opened a door. My studio had its own washroom. En-suite, as they say. The look on my protector's face told me I was meant to be pleased by this. I found a dustcoat and wrapped myself inside it.

When I came back, there was Eric, and the tea

chests. I was suddenly certain it was some awful tribe of clockwork monkeys blowing smoke. Sir Kenneth Claringbold had a horrendous collection of automata, clockwork Chinamen and singing girlies of all sorts. In fact my first assignment at the Swinburne had been his gift to the museum: a monkey.

That particular monkey had had a certain elegance, except for the way it drew back its lips to smile, but for a person raised on the austere rational elegance of clockwork it was creepy beyond belief. I got headaches and asthma. Finally, in order to complete the restoration, I had to cover its head with a paper bag.

Later there was a smoking Chinaman who was not quite so horrid, but there was always, in any circumstance, something extremely disturbing about these counterfeits of life and I sniffed around my new studio more and more irritated that this was what Eric had chosen to console me with – eight tea chests were much more than you needed to contain a clock.

'Aren't you going to see what it is?'

I imagined that I detected some secret in Eric's mouth, a movement below the fringe of moustache.

'Are there textiles involved?' I demanded.

'Why don't you look at your presents?'

He was talking to Catherine Gehrig who he had known so very well, for years and years. He had seen me in very stressful (dangerous, in museum terms) circumstances and I had never given him cause to see me as anything other than calm and rational. He liked that I never seemed to raise a sweat. Eric, by contrast, loved big emotions, grotesque effects, Sing-songs, the Opera. Whenever he found fault with me it was for being too cautious.

So dear Eric had no idea that the present beneficiary of his kindness had become a whirring, mad machine, like that sculpture by Jean Tinguely built to destroy itself.

He wanted me to inspect his gift to me. He did not know it would blow me wide apart.

'Eric, please. I can't.'

Then, I saw the blood rising from his collar. He was cross with me. How could he be?

And then in the stinging focus of his gaze I understood that he had pulled a lot of strings, had pissed off a lot of people in order to get the back-street girl set up where her emotions would not show. He was looking after me for Matthew, but for the museum as well.

'Eric, I'm sorry. Truly I am.'

'Yes, I'm afraid you have to go through Security if you want to smoke. You are still smoking?'

'Just tell me it's not a monkey,' I said.

Tears were welling in my eyes. I thought, you dear moron, please just go.

'Oh Lord,' he said. 'This is all awful.'

'You've been very sweet,' I said. 'You really have.' For a second his whole face crumbled but then, thank God, he pulled himself together.

The door closed and he was gone.

## 3

In the middle of the night I lost Matthew's hat and got in a mad panic, stripping the bed, knocking over the reading light until I found what I had lost. I took a pill and had a scotch. I ate some toast. I switched on the computer and the museum email was functioning again.

'I kiss your toes.'

An insane fear of my employers prevented me replying. I filed: 'unread'.

I wrapped myself up in his shirt and took his hat and went to bed and snuffled it. I love you. Where are you?

Then it was the morning, and he was dead. The server was down again. Matthew was completely gone forever. His poor body was lying somewhere in this stinking heat. No, in a refrigerator with a label on his toe. Or perhaps he was already trapped inside a coffin. The funeral was at three o'clock.

I had sick leave and sleeping tablets but I would go mad alone – no church, no family, no one to tell the truth, nothing but the Swinburne which I had stupidly made my life. By noon I was back inside the claustrophobic underground. Three trains later, I surfaced at Olympia with unwashed hair. There was a yellow misty haze.

My colleagues at the main museum would, by now, have dressed for the funeral. It was too early for them to leave so they would hover in their workrooms, surrounded by their lives, their personal knick-knacks, photographs of their kids, lovers, holidays. My own workroom would tell nothing about its former occupant: the pin board displayed a photograph of a tree in Southwold and an empty street in Beccles, the true meaning of both images being known only to us two. Us one.

The walls of my old studio were cream and the lino was brown. The room contained me as if it were a lovely old chipped jug. My Olympia studio, in contrast, had polished concrete floors and the blinds were down because the view was so depressing. I thought of those nineteenth-century prisoners escorted to their cells with bags over their heads, locked up with their looms to work and work and never know where they were. In my case, it was the tea chests, not the loom.

There was a brand new Apple Mac on the bench. Gmail was working quite normally but the museum server, typically, was suffering from 'Extreme Weather' once again.

My head was furry and my chest thick, but I lined the tools up like a surgeon's instruments upon my bench – pliers, cutters, piercing saw, files, broaches, hammer, anti-magnetic tweezers, brass and steel wire, taps and dies, pin vice, about twenty implements in all, every one tipped with an identifying spot of bright blue nail varnish. Matthew's idea.

What can we do? We must live our lives. I opened the first tea chest and found a dog's dinner, everything wrapped in the *Daily Mail* on which I could make out the dome of St Paul's cathedral and the clouds of smoke on the yellow front page. So: it had been packed by amateurs, during the Blitz; evacuated from London to the safety of the country.

I thought, please God let this 'thing' not involve clothes or any sort of fabric. Apart from the nasty way it lifted its lip to show its teeth, it was the silk velvet I had most hated about the smoking monkey – faded and fragile, cracked and bruised. When the clockwork turned it was this faded shabbiness that made the undead thing so frightening.

But really, truly, anyone who has ever observed a successful automaton, seen its uncanny lifelike movements, confronted its mechanical eyes, any human animal remembers that particular fear, that confusion about what is alive and what cannot be born. Descartes said that animals were automata. I have always been certain that it was the threat of torture that stopped him saying the same held true for human beings.

Neither I nor Matthew had time for souls. That we were intricate chemical machines never diminished our sense of wonder, our reverence for Vermeer and for Monet, our floating bodies in the salty water, our evanescent joy before the dying of the light.

But now the light was gone. In one hour it would be suffocated in the earth. I dug into the rat's nest of newspaper and came across a very plain tobacco tin. It was yellow, had a brown legend – 'Sam's Own Mixture' – and a picture of a dog who I assumed was Sam, a gorgeous Labrador, gazing adoringly upwards. I should have a dog. I would teach it to sleep on my bed and it would lick my eyes when I cried.

I tipped the contents into a metal tray. That they were small brass screws would be obvious to anybody. The horologist's eye saw more – for instance, most of them had been made before 1841. The later screws, about two hundred of them, had a Standard Whitworth thread with a set angle of 55 degrees. Could I really see those 55 degrees? Oh yes, even with tears in my eyes. I had learned to do that when I was ten years old, sitting beside my grandfather at his bench in Clerkenwell.

So I immediately knew this 'object' had been made in the middle of the nineteenth century when Whitworth thread became the official standard but many clockmakers continued to turn their own screws. These different types of threads told me that Crofty's 'object' was the product of many workshops. Part of the restoration would involve matching holes and screws and this might sound maddening but it was exactly what I liked about clockmaking as I had learned it from my grandfather Gehrig – the complete and utter peace of it.

When I wanted to go to art school, I thought it must feel like this, to paint, say, like Agnes Martin. It never occurred to me that she might suffer from depression.

I hope my father knew this blissful feeling as a young man, but now I doubt it. He had certainly lost it by the time I understood our family secret. That is: my father was an alcoholic. He fell off his stool without me understanding what the problem was. His unannounced trips 'abroad' were benders, I suppose, or detox. Did they have detox then? How will I ever know? Poor, poor, dear Daddy. He loved clockmaking, but he was destroyed by what it had become. He hated these city louts coming into his shop demanding to have their batteries changed.

Go away with your damn batteries.

What my father had lost was what my Matthew was always blessed with, the huge peace of metal things. Scientifically, of course, this is a stupid way to speak. Metals don't relax until they have rusted or otherwise been oxidized. Only then can they rest in peace. And then someone like Eric Croft wishes to *shine them* in which showy crowd-pleasing state they are poor creatures with their skins removed, naked in the painful air.

Not only Eric, of course. When Matthew and I first became lovers, I helped him strip a Mini to the bare metal. Who would have thought that love would be like that?

Removing the thin ply lids of tea chests with my rather shaky hands, I came across a great number of twisted glass rods which told me this clockwork thing was probably not a monkey.

I began rootling around in a most unprofessional manner. I turned up a nasty coin-in-the-slot mechanism from the 1950s and a number of school exercise books tied together with raffia.

These I carried to the bench, and then I closed the tea chest.

And that was the moment, perhaps thirty minutes before three o'clock, that I began to drift from the straight and narrow. If I had followed the correct protocol I would not have touched this paper until Miss Heller (who did not like me) got the exercise books to the 'Paper People'. I would not have been permitted to read a word. I would have had to wait – she would have enjoyed that part – perhaps a week, or even two, before the scanned images were made available. By then each page would have endured, first Miss Heller's aggressive protection and then the conservator's treatment – an intense assault of white light (3,200 degrees Kelvin to be exact) which is known as 'the final insult'.

His body was surely in the hearse.

The cortège was in the traffic, heading north on the Harrow Road. I sat down. I registered the fact that the notebooks came from the 'werks' of one Wm. Froehlich in the City of Karlsruhe in Germany.

Then, as my darling was conveyed into the maze of Kensal Rise, I held, in my naked hands, eleven notebooks. Each one I examined was densely inscribed in a distinctive style. Every line began and ended at the very brink, and in between was handwriting as regular as a factory's sawtooth roof. There was not a whisker's width of margin.

I was in a state of course. All my feelings were displaced, but it was definitely this peculiar style of handwriting that engaged my tender sympathy, for I decided that the writer had been driven mad. I did not yet know his name was Henry Brandling, but I had no doubt he was a man, and I pitied him before I read a word.

# HENRY

## Twentieth of June, 1854

No matter what circumstance might require a man to travel abroad, it will always be pleasant to be awakened by the morning sun and to find, in the chamber of a German hotel, say, safe on the chair beside you, a portmanteau and sac de nuit, and your pleasure will be so much the deeper when you recall that you have survived the inspection of a customs agent who had it in his great German block-head that you were smuggling plans for what exactly? A very comic instrument of war?

Blessed morning.

I had crossed into Germany with the full assurance of my family that all but the peasants spoke perfect English. Having endured the customs agent I understood that the peasants were very widely distributed and I therefore procured a German Grammar at the railway station.

As I walked about my quiet white-washed chamber next morning, I had a good go at learning German. This was not my métier exactly, but never mind – I was a Brandling and even if I must converse in dumb-show like a circus clown, I was determined to return home carrying that trophy I had come to find.

My son had been in the dumps with his hydrotherapy. It was awful to hear the little fellow's shrieks and know the cold wet sheets were being wrapped around his fevered body and another day of treatment had begun.

From the first bronchial event, two years before, my wife had been waiting for the worst. Our first-born's death had exacted a dreadful toll on her so that now, in all her wary relations with Percy, it was clear as day, she dared not love the little chap. And I? I acted like myself; I could not help it. I persisted with my optimism with the awful consequence that the dear girl who had loved me with all her heart became first irritable and then angry. Finally she established her own separate bedroom on the gloomy north side of the house.

I made every effort to please her. Indeed it was I who commissioned Mr Masini to paint her portrait and encouraged him to bring his assistant and whatever entertaining friends he wished. I was not wrong in this and the library was soon a regular salon and during all that chatter the portrait did indeed progress. Hermione is a handsome woman.

But I would not abandon my son to pessimism. I had the hydrotherapeutic cistern constructed and employed the Irish girl and gave up my office at the works and slept on a campaign bed in the nursery where, according to the recommendations of Dr Kneipp, we kept the windows open throughout the fiercest storms.

Each morning when the hydrotherapy was complete and the nursery floor had been mopped dry, Percy and I sat together with our fruit and grains and planned our 'Adventures of the Two True Friends'. In the village, apparently, I was thought to have become 'potty' because I had been seen to climb an oak with my sick son in my arms. Potty, perhaps. But I was the one who witnessed dear Percy's face as he beheld the four pale eggs of the Great Spotted Woodpecker.

Dr Kneipp was in Malvern but we were in constant correspondence, and there was never an instance when he did not judge my instincts sound. And I specifically include those cases which were reported as 'insane' – for instance, carrying the naked invalid across the raging River Race. 'Always remember,' Kneipp wrote, 'that almost any treatment is safer than the condition you are treating.'

I was slow to understand that, in spite of her portrait and her new amusing friends, my optimism was worse than torture to my wife. Only when it was too late, when I had alienated her completely, did I appreciate what damage had been done. But I am who I am. I would not give up, and I still cherished the hope that, when Hermione finally trusted we would not lose our son, her heart would burst with happiness and she would love us, both of us, again.

I made definite progress with his cure although it often seemed that only Kneipp and I could see the signs. Then, quite by accident, I came across the plans. They had been already a century old when they were published by the *London Illustrated News* but I immediately saw their possibility and I had one of my brother's draughtsmen draw them afresh and by the time he was finished with the transverse sections and so on, it might have been part of the offering plan for the new Brandling railway.

When my little fellow saw the design for M. Vaucanson's ingenious duck, a great shout – huzza – went up from him. It was a tonic to see the colour in his cheeks, the life brimming in his eyes where I observed the force of what Dr Kneipp calls 'magnetic agitation' which is a highly elevated form of curiosity or desire.

I thought, dear Lord, we have turned the corner.

The ten sheets of plans covered his bed. 'Oh Papa,' he said, 'it is a wonder.'

Then I knew that he would live. How alert he was when I explained that, by following the precise instructions on the plans, a clever soul-less creature would be made to flap its wings, drink water, digest grain, and defecate, this last operation being the one that most amused my son and would offend his mother, who, even as she was outraged by the duck's vulgarity, could not help but see the good result.

★   ★   ★

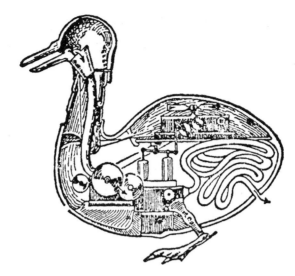

*Brandling. Cat. No. MSL/1848/.V31*

The consequence of this was not exactly as I had wished and I must say that for a day or two I did not quite understand what had happened to me. In Hermione's mind, however, there was no question that I had guaranteed Percy I would have the duck constructed.

'You don't know you have made your son a promise?'

'No.'

'Then you were just teasing him. Could you ever be so cruel?'

'But Hermione, I would have to go abroad.'

'I am sure you know best how it should be done.'

She was a Lyall which is to say, she was driven by a hot engine. This seemed to be a family characteristic, as if the heat of the Lyalls' bodies was part of the fermentation process that underwrote their Newcastle ventures. Now, at a lonely dinner

I will never forget, I understood that this heat was being applied like a blow torch to encourage my departure from my own household.

## 2

Next morning at the Two True Friends' breakfast table, my son asked me, 'When will you leave, Papa?'

So his mother had been at him already.

'Would you not be sad to see your papa gone?' I asked him.

'You should not be sad, Papa,' he said and in his frown I saw the risk that he might glimpse the dire state of his parents' marriage. I had never lied to him before but now I was a jovial clown, so much so that, by the time I poured his cocoa, he believed I could not wait to start my quest.

'Huzza,' he cried. 'What an adventure you will have.'

Of course I did not depart until I had made complete arrangements for his proper care. That is, I acquitted myself with character, although my wife, being a Lyall, would not accept her victory graciously. She refused to understand why, if I was so keen on M. Vaucanson's invention, I would not travel to the nation of which Vaucanson had been a citizen – there was no question in her new friends' minds that the French were in every way superior to the Germans – but I had had enough of them and their opinions. Quite sensibly, my chosen destination was in the Schwarzwald or Black Forest south of Karlsruhe, where the cuckoo clock had been invented. Deep in the Breg Valley there nestled tiny farms – or so I learned in the encyclopedia – for all the world like dolls' houses set in children's plantations and apparently inaccessible save by climbing down rope ladders from the heights above. Here lived a mighty race of clockmakers, notorious not only for their physical strength but the dexterity of their fingers and the unexpected ingenuity of their peasant minds. Here were enough brains and fingers, an embarrassment of riches, any set of which might make my duck.

In Karlsruhe I took rooms at the *Gasthaus an der Kaiser Straße* knowing I would need some time to practise my grammar. Also, having left Low Hall in an awful rush, I needed time to still my injured heart, to sit myself down and understand the situation I had arrived in.

To that end I bought a child's exercise book from the printer Herr Froehlich who must have been, by my brother's calculation, a peasant – that is, he had no English. It was my intention that I should make an 'adventure' of my sad situation and that Percy should feel himself a constant partner. I would keep a day journal to serve as raw material for a continual stream of letters that would place me always by his side.

3

One cannot claim that sanity has been, so to speak, one's *birthright*. There were several aunts who proved a little wobbly and my uncle Edward, an exceptional athlete, returned to his bed for thirty years after rescuing a young boy from the German Sea at Aldeburgh. If we Brandlings have sometimes lost our wits or our fortunes on the horses we have also – this is the other side of the coin – known that the impossible was possible nine times out of ten. That was the basis of our fortune. If the pater had not believed that the steam engine was possible he would not have plunged so much on Stephenson. He therefore ruined himself, or so it was said for a number of years. But of course the impossible was possible and because of that there was now a Brandling Railway and a Brandling Junction, and as a result of that triumph he could order the draughtsman to conjure up that extraordinary spectacle, of the swift trains rolling sweetly through the glass tunnels in the middle of Fortnum & Mason's.

In this sense I was, if only in a modest sense, a Brandling.

Of course no one in Karlsruhe knew what a Brandling was or how he should be treated. Certainly no English soldier would dream of ordering me to vacate a park bench so he might occupy it, and when a German did so, my dictionary was no use at all. Likewise the town's clockmakers did not seem to know how they should treat me. After some four or five unsatisfactory encounters I was cheered enormously to spy, through green panes of ancient glass, a very clever music box made in the form of a merry-go-round. The horses were moving up and down and the riders themselves responding in the most original and lifelike manner, raising an arm high, or slipping sideways in a saddle. Entering a door so low I had to stoop, I beheld the watchmaker himself scuttling out of the shadows of his workroom still buttoning his frock coat. In the light he revealed himself to be slight and very fair, with those pale watery eyes so common in those who spend their days peering into complex engines. He was not a young man and suggested, by his general manner, someone who had found the life of solitude he sought.

At first everything seemed very promising, and he examined my plans with interest. Would he accept them? His feelings were not clear. Yet he was a watchmaker with an ingenious automaton in his window. I had brought him a project worthy of his peculiar intelligence.

'You wait,' he said in English. I thought, thank God, but he spoke no more, using mime to indicate that he would leave the shop, but not for long. Far from being offended when he locked the door behind him, I was encouraged.

While I waited I contented myself with the queer facsimile of life, so dead and not dead it would give a man goose-bumps. All its details I would remember for my son. There were perhaps twenty riders and each one must have, at the heart of their magic, a series of brass cams of the most ingenious construction. It is no small thing to be able to turn these curiously shaped parts, but that is not the half of it for the watchmaker must be an artist who can observe the natural movement of the human figure, and then know what cams he must cut to achieve his counterfeit.

So there I was, the Second Friend – all knees and moustache, happily crouched beside the door, observing the wonderful machine like a tail-flicking cat – when my man returned. Behind him was a very homely-looking fellow, a policeman in fact.

He had been conscripted to translate, and began his service by telling me I was a Respected Sir, and as Karlsruhe seemed to be a place where one must be a Respected Sir, I was very pleased to hear him say so.

I told the policeman that M. Vaucanson's original no longer existed. His countryman Goethe had seen it, did he know of Goethe?

'But of course Sir, we are Germans.'

'Yes,' I said. 'Then you will understand Goethe saw the duck after Vaucanson's death. He said it was in the most deplorable condition. The duck was like a skeleton and had digestive problems.'

I thought, they have never heard of Vaucanson.

The policeman told me, 'I will take you.'

What was happening was not clear, except this clockmaker would no longer meet my eye. There were no farewells, whatever that might mean. My interpreter and I passed Herr Froehlich's lean lop-sided printery and then entered a street of medieval gables, thence into a narrow laneway. Here, at a door I had never entered, my guide ushered me inside my own inn.

What was one to think? What could I do but wait while the policeman took my plans and explained the workings of the Duck to one Frau Beck, the rake-thin inn-keeper. This service done, he clicked his heels and bade me farewell. Then seeing my confusion he went so far as to shake my hand which he seemed to imagine was the custom for constabulary in their dealings with gentlemen.

Frau Beck, meanwhile, was rolling up my plans and shaking her head in a most severe manner. I thought, Lord help her children if she has any.

'No,' she said, and waved a bony finger at me. 'No, Herr Brandling. You must not. You do not show this to Herr Hartmann.'

'Who is Herr Hartmann? The watchmaker?'

She clicked her tongue in such a way as to suggest I could not be more wildly wrong. I should have been home in Low Hall taking German lessons.

'Then who?'

'Then no one! Not one! You are very fortunate that this is all.'

'Why?'

'You have been noticed by everyone,' she whispered. 'Why did you not give up your seat to the Captain?'

I was appalled that all of Karlsruhe seemed to know my business.

'Herr Brandling I must ask you to behave yourself politely. Here,' and with this she delivered me my rolled-up plans and stood to one side to make it clear I should go up to my room. I fancied I chuckled to myself as I obeyed her, but it was not at all funny, and the people of Karlsruhe were clearly not a congenial lot.

I returned to my room. I threw down my plans on the dresser and myself on the peculiar German bed. Then of course the housemaid arrived, accompanied by a boy of perhaps ten. He was hard where Percy was soft, and very fierce and blond, but he was a boy of an age and I felt I knew him.

I greeted him *Guten Tag*, and gave him a Pfennig. How I missed my friend.

The boy's mother – and she could only be his mother – placed her hand upon his shoulder and whispered in his ear. She was telling him to thank me, obviously, but it was the hand on the shoulder that moved me.

'*Danke*,' the boy said and when I saw he was partly lame I was suddenly, unexpectedly, affected. Childhood is so cruel.

It was still only a little after nine o'clock and I could no longer avoid the first meal of the day which had evidently been conceived with the firm belief that a man should stuff himself like a pig before he left the house.

I could find no kipper in my dictionary.

# CATHERINE

My father, when a boy, had read right through the terror of the Blitz. At three o'clock, as they buried my beloved man, I too was reading: Dr Jessica Riskin, 'Artificial Life and Intelligence, *circa* 1730–1950'.

> Cams in the upper cylinder activated a frame of about thirty levers. These were connected with different parts of the Duck's skeletal system to determine its repertoire of movements, which included drinking, playing in the water with his bill, and making a gurgling noise like a real living duck, as well as rising up on its feet, lying down, stretching and bending its neck, and moving its wings, tail, and even its larger feathers . . .

I also read Abbé Desfontaines who described the duck's wings: 'Not only has every bone been imitated, but also the Apophyses or Eminences of each bone . . . the different joints: the bending, the cavities, and the three bones of the wing are very distinct.'

Had Henry Brandling any inkling of the size and

expense of the object he had promised to his child? The Karlsruhe clockmaker had surely known – the plans published in the *London Illustrated News* were only the tip of the iceberg. Below the preening 'actor' there would have to be a main-frame 'chassis'. The chassis would be at least the size and shape of an English telephone box. That was the revelation: a telephone box will not fit inside a tea chest.

I was no equal to my father. At a quarter past the hour, I had retreated to the studio where I felt Matthew's absence in the hollow of my bones. My lungs collapsed. I could not breathe.

Eric Croft was at the graveside. He had his Blackberry tucked inside his pocket. I was sure he imagined the duck would be a crowd-pleaser, something to satisfy the Ministry of Arts. *But the chassis is not here, Eric. The guts are missing, so there is no point.*

To: *e.croft@swi.ac.uk*

'Hi Eric,' I wrote, as people do, even in the Swinburne.

I then informed the man who dared stand at my lover's graveside that the automaton was disastrously incomplete, and until such time as its chassis was found there would be no point in even unpacking. Then, because I was under the influence of Lorazepam as well, I told him that it was highly 'inappropriate' to give a grieving woman the task of simulating life. If he had wished to give me nightmares he had already had a huge success.

I pressed 'send' and turned off the computer.

It was then, high on grief and rage, I stole two of Henry Brandling's exercise books. What would happen if I was caught? Burn me alive, I didn't care. I tucked them inside my copy of *Antiquarian Horology*, and walked straight past Security and out into the London street which was now, in late April, hotter than Bangkok.

It is beyond argument that at the moment I unlocked my own front door, Matthew's body was beginning to decay. Inside the flat it was awful, awful, hot and stuffy. Effluvium. Booze and cigarettes. I threw open the windows at the front and back. I sprayed Aveda lavender in every corner, lit a cigarette and stabbed it out, poured a glass of whisky and retched. I did not like red wine, but I uncorked a bottle of Matthew's Bourgueil and smelled him. I closed the windows so no one would hear me cry.

I had owned, since my dear grandfather died, this basement flat. It was on Kennington Road, diagonally opposite the Imperial War Museum. I have heard north Lambeth called an 'unlovable' corner of London, but I have always known myself blessed by the walled garden which, as the wealthy New Labour owners of 'upstairs' were mostly in Ibiza, was often mine.

In the days when there was still a future the garden had been magical. As recently as last week we had lain in bed and watched a family of foxes frolicking in the backlit uncut grass.

'Look. Watch. Shush.'

The foxes were not exactly cute. Their earth

stank and they brought fast-food wrappers and soaking Pampers onto the lawn. We knew we were meant to telephone 'Bert in Putney' who would come and shoot them. Of course we disobeyed.

Now I read, slowly and carefully, giving all my attention to the evasive puzzle on the page. I could not doubt Henry Brandling's real desire to keep his promise to his son. But he did not seem to have imagined what would happen when the duck was finally made. Did he really expect his wife to fall in love with him again? Or was he, without knowing it, building some mad monument to grief, a kind of clockwork Taj Mahal? Or was that me?

Henry Brandling did not seem hugely bright, but given that some of England's most unpleasant men have Firsts from Oxford, I was not at all put off.

The more I read the more I drank, the more I drank the more I was moved by Henry Brandling. He, like my beloved, suffered for his children heart and soul. I began to imagine that he had anticipated me, that he had bequeathed these notebooks personally. I finished the scotch. I began to drink Bourgueil. The tea chests could go back to whatever dark hole Crofty had found them in, but before they left my studio I would remove each and every exercise book and bring them home and keep them in a place where they would be loved and understood. My sense of ownership was like that created by my first viewing of Fellini's 8½. Then, like now, I believed I was the only person on earth who could understand the thing before my eyes.

# HENRY

I had abandoned Percy. I could not hear him cry or even breathe. Thus I slept deeply, and woke slowly, feeling the backs of my calves move against the smooth cool sheets. What vile luxury. When, after breakfast, I returned to my room I was comforted to feel the usual pain return.

The strange German bed had been severely tucked in, eliminating the history of my body from its reckoning, and this effect was all the stronger as Karlsruhe itself seemed intent on excluding me. I had no purpose in Karlsruhe, no reason to be born at all.

How I missed my true self, the smell of the salty sulphurous cistern, the musty drying mops, the red-eyed child scraping his hob-nailed boots beneath the breakfast table.

Seated on the hard uncurtained bed I saw that any evidence of what and who I was had been scrupulously removed. The only sign of character was that of a maid who clearly had foibles which I had previously considered English. That is, she had artfully rearranged those small private objects I had left sitting on the dresser. Such altars were built at Low Hall continually. Indeed, it had been a matter of acute distress that both Maisie and Elsie had continually interfered with my wife's own deliberate arrangement of the nursery. For instance (to take just one of twenty possible examples) the small brass lantern clock which had so soothed our daughter in her final stages – 'Alice's Clock', so called. My wife preferred this small memento be positioned to left of centre of the mantel and, in her grief, she became quite fierce about what exactly was its place – just to the left of centre and then twisted on an angle so it could be seen clearly from the bed.

Yet maids do not listen. And maids love to fiddle, and two maids are twice as bad as one for each in their turn (Maisie had been 'sent packing' before Elsie had been engaged) would shift the clock to the centre of the mantel and line it up directly parallel with the wall. Elsie's action left my wife with the choice of dismissing her or doing without the clock. All in all she thought it simpler to have the clock 'go missing' with the result that poor Elsie, who was given to nervous conditions, spent her five years in our employ worrying about that 'blessed clock' and having dark suspicions about which departing servant had been 'the one'.

I have left out all the other maids' arrangements, the consequences of which finally spread well beyond the nursery. So when, in Karlsruhe, I finally comprehended that my cuff links, my compass, the enamelled miniature of my son, my pack of cards, my pens, sovereign case and all the little accoutrements of life, had been arranged as by a magpie, well, I was – from habit? – somewhat apprehensive. Oh Lord, I thought, there will be trouble now.

In the very centre of my dresser, much in the manner of Nelson's Column, stood my rolled-up plans, and around this obelisk these objects had become subjects paying homage. The plans themselves now bore the simplest of decoration, a royal blue thread which I was slow to realize served the purpose of attaching a small sheet of notepaper.

I was loath to touch the composition, but how could I have no curiosity about the message there attached? Being the Two Friends champion at pick-up-sticks I had the steadiness required to slip it free. There, in a childish but not ungraceful hand, I read: *Wir bauen die Ente.*

Why this should make the hair stand on my neck I could not say. Was I frightened of my wife or of the maid? I rushed to my dictionary and you might consider my feelings (in this city where everyone knew everything about me, where the most innocent action created hostility and suspicion), you might imagine my racing heart, when I learned that *Ente* = 'duck'.

Yet the dictionary was just a little thing, and I rushed off to seek a live translator who was, of course, alas, Frau Beck.

She looked up, smiling, from her ledger, and I noted, for the first time, that despite her whole presence being like a dry and wrung-out cloth, her little brown eyes were soft and rather wary. I thought, you are a widow.

43

'Who is *Ente?*'

'Sir, it is a duck of course.'

'What does it say about the duck, Frau Beck?'

She placed the small note on her counter, dipped her pen and – all the while smiling – corrected the child's handwriting.

'Herr Brandling,' she said, 'we will make your duck, of course. It will be ready in two hours.' Her misunderstanding was clear enough, but I did not wish to argue with her. So rather than further damage her opinion of me, I contracted to pay her for a duck I could not eat.

'Now you must walk, Herr Brandling. You must be healthy. You are in Germany, you must exercise. In two hours you will dine again.'

I would have interrogated her further, but the major-domo – an awful creature with a limp – chose that moment to begin an argument with the old woman who was mopping the front steps of the hotel. 'Walk, Herr Brandling,' Frau Beck cried, rushing to the scene of the conflict. 'You will be pleased.'

I began my stroll with no particular plan, wandering the little streets as many visitors had done before me. I had no curiosity about anything except the meaning of this note. I rather feared it was belligerent.

There were just as many clockmakers' shops along the streets as yesterday but I had no stomach for them, and so chose streets that took me out into the countryside or to the church which I believed

I could not be blamed for entering. Then of course it was Catholic so I thought it best to leave.

The backstreets were not so different from a provincial English town where the shopkeepers chalk their wares on the door posts. So it was, by luck, I recognized a stationer's where I managed to negotiate the purchase of an envelope and a stamp ('*Brief-marke*') which I understood to be of sufficient value to get a letter to my boy. In an empty beer garden, I found a single chair beneath a chestnut tree. I tore a page from my notebook and described for Percy the tiny merry-go-round. As my memory is rather good, I managed to fill both sides and then a third with a full account of all the little figures and their motions. I encouraged him to see this as a promising start. I was hopeful, I wrote, of more good news in the next letter. I was a liar, but what choice did I have? It was essential, even in my absence, that his magnetic agitation be maintained as much as possible.

I returned to the inn with no appetite and Frau Beck led me immediately to a parlour adjacent the main dining room. This was panelled in dark wood and hung about with a number of fusty tapestries depicting what were said to be 'Rumanian Hunters'. The windows being rather small, the light distinctly funereal, it required candles even in the middle of this sunny spring day. It was some time before I made out the considerable figure of a man seated in the corner.

He addressed me in a deep voice, '*Guten Tag.*'

He looked like a soldier, a major uncomfortable in his mufti.

A waiter arrived, his head lowered in such a way that, had he been a dog, his ears would have been flattened on his head. I was by now in a panic about the duck which I attempted to cancel by ordering an omelette.

'Of course,' he said. '*Immédiatement.*'

'How do you enjoy Karlsruhe, Brandling?'

Brandling? The hair rose on my neck. He was a large man, with a neck as wide as the gleaming head which he kept completely bald. His brows were black and heavy and clearly kept in shape with the same mad barbering he brought to his moustache.

I thought, was it you who wrote the note? At the same time I thought, this is ridiculous.

Two waiters arrived (*Immédiatement*, indeed) to present me with – no omelette, no beer – but a duck which had been prepared with fruit and cinnamon and other ghastly ingredients that would more properly be found in pudding.

The stranger kept on at me, stretching his arm along the back of his banquette. He had nothing before him but a book in which he appeared to sketch. It occurred to me that, although his broad shoulders suggested a plebeian, he was a pretender to the role of artist. That is, he exhibited a sort of insolence not unlike various individuals who had dined at our table when Mr Masini was finishing his first 'portrait' of my wife.

'Your meal is agreeable,' he demanded.

I did not reply.

'You are the bloke who went to Hartmann with your plans?'

Bloke was I? Indeed. 'I'm afraid I know no Hartmann.'

'Hartmann the clockmaker,' he insisted, using English as if he had been wet-nursed by a cockney. 'You spoke to him about your plans. You are Mr Brandling, I believe?'

'Am I?' I said. 'Indeed.'

'You scared the pants off Hartmann.' A cigar was ignited and in the flare I saw how his jacket strained against his arms.

'Herr Hartmann is not from here,' he said, 'but if he was from Karlsruhe, what would it matter? The idiots have no idea of who they are. They spend their time trying to be Prussians. They are living in a dream,' he said.

I was doing my best with the meal, that is, not very well at all.

'Do you know what I am talking about?' the ruffian demanded.

At home, I would have confidently become deaf and blind. In Karlsruhe I did not know the form.

'They are living in a dream,' he insisted.

So then, finally, I spoke to him. 'I do not understand you, Sir.'

'Then,' said he, rising as he spoke, 'I think it is time for me to join you.'

I was appalled to see the giant come towards

me. My brother, doubtless, would have left the room. But I, Henry Brandling, sat like a great big English bunny, and permitted the 'bloke' to deposit his leather book beside my meal. This ill-treated volume held, between its pages, countless numbers of other sheets, all of different sizes and colours. The whole was tied together with a leather thong.

He shouted in German at the waiter, demanding what turned out to be an ashtray. When that wish was satisfied he turned his attention to my meal. No question of consulting me. I should have pulled his nose for him but I sat like a dressmaker's dummy and permitted him to use *the handle of the butter knife* to deftly, one might say surgically, separate out the elements in the sauce, and with each of these excisions he asked a question, not of me, but of the servant. Finally he ordered it removed, or at least that seemed a consequence of what he said.

'Next we will have cognac,' he announced.

I thought, perhaps he is a mayor, an ill-mannered farmer risen through the ranks. I thought, Good luck with your cognac old chap.

'Why do you smile, comrade?'

'They serve only beer.'

He smiled, but not offensively. 'Comrade, they are living in a dream.'

I shrugged. 'When it comes to cognac, might I say the same to you.'

Now he was opposite me, there was no doubt that his tailor had done a poor job accommodating him. However that tight jacket had a pocket for everything, one specifically, it seemed, to fit a deck of cards.

He dealt one card, face down. 'Do you know what this is?' he demanded. Was he smiling in the shadow of that large moustache?

Clearly I had fallen into company with a card sharp, but I would not be the easy victim my friends all feared. 'If you expect me to turn it over, you are quite mistaken.'

'No,' he tapped the verso. 'It is this I show you. This is the dream you are living in the middle of.'

For the first time I looked into his eyes. They were a very dark brown and one could almost call them black. I was not afraid of him, but he was certainly a beast both fierce and strange. 'This is a picture of Karlsruhe,' I said.

*Verso side. German playing card c.1820*

'In English that would mean Karl's Rest. You see that of course. But what you cannot see is the Karl who dreamed Karlsruhe. That is, Karl III Wilhelm, Markgraf von Baden-Durlach. He fell asleep and had a dream, and what he dreamed is what you see on the back of this card. So what do you observe?'

'Clearly it is in the form of a circle.'

'Clearly, Mr Brandling. A wheel in fact.'

I thought again, how in the devil does he know my name? From the awful jumble of his leather book he plucked an illused sheet, a kind of catalogue, of clockwork wheels and gears.

'You are not a clockmaker,' I said – the hands upon the table were too large to decently tie boot laces.

'Why on earth did you speak to that idiot Hartmann? You come to the home of the wheel, and you talk to that dull bourgeois little shopkeeper. Do you not know where on earth you are?'

I thought, perhaps they all address each other in this tone.

'You want a cuckoo clock.' He almost sneered.

'No,' I said but he was insisting I consider an engraving of clock wheels, all the time staring with that senseless excitement you see in the eyes of people who have lost their wits. He had a theory, I understood. If you were from Karlsruhe you had spokes and metal rims.

'Have you ever seen a running machine?'

'A machine that runs?' (My goodness, I thought, that would be really something.)

'For God's sake, drink, no of course not. If such a machine were to be invented, where would the most propitious place be?'

'You will say that it is Karlsruhe.'

'Here,' he cried, plucking one more item from his collection, and offering it with his enormous hand – a card like the ones manufacturers sometimes slip inside their tins of pipe tobacco. 'Study it,' he commanded. 'You spend too much money on your tailor and not enough on books.'

It was a coloured engraving of a fellow with a two-wheeled contraption.

'This is Herr Drais of Karlsruhe.' He tapped the fellow's head with fingernails as square and dirty as a gardener's.

I said, 'Why are you showing me this?'

'It is named after him. It is a Drais.'

'Why are you showing me this damned Drais?'

'So you will not die of duck,' he said, and threw back his head and roared with laughter. I shoved his papers back at him, but he had one more to give.

'And what is this?' I demanded.

'How should I know everything?'

'Then why should you give it to me?'

*Silk paper, organic inks and dyes. Provenance unknown*

'In trust.'

'In trust for what?'

'If I have your plans,' he said, 'it is only fair that you have mine.'

'You do not have my plans,' I said. 'And do not call me Brandling.'

In return he folded his arms across his broad chest and revealed the white clean line of his teeth beneath his big moustache.

'Excuse me,' I said. 'I have an appointment.'

'Then you must go.'

He made no attempt to say farewell, but sat there very placidly poking his great big nose into his strong drink. A few moments later, having found my way along the dark and twisting corridor to my room, I discovered my plans were missing.

I beheld the likeness of my poor dear boy, the sloe eyes, the residual sadness, and knew it was a crime to have left him. I rushed back down the stairs. I had a mind to take the butter knife and stab the scoundrel in his staring eyes. But of course you can see already what had happened. As usual I was the last one to understand. Yes, I found the parlour now deserted, no sign of what had happened, nothing but two empty cognac glasses and, beneath the table, a single playing card.

I was never an adventurer. I was not suited to adventures. If I were really a True Friend I would have stayed at home.

# CATHERINE

I was very frightened of visiting the cemetery. But I would not abandon my beloved. I made the bed and threw my clothes in the wash. I swept the cornflakes off the floor and washed out the whisky glass. I cleared away the bottles and made myself a cup of tea. I sat back at my table. I found my Lorazepam and chewed one up. It was only eight o'clock so I thought, just for a little, I might spend some time with Henry Brandling. I turned the next page of the notebook and discovered a postcard of Karlsruhe held there by a rusty pin. There were also, between the next two pages, a few other bits of floating scrap, but the following sheets were all blank, each and every one. Only then, as my throat closed on itself, did I understand I had been relying on Henry to continue. Now I saw that he might not. For all I knew, the books inside the tea chest would be empty too.

I was finding clothes for work when I realized it was Saturday and there was no telephone call I could make, or story I could invent to get access to the studio.

'Weekend work in studios is not undertaken without an exceptional reason.'

So I ran a bath. I lay in the tepid water and looked at my poor scrawny unloved body with its seaweed hair. I cried. I shampooed and conditioned and cried again. Even inside the bathroom you could feel the heat wave, all the car engines and motorways to the horizon and beyond. I dried my hair. I had good hair, I had been told. I used Preparation H to reduce the inflammation of my puffy eyes.

I didn't know where they had hidden Matthew, but then I called the cemetery and was almost brought undone by kindness. I had been so armoured. I had thought they would ask me was I 'the wife' and prove it. But this young man was not like that at all. He had a lovely West Country way of talking, and he was patient while I found a pencil to write down the lot number and the directions. He said it was a very pretty part of the cemetery. He had walked there yesterday. It was really rather wooded, 'a real refuge' in the heat.

I would still have put it off, but just after ten I realized that 'upstairs' had returned and the former Speaker of the House had decided he would cut his lawn. The noise was awful. So I went.

I could get to Kensal Rise on the Bakerloo line. I have never liked the tube, but today seemed particularly unpleasant. Later I discovered it had been the hottest April day in forty years. It had been 117 degrees on the platform, but I did not know that and when I began to panic I felt the claustrophobia was my own fault. I thought, I must not give in to this.

But at Marble Arch I fled, running up the escalators. I told myself I was getting flowers, but there were flowers at Kensal Rise and none at Marble Arch. Then I decided I would go by bus. Being too agitated to read the map, I got the bus to Westbourne Grove, because I knew that it passed the Harrow Road and the cemetery was up the Harrow Road.

I missed the stop at the Harrow Road and got off further up. I thought, I can take a break, and calm myself. Matthew was trapped beneath the earth, bloating cruelly, all his beauty turned into a factory, producing methane, carbon dioxide, rotten egg gas, ammonia. I was afraid of what I knew.

I could have walked to visit him in forty minutes, but I did not want to see the broken earth. I decided I would return when the grass had grown. So I turned my back on him and headed toward Notting Hill Gate. Matthew, I thought. Forgive me. You would never have left me alone like that. But of course that's exactly what you did.

Englishmen with white skin and stout legs were parading in their shorts. Matthew was tall and slender. He had the most gorgeous legs. It was horribly humid and the sky was low and feathery and very very sad.

I was frightened to go home to my nothing. I

was scared of the afternoon and the night ahead. So I decided I would make an attempt to talk myself into the Annexe. I finally got myself to Earl's Court, but the Olympia shuttle had committed suicide. I walked north from there towards Olympia, not noticing how dark the sky was getting behind my back. In this way I stumbled into what estate agents call Brook Green.

And my man in the pleasant wooded shade of Kensal Rise was the finest of the fine, and I thought how he would have liked this – the little wine bar most of all. The shops looked very pretty in the golden light and I came into a very quiet street of grey and pastel houses and there was one shop, on the corner, and I thought, that looks nice, and as I got closer it was clear it was a very particular shop, and it had some very, very simple bags for which I now had a pressing need. It was closed. But then I saw there was a woman inside, and she turned on the lights as she walked toward me. She was a strange and honed-down thing, perhaps fifty, but terribly thin, and petite, with the sort of severe and interesting character one normally thinks of as French. Her hair was strong, grey, cut short, but quite expensively. She opened the door, frowning, as if she knew my darling was dead and I was a disgrace to even think of shopping.

'You must be hurried,' she said. I did not know she was talking about the storm.

She turned back into the shop where, looped casually over a locker-room hook, was the simplest bag I ever saw. The leather was black, and very soft and light. I put it over my shoulder and it disappeared beneath my arm as if it might dissolve. Inside there were two perfect pouches, one zippered, one not. Best of all, it was lined with a peacock sort of silk. This was the bag whose sole function was to steal Henry Brandling from the Annexe.

She was Italian, not French. She said it was a hundred pounds.

She said she was sorry, but would I mind paying cash? I had just enough.

She gave me the bag without wrapping it and then, firmly but politely, pushed me out the door.

There was an awful crack of thunder and a sizzling sort of noise. It was not yet raining, but the sky was black and bleeding like a Rothko. And then, from around the corner, there appeared a taxi, with a lovely yellow light. I was no sooner inside than the rain began, great fat splats like glycerin against the windscreen. I saw lightning hit the Natural History Museum, or that is what it looked like.

At Kennington Road, I should have run straight inside, but I had the cab drop me at the off-licence, what Matthew called the offy, where I put a bottle of cognac on my MasterCard. As I came outside everything was dark except for a weird yellow sheen across the houses. I thought the rain had let up – maybe it really had – but when I was half way across the road the hail arrived, lumps like hotel ice blocks, river stones, cruel, unforgiving pelting against my naked head and unprotected shoulders. I arrived in my kitchen, stinging sore, drenching wet. I watched the monstrous hail pile up across the garden. Why hast thou forsaken me?

## 2

Hail and hate, roaring like a train, the entire back garden stoned to death, crushed glass or ice now two inches thick. The geraniums were flat, the daphne devastated. God knows what had happened to my neighbour but he had abandoned his lawn mower in the middle of my view.

In the bathroom I examined my blooming injuries, but none of this took very long and soon my hair was dry and I sat in my dressing gown, at the kitchen table. Here I slid my Brandling books inside the new handbag. I paraded, and it was as I thought – the bag fitted so snugly between my arm and chest. I was so absorbed, so impatient to retrieve the notebooks that I might not have seen the peculiar mist lying above the field of ice. But I did look up. And the sun came out. And all the garden turned to gold sublime, unearthly and very strange.

For just that instant I felt wonder. For that moment I forgot my grief. I reached for my open laptop. As it slid toward me, I recognized the nature of my expectation – I had been about to tell Matthew.

I kiss your toes. Mark unread.

There was a new email from Crofty. He wrote, 'I've fixed it.'

I thought, how can you fix anything? Then I understood, he had read my ill-mannered email and thought: I am without doubt a wretched stupid man. So he had discreetly, sweetly, secretly, removed the bloody tea chests and their contents from my studio.

He had done exactly what I had asked – taken my project from me. And he had paid overtime for weekend work. It was like a fairy story with a moral. Due to my own bad temper, all of Henry's notebooks were now beyond my reach.

I opened the cognac and took a slug straight from the bottle. I found the Swinburne staff directory.

'Hello, is that Arthur?'

'Arthur's just stepped out.'

'This is Miss Gehrig from upstairs in Horology, I'm working on 404.'

'You missed them, Miss Gehrig, by, I would say, thirteen minutes.'

'Did you get the hail?'

'Well to be exact, Miss, I would say Arthur must have got the hail. Shall I give him a message if he's still alive?'

'Is Mr Croft there?'

'He was here with Arthur for a good three hours. Then they stepped outside.'

'And now he's at the Fox and Hounds?'

'Licking his wounds I would say.'

I had no doubt the men had spent the afternoon removing my tea chests. I would never have a chance to read the notebooks. I could not speak. I hung up. I phoned back and apologized for dropping the phone. I said I would see him on Monday.

I did not think, the Head Curator of Horology has turned himself into a manual labourer on my account. I saw only that I had all of Sunday to suffer this new agony. Very well then, I must not wallow. I unlocked the French door and forced it open against the weight of ice. I climbed the three crunchy steps to the garden, and moved the ugly mower from my view.

This served to put the smell of the oil and rubber on my hands. That is, the perfume of my nights in a little stables in a copse in Suffolk, not far from Beccles, in a snug loft bed above a Mini Minor we spent years restoring. That was Matthew's place, his own. That is what our love smelled like – oil, rubber, the musty rutty smells of sex. I had spent the happiest nights of my life with my body washed by leafy shadows, headlights from a bend in the A12.

When I sat in Kennington Road and smelled my oil and rubber hands, I was no longer thinking about Henry Brandling and his duck. The ice had melted. The air was moist. As the grassy breeze blew through my open kitchen window I recalled lying in bed in that little stables with the sweet Suffolk rain upon our fragile roof.

## 3

On Monday morning I rang the bell beside the Annexe gate and the turnstile pivoted at the centre of its ungiving heart. From that moment a camera held me.

Reception was to my left and there was Arthur. I could not reasonably ask him where the tea chests had been stored.

'Good morning Mr Phelps.' He lifted his face and I saw the puffy boozer's eyelids.

'You were working on Saturday on my behalf. I am in your debt.'

The old codger rubbed his foxy silver hair. 'I would say that Mr Croft has settled that, Miss Gehrig. He nearly killed me with his bleeding settlement, if you'll forgive me saying so.'

I swatted my ID card. A second turnstile. The camera observed me, but there was nothing in my bag except a pashmina, purse, and Lorazepam. I carried emptiness. Doors opened. Another camera recorded my progress. Doubtless there were thousands of my days repeated thus, interred digitally in limbo. I ascended two steps with nothing to look forward to, and swiped my card one final time.

I opened my studio door to meet, not emptiness, but tea chests.

I think I made a small cry. Perhaps it was recorded. A moment later the rat's nest of *Daily Mail* opened up its crumpled innards, and there were Henry Brandling's notebooks in their careful raffia string.

At my bench, I found the first book completely filled with handwriting, every page. All the books, every one. In all that sharp sea of waving lines there was not one blank. Although I wanted all of them at once, I slid only four of them inside four ziplock bags and these I hid inside my handbag. Then I shifted the remainder to the high shelf above the fume cupboard where no one would ever think to look. There were precisely nine more instalments for me to read.

Only as I hung my booty on the hook behind the door did I realize things were not at all as they had been on Friday night. In the left-hand corner of the room, nearest to the door and therefore behind my left shoulder when I first entered, was an iridescent grey tarpaulin thrown across some objects, the largest one of which stood about four foot high.

I thought of a beached sting ray, some undead thing washed ashore in *La dolce vita*. When the rational brain woke up, I understood what *must* lie beneath the tarp – an upper and a lower cylinder driven by a weight, thirty levers that could be connected with different parts of the duck's skeletal system to make it drink, et cetera, à la Riskin. This was not going to be a smoking monkey, that was clear when I took away the shroud. If, a moment later, I was replacing it, it was not because of the ingenious mechanism, but because of a wooden object placed beside it. Even that was nothing, of course, nothing at all. It was just a sort of wooden hull that had probably once contained the mechanism, but I was in a waking nightmare and the brain reported a failed cremation, a burned roast dinner, a black and formless fear. Professionally I understood the pitch-black underside, but what I saw was the shell of a huge bivalve, crusty, flaking, disinterred from tar. I smelled napalm, creosote, burned pig, death.

TO: *e.croft@swi.ac.uk*
FROM: *c.gehrig@swi.ac.uk*
SUBJECT: Bronchitis
Sorry. Diagnosis confirmed.

A very short time later I was signing out downstairs.

'You're shivering,' Arthur said.

I hurried through the turnstile with my booty tight beneath my arm. I thought, Henry Brandling, what happened to you? How much money did they steal?

# HENRY

Although firmly interrogated, Frau Beck affected to have no memory of the man in the parlour.

'If Herr Brandling means the Englishman, that gentleman has settled his account. That is all I know.'

'I am the Englishman.'

'Yes Herr Brandling,' said Frau Beck (rhymes with peck, a pecking little person). 'Mr Brandling you are also an Englishman. But *that* Englishman.' She held apart her wiry little arms to indicate the scoundrel's shoulders. 'He paid.'

Clearly I had been duped by a confidence man of the type that preys on travellers. I slammed my hand down on the counter and this displeased Frau Beck.

'He was a German,' I said.

'No, an Englishman.'

I was eviscerated. I had abandoned my son for what, a playing card?

'What of the maid?' I asked.

The maid? What maid? Etc. Was Frau Beck a member of the gang?

'The maid of my room.'

'The maid of your room,' Frau Beck said, as if mocking my English grammar. 'The maid of your room has departed.'

'Clearly,' I cried, seeking her behind her lenses. 'Clearly, these criminals do not work alone.'

'Herr Brandling, it is the springtime. The maid goes to her family in the Schwarzwald. It is to be expected. Each year the same.'

'She has taken my plans to the Black Forest!'

'Herr Brandling, we know this is not possible.'

'It is so, Frau Beck, believe me.'

'And these plans, were they the same plans you showed Herr Hartmann?'

'They are my plans. I have no others.'

Dipping her pen in her ink well, Frau Beck dismissed me.

At home I would have sent a man to summon the police, and they would have frightened all the servants (as they did both times my wife lost her wedding ring).

I informed Frau Beck I was going to my room to write a complaint. I doubt she knew what I meant, and how could I know myself? What would I write? In English? To whom would I address my charges? No, I must bite my tongue. I had no recourse but to order new plans, and of course the firm's draughtsmen would copy the *London Illustrated News* again, although my brother would make it clear to them that 'Mr Henry's' request was even less welcome than the first.

And yet, was not my little boy himself the most important family enterprise? He was a Brandling, which is also the name of a salmon before it has gone to the sea, a parr, a pink, a smolt, a smelt, a sprag, or brandling. My brother must be made to see that Percy was our future. He had none of his own.

I returned to my eyrie and lay upon my bed. How long I slept I have no idea. I was roused by a mousey skittering as someone attempted to slide paper beneath my door. I was on my feet in a trice.

I surprised the maid's son kneeling, envelope in hand, blue eyes wide with fright. I caught him by his long white wrist and hauled the limpy creature into the room. I felt his magnetic life surge as it shook my arm, jolting, kicking like a hare or rabbit in a trap. I booted the door shut as I shackled his other wrist as well – if he had lice eggs under his fingernails they would not find a home beneath my skin.

Trapped – my little criminal, in the middle of the white-washed room, shaking, crying, crumpled letter in his hand. Then it was knock knock knock and rattling on the handle and here was the accomplice, 'The maid of the room', a red kerchief around her wheaten hair. This second party required no dragging. Indeed she rushed to embrace her offspring. There, by the foot of the peculiarly austere bed which she had so recently made herself, she kissed his crown and glared at me. I was a brute. The boy pressed himself hard against his mother and regarded me with fear and hatred, his fierce eyes revealing a will much stronger than my own. I wanted him to like me even so, this tiny enemy.

The mother I had earlier thought to be quite pretty, but now I saw, in that wide and delicate mouth, the knowledge that all happiness was conditional. Her complexion was as fine as an English woman's but her thief's hands were used and hard.

'Give me back my plans,' I said.

She showed the perfect understanding of the guilty.

'Sir, your plans are safe,' she said, and the quality of her English was not of the natural order. That is, she was revealing herself to be a maid so dangerously well educated that, apart from the eccentric Binns, no one of my acquaintance would have employed her.

I said: 'They will be safe when they are with their lawful owner.'

She dared to contradict me.

Said she, 'They must not be allowed to remain in Karlsruhe.'

I fear I may have snorted.

'It is better the plans go to where they can be understood.'

Her craven manner had slipped from her. I thought, yes, I am correct, a gang.

'And where might my plans be understood?'

'In Furtwangen.'

Who had ever heard of such a comic place?

'But even Furtwangen is filled with mediocrities.'

I would have grilled her on the sources of her strong opinions had not the child slyly produced a number of small brightly painted wooden blocks, and then – from where? – a length of thick steel wire perhaps a quarter of an inch in diameter. I watched in silence, while he swiftly assembled an ingenious bowed bridge along which his red and yellow blocks were made to slide and hop, all under the power of their invisible or magical engines.

It was a delightful contrivance. What lovesick father would not be charmed by such a child?

The boy had a voice like a little bell. When he spoke he was so tuneful that I did not immediately understand he spoke my tongue.

'He has made it for your son,' his mother said. 'You will send it to England and your son will play with this while he waits for his father to return.'

How do they know I have a son?

'It is very kind,' I said at last, 'but your son does not need to buy toys for mine.' They had seen Percy's likeness. That was it.

'He does not purchase,' she said, cupping the back of his head with her hand. 'He makes. In the night.' How she loved him – she was alight with it – but given the dexterity of the manufacturer and the ingeniousness of the invention, I had to make clear my scepticism.

'You wrong him,' she said, all respect now

vanished. 'He made it. He cut himself and he will be punished for his carelessness.'

He was clearly a very serious boy and he wore a white bandage on his forearm. Indeed his unwavering gaze defeated me and I retreated to the contents of the envelope, a very calligraphic English – 'Herr Brandling, we will make the duck. A coach we have prepared to take you to the clockmaker.'

'There is no cost to you,' the woman said hurriedly. 'We will take you to Furtwangen and there your duck will be constructed as you wish.'

What could I do but laugh at her?

'Why would I lie to you, Sir? You would put me in prison if I cheated you. I would be ruined. Please, Sir, do come. You cannot have a fine machine constructed by a common shopkeeper.'

'How could one manufacture such a thing *without* a shop?'

'You will meet him. He is Herr Sumper.'

'It is Mr Sumper has robbed me?'

'No, he is gone to Furtwangen to await you.'

Since my first day at Harrow my trusting nature has been a source of amusement, and it is curious to me that these judgements have inevitably been passed by those who are untrustworthy – why be so boastful about your own appalling character?

But consider a moment. Would you, in my place, have refused to go with the thieves? Then what injury you would have caused your son. What an extraordinary journey you would have missed, one such as many have trouble crediting, and the very first stage of it, south along the Rhine, was both aesthetic and pacific. That is, I gave charge of my life to a child and his mother, and permitted myself – a rather dull chap really – to be transported, nay, elevated into the Black Forest which I had previously known only from the Brothers Cruel, as my mater called them. A great deal of my journey – which I experienced alone inside the coach while my little gang sat on top, often singing at the tops of their voices – was rather lonely but so much more peaceful than the previous two years during which I had dreaded the appearance of blood stains on the nursery pillow.

The first inn was hospitable although not clean. I called for candles and wrote to Percy, telling him all about the clever crippled boy, his luminous invention, the adventure that would take me into Ali Baba's cave. By previous arrangement I sent this letter to my friend George Binns who had agreed to come and read to Percy on Saturday and Thursday afternoons.

On the second day we journeyed deep into the Schwarzwald. The forest road was picturesque, although very steep. All was particularly un-Grimm. Everywhere was beauty and delight – dark green forests, bright meadows, the well-kept gardens, an extraordinary abundance of mountain streams, brooks and rills, not to mention the quaint houses with their heavy overhanging roofs, bright rows of glittering windows, carved verandahs, and their inmates – a distinct and peculiar race of people

– the women with bodices and bright skirts, aprons, neat little pointed caps from which dropped those massive plaits it was their husbands' privilege to see set free. I wished I were once again a husband in that private sense.

So, sad sometimes, often lonely too, but never in my entire life had I essayed a real adventure and I thought a great deal about my automaton and how, before it had been brought to life, it had already proved its power to realign the stars.

The swaying coach continued upwards until the sunlight showed that melancholy whiteness distinctive of the very highest altitudes. Then we were in country which forbade all growth except of grass and shrubs. Silence reigned upon the roof and I began to fear that the landscape of our destination might be in no way like that of the journey. Now the grass was blighted. We were in a land of peat, although as far as I could see the inhabitants had found no use for it. The timber houses were bleached like bones. And in the queer white light I became my own worst enemy, my own best hope, one of those unstable Brandlings who would always be in the market for a miracle.

## 2

It was once said: 'Brandling would see the glass half full even when it lay in shards around his feet.' Ha ha, indeed. But has no one bothered to observe that the optimistic view is commonly correct? That is why our fearful prayers are so often 'answered'. That is why, when we descend from one of life's barren mountain tops, we almost always enter a pleasant valley where there is an inn, very clean and white-washed, its window boxes filled with flowers in bloom.

And to that inn I surely came, and my natural 'naïve' spirits were immediately restored. And from that inn's airy stables the wall-eyed coachman would soon set off, carrying my trunk on his broad back. First, however, he joined us around a bowl of moist ham hocks and mugs of creamy beer. There were no fearful intimations, no mortal shadows; every leaf of privet was bright and green and barbered.

Not even the weight of a Harris tweed suit could distract one from the pretty harvest scene through which our little party strolled and stumbled. And who could not be affected by the mood of one's companions, particularly the boy who ran and limped and gambolled and called to the harvesters? They knew him – Carl.

We were now on our way to the place where a powerful cure might be constructed. I was a-tingle with impatience yet also, paradoxically, much elevated by the delays. Who would not be happy to see a much-loved boy have his weight guessed? When he performed a clever tumble, he never once pitied himself his crippled leg. Yes, I felt the absence of my own son – an awful ache – but only love provides the lucky man such symptoms.

As for the German mother? Who would ever

imagine that distant figure in the wheat field to have poor hard hands, red elbows, and a mouth that did not dare hope for very much at all?

In the winter (as was apparently well known to everyone but me) the Furtwangen men all worked on their cuckoo clocks, and in the summer they laboured beside their wives. They were Alemannians and Celts and they were large and strong and showed a bright and cheerful speech and temperament. I liked them even when they clearly did not give a fig for me.

Our path soon joined a brook and young Carl paused by the muddy bank to once more display his wooden trick; the leap of red and yellow produced the desired effect; the performer said goodbye; and we followed the brook as it traversed two pathless valleys and a cool ravine where the black needles of the tall silver firs massed in whole mountains or sometimes mingled with the brighter green of oak and beech. A narrow path then led us down a cliff at which point the gentle stream soon revealed its secret nature as a roaring beast, rushing, and foaming, and hurling itself into a deep cleft, where it spun the high wheel of a mill. From here we followed steps cut in the living rock.

At the top we found the mill stretching itself across the plateau, a muddle of high-pitched deep-eaved roofs. The air was unseasonably damp here, and green and mouldy. On the shadowed fascias were visible many carvings, a clear evocation of the cuckoo clock and, in this sense, encouraging to the seeker.

'Sumpy,' the boy cried.

Although it was now early summer and therefore past the season for logs to be floated to the bigger rivers, we found abandoned fir trunks stacked untidily. In the deep shadow between mill and dwelling everything was sour and damp. Piles of old grey sawdust and freshly murdered logs sometimes blocked the path. Copper cables, like guy ropes, ran from the peak of the mill house to the surrounding earth at which point they were enclosed in wooden boxes. Not everyone, I realize, would be comforted by this unscientific mess, but to me it was further evidence that my thieves might be angels in disguise.

'Sumpy, Sumpy.' The boy's eyes were bright with expectation. I thought, how wise I had been to accept this new adventure. I felt like G. L. Sanderson:

> When life was all but over,
> so this silver seam began.

We opened a bright black door and, without so much as an elephant's foot or coat rack to prevent our immediate arrival at the heart of things, stepped inside a cavernous kitchen with a low ceiling and small deep windows. It was the middle of the afternoon but two candles and a lamp were already burning. Various pots steamed on

75

the stove and I detected the very welcome aroma of baking apples.

'Sumpy!'

At a large square table beneath a window, sat two men, one as small as a pixie and the other – well, it was, of course, the big thick-necked fellow from the hotel, he who espoused the romantic doctrine of the Karlsruhe wheel. That improbable creature, with his bumpy bald head gleaming in the candlelight, was the object of Carl's love. I adjusted. It was my character to do so.

Then off, hey, ho, and up the stairs, the pair of them, man and boy, in a great rush together, like chums reunited after hols.

No one had cared to introduce me to the delicate man in lederhosen, so I did the honours myself. I presumed him a clockmaker, and his high-pitched precise way of speaking was exactly what one might expect – one does not anticipate wonders to be made by men with gardener's hands. He said his name was Arnaud.

Henry, I thought, you have arrived at a place you could never have pictured. I began to mentally compose another letter to my son.

A balmy breeze flowed through the open shutters. One could hear the hissing of the apples, the persistent river, the unrelenting echoing conversation between Herr Sumper and the adoring child.

The coachman delivered my trunk somewhere or other. I tipped him and he set off. Frau Helga busied herself around the kitchen and I sat at table to play host to myself.

The small Huguenot – as he let himself be known – spoke an excellent English in which he informed me that a fierce and peculiar race of men lived in these mountains. If he thought to frighten me, he did not succeed. Fierce and peculiar was what the doctor ordered. For now, however, the air smelled of chaff and mellow pipe tobacco.

It was a good half hour before Herr Sumper and Carl descended the stairs, hand in hand, clearly happy to be reunited.

'Well, Herr Brandling,' said Herr Sumper finally, 'you and I have a spot of business to discuss.'

*Spot of business, spot of business.* How strange to find the cockney intonation pleasing. I asked the German why he spoke my mother tongue this way, and I do not doubt he answered me sincerely but he was already charging back up the stairs.

When I caught up with him he was striding along a windowless corridor. The floor inclined downwards like the murderous chute of the Brandling Railway Co.'s gravel crusher but if this was an omen I was very far from seeing it. At the lower end awaited my true destination, a sturdy pine door fastened with three quite different locks. Of course, of course, *it must be locked*. I would be the last to disagree.

With a fortune of one's own, I belatedly realized, a chap could travel into any realm he dreamed. How peculiar I never thought of this before. Here I was – inside the sanctus sanctorum, the vision made concrete, and every small detail of the workshop's physical existence, its concrete fact, stood at the service of Hippocrates. I saw machines, of course, as I had dreamed, but I had never had the wit to anticipate that the workshop might somehow hang above a wild chasm whose stream would provide the engines' motive force. Everything was exceptionally clean and ordered, a number of shining lathes, for instance, one quite large, the others of the size traditionally used by clockmakers. The smallest lathe had a canvas belt attached to a spinning cylinder and this, in turn, was connected by a wider belt to the spring-wheel of the sawmill.

To my ear, we were behind a waterfall, against a rock.

I called out to say that Vaucanson had invented a lathe almost identical to this pygmy version.

Herr Sumper glared at me.

I thought, my goodness, do not offend him now.

Then, in an instant, as if his own drive belt had slipped onto a faster wheel, he was grinning and gesturing at the wall behind my back.

'This is the only Vaucanson we need.'

And, you have guessed already – here were the Two Friends' plans, tacked onto the wall.

In the roar of water I heard the voices of my father and brother, in chorus, shouting that I must not give family money to this rogue.

But I was not their creature. And when Herr Sumper showed me exactly how much he would require for materials, I was so far removed from

Low Hall that I praised the thoroughness of a shopping list I could not read. Confused and jubilant in the roar of water, I paid him every Gulden and Vereinsthaler he required.

With each coin I placed inside his deeply lined palm I was closer to the object that the supercilious Masini had called the 'clockwork Grail'. So let it be a grail. I emptied my purse. And it was triumph I felt as I strode back up the sloping chute, thence to a half-way landing where I was to make my bed. With what joy I entered my lodging, so SPARTAN, so much superior to my own home which had been redecorated by the youngest daughter of a family of brewers. God forgive me, that is an ugly unworthy way to think. It is enough to say that henceforth I would require no oils, no pastels, no Turkey rug, no artistic clutter, no dresser, no cupboard, no commode, only this extraordinary fretwork bed and a series of ten black wooden pegs – I counted – driven in a line across one wall.

I swung open the shutters and what a violent shock it was after the gloomy green light of the kitchen – the azure sky, the dry goat paths like chalk lines through the landscape, the bluish granite which contained the stream, the harvesters still swinging sweetly on their scythes as if it required no effort in the world.

I asked my clockmaker, 'When will it be done?'

But he had already vanished. I descended the stair with some happy trepidation, grasping the rail in order not to fall.

More candles had been lit and the males were at table, the boy's hair filled with golden flame.

'Are you hungry, Herr Brandling?' Sumper asked.

'Make no fuss on my account,' I said.

Frau Helga, however, was stoking the firebox with crackling yellow wood. Her face was very red.

Herr Sumper's countenance, in contrast, was cool. He nodded that I should be seated next to him.

'How long will it take?' I asked.

He placed his considerable hand upon my own as if that sign could be an answer.

I told him: 'In England we would say, time is of the essence.'

'You are, as they also say in England, "in good hands".'

'Indeed, but surely you have some idea how long those hands will take to do their job.'

'I have a very definite idea,' he said, accepting a dripping green wine bottle from the child. He boxed the boy gently across the head and the latter squeaked happily and ducked away. 'I have a very definite idea that you will achieve your heart's desire.'

'Vaucanson's duck.'

'Your heart's desire,' he said.

He was slippery, of course. I watched as he shared the wine, giving the boy a thimbleful before emptying a good half bottle into his stein.

'And what is my heart's desire?'

'Why, the same as mine,' he said and poured for me.

'*Spargelzeit*,' said he.

'*Spargelzeit*,' I said, and raised my glass.

'In English,' said the precise little Arnaud, who had been left to fill his own glass, 'you might translate *Spargel* as *edible ivory*.'

'*Königsgemüse*,' said the musical boy, and happily suffered being squashed against the clockmaker's massive chest.

'It is the King's vegetable,' announced Frau Helga placing in front of me a plate of white asparagus and small unpeeled potatoes.

So *Spargelzeit* was not a toast. Far from it – a curse – I cannot swallow egg whites, liver, brains, cod, eel, anything soft and slimy. If they had given me a plate of maggots it would have been the same.

My companions at Furtwangen were hogging in, sighing and making very personal noises. Frau Helga, in particular, was so emotionally affected by this spectral *Spargel* that she made me quite embarrassed.

I selected a small unskinned potato and scraped the sauce away.

'Eat up,' instructed Herr Sumper, picking up the long white vegetable, the secret organ of a ghost which he sucked into the maw beneath the bush of upper lip. 'We have yet to agree on what you will pay for board. But at this meal you are our honoured guest.'

The potato tasted of wet jute. The asparagus lay before me naked. I cut its tip off and washed it down with wine.

Sumper narrowed his eyes.

'You like it?'

'Immensely.'

He considered me closely.

'You don't know how to taste it,' said Herr Sumper, 'I can read your thoughts.'

I did not comment. He winked at the boy, who squealed with laughter. I was not sorry when Frau Helga slapped his leg. I thrust my plate away from me.

'The more for us,' he said, dividing my meal between the other diners. When the gluttons had eaten my meal, Sumper wiped his mouth and spoke to Carl behind the napkin.

Immediately the boy sprang from his chair and up the stairs. To work, I thought. I put aside my pride and followed him.

There is nothing better to soothe the stomach acids than the company of an artisan when he is at his careful labour. When my wife's first 'portrait' had commenced, I would often walk into the village to the workshop of my widowed friend George Binns, whose father had been the clockmaker to Her Majesty the Queen. There amidst all the quiet ticking I found some peace. So I expected it would be in Furtwangen. The child slipped through the workshop door but a large hand restrained my shoulder.

'You are the patron,' said Herr Sumper, dancing me around then blocking my path through his doorway. 'I am the artist.'

Well, of course this was preposterous. He was not an artist, he was a clockmaker. I had already endured a surfeit of *Artist* in the place from which I had been sent away. I thought, you damned rascal. It would serve you right if I was sick all over you.

'I cannot work with you at my shoulder.'

So I must eat insults too.

'I wish to assist,' I said.

'Yes,' he said. 'I have brought you this.'

He placed in my hand the sort of ruined book you find in barrow carts, its pages freckled brown, its boards bowed.

'It is *The Life of Benvenuto Cellini*. In English. This book will teach you how artists suffer from their patrons and will instruct you on how to play the important role you have chosen for yourself. By the time you have read it, I will be able to tell you when the work will be complete.'

Thus did I abase myself to achieve my end and I, Henry Brandling, not only permitted a foreign tradesman to pretend he was an artist, but allowed myself to be sent to bed without a decent meal.


3


No sleep, my mind a carousel of memory. For instance: the night before my departure from home I informed Percy that I might not return until Christmas. 'How lovely, Papa,' he said. 'What a Christmas we will have.'

Round and round I saw it once again, our conversation then, the following morning when I bade my brave red-eyed boy goodbye. I should never have mentioned Christmas. I had been too whimsical. But I could not say to him: your True Friend's heart is bursting. I did not know the terms wherein I might be permitted to return.

'Goodbye, silly Papa,' he had said.

I thought, who told you that? I kissed him twice. I could not be certain I would see him in this world again.

In Furtwangen my allotted room was filled with the roar of water, endless torrent, the drowned squealing of a silly turning wheel.

Hour after horrid hour I thought of the nights when his mother and I were first married, till death us do part, I never doubted it, round and round, and how she shuddered beneath my human weight. Hard heavy man, she called me recklessly, round and round.

I was a god for really quite a while. Only at the end did she say that cruel thing about my breasts. I had been foolish enough to think aloud, wondering could it be that wet nurse who sickened first our girl and then our little boy.

'So you blame me,' she hissed. 'How dare you.'

'No,' I cried, 'a thousand times no.'

I was the one with the breasts, she told me. I

should have been the mother, which I clearly wished to be. My breasts were disgusting and hairy like a dog. How could I continue to be alive? she wished to know.

Only in the heat of battle did I blame her for her famous breasts, those false promises which would never touch her Percy's hungry mouth.

In Furtwangen I slept while imagining myself awake. I woke inside a realm of gold, dawn, floor, an effect of light. In truth, the dawn in Furtwangen was so much less a wonder than my True Friend's own white room in Low Hall where the plain and decent Irish nurse would presently arrive with a cup of beef tea. Then they would sit together and wait for dear George Binns to bring the mail in through the garden gate.

Oh dear, I was hungry as a tank of acid, but Percy must know exactly where I was. I found my pencil and wrote my letter in the form of directions to my present home. If he followed these instructions he would find Furtwangen on a map and then he would know exactly where the duck was being made, for him alone. No other child in England would own such a thing, no child in all the world. I promised I would describe the manufacture in its fullest detail so he would imagine he was at my side, or perched up in the rafters like a clever bird, looking down on the miracles performed.

Then, I addressed the envelope to dear old Binns. With no inn-keeper to entrust my letter to,

I must now discover how the Germans sent their mail.

My first day in Furtwangen began.

No chamber pot, so it was Adam's Duty, after which I washed in the stream and was observed by a surly sawmill worker. I might have tipped a peasant to post my letter but no, not him.

There was nothing for breakfast but some small bitter strawberries which made the hunger worse. No life was evident except the Huguenot writing by a window.

I asked him when was breakfast served.

'Sir,' said he, 'one becomes accustomed to it.'

He continued with his scribbling.

'You wonder what I am doing?' he said.

I had not.

'I am a fairytale collector,' he said.

How extraordinary, I thought, I have met a fairytale collector. Whatever will happen next?

I set off to find the village of Furtwangen where I was intent on posting my letter. Awful morning. No need to describe my humiliations. Foreigners not liked, obviously. A boy threw a stone at me. Not even the priest would understand what I needed with my urgent envelope and by the time I had been forced to stand aside to permit the locals right of way, had tramped along a rutted road and then a highway, I was completely lost. It took me all afternoon to find the sawmill by which time I was suffering the most painful bilious hunger. My stomach was tight as a drum, filled with sloshing river water.

It was late afternoon, nothing but a boiling kettle on the stove. I would not steal food. I would endure, but what of Percy? How long can a small boy wait?

Carl came to fetch me in due course. He held my sleeve, which small show of kindness I was grateful for. The dinner was the same as the previous night. What I would have given for all the old boarding-school favourites I once reviled – toad-in-the-hole, stewed beetroot, fried bread, frog's spawn. I was so hungry now I could have swallowed maggots and asked for more. My hosts looked down at their plates, and I knew they were embarrassed by my manners, but I was in a rage. I turned my eyes upon them one by one and dared them return my gaze.

Finally they retired and when Sumper retired from the field, I scraped his plate, the last skerrick of cheese sauce as well.

Then I stepped out into the dark, my guts in agony.

I lay on the damp path and listened to my hosts – grotesque moustached hens setting each other off, exploding bass and treble, sighing. Sometimes I woke and heard them laughing, and then I understood I had been snoring.

The stars were out. Beneath the icy constellations, I was damp with dew, too shy to walk through the kitchen to my bed.

They spoke excellent English except when singing and composing lists which was a passion it would seem. What lists these were I could not know. Men's names, or perhaps villages or landmarks which would assist in finding where an individual lived, or so I guessed. The so-called fairytale collector's thin voice remained dominant. Why this was, I could not imagine, unless he was like those tramps who knew the names of farmers, which one is a 'soft touch' etc. On and on they went. When not lists, then folk songs. When no songs, then crickets.

'For God's sake, you will die.'

Sumper helped me to my feet, and led me to the kitchen. Here he sat me at table and watched me as if he was my mother. Frau Helga served me a sort of porridge. Sumper remained watching while I ate it.

'What are you up to, Herr Brandling?'

'It is urgent that I send a letter to my son.'

'Tomorrow,' he said, having no notion of the life at stake.

In the mornings, from my bedroom window, I observed how strange bright-eyed Carl went trotting off, hopping along the goat path, waving to the harvesters, returning in an hour or two with a package or a basket or no more than a bulge in his pocket, which mystery would be delivered up the stairs, across the chute, knock knock, and greeted with exclamation either of triumph or reproof.

He had the most extraordinary hands, Carl, so

long and thin you might think he needed another set of knuckles. Sumper treasured this boy. He called him Genius and Spirit and other extravagant expressions that led me to believe that it was with those unworldly hands that Percy's machine was being constructed.

Without looking up from her darning needle Helga said: 'Show him our new post box, M. Arnaud.'

'Directly,' Arnaud replied, but then he wandered off. I was still in that same room at supper when he finally returned.

After the remains of the meal had been cleared away, I announced that I would leave to find the post box by myself.

The fairytale collector leapt to his feet.

'Do you have your letters ready, Herr Brandling?'

I saw that the wretch was now dressed 'for town', with waistcoat and breeches of dark green velveteen, stout boots, and a broad leather belt which he now took in a notch around his narrow waist.

'I do not have stamps,' I said.

'We have stamps in beautiful colours,' said the fairytale collector. 'It is for England that they are required. Two letters I think?'

You have known this all day, I thought. Soon it will be dark.

'We will need a lantern.'

'No need.'

'There will be a moon?'

'I have the eyes of a cat,' the queer man said.

And we descended into the spray and chaos of the gorge.

When, minutes later, we emerged, the world was alight with golden straw. One could hear the birds again, the light clink of the chain that tethered three dwarf goats beside the stream.

'My mother was a cat,' said the fairytale collector, as if he had made the most common observation.

I made no riposte but in truth I have a horror of fairy stories not because I believe them but because I cannot stop myself imagining the evil stepmother, say, being forced to dance inside her red-hot iron shoes. What cruelties we humans practise every day.

The village turned out to be very near. I deposited Percy's letters in an iron box with golden tassels like a General. Then we turned the corner of a lane and I beheld the quaint houses pressed together, the pointed roofs with their projecting eaves, the wooden staircases, and, drenched in the last rays of the setting sun, a glorious yellow inn, now glowing golden.

'The inn is not too far, Herr Brandling,' he said shyly, and I finally understood why he had made me wait all day.

4

The collector of ancient cruelties was a mere smidgen, a tiny creature, with a mass of curling salt-and-pepper hair. At the sawmill he had not

90

seemed any more eccentric than anybody else, but at this village inn he cut a most unusual figure, soft-skinned, half man, half child, with his head in perfect proportion to the whole.

At the sawmill he had been completely at his ease. At the inn he was as nervous as a bird, its heart always pattering as if everything, even a single grain of wheat, might pose a mortal risk. Perhaps he saw the possibility of violence in the schnapps bottles, or perhaps it was his Protestant bones in a Catholic atmosphere, or the excessive smoke, or the fearsome physiognomies – Jews and Germans playing cards, arguing, in too many languages to count.

The mistress of the inn, a stout bustling little missus like you see in the old engravings, greeted M. Arnaud very fondly, found him a table, and brought us cheese and small beer before we had a chance to ask. I said how very nice she was.

Arnaud leaned close toward my ear.

What did I know of Herr Sumper? Why had I brought my plans to him? Why had I not commissioned a Karlsruhe clockmaker where the sort of work I wished could have been more surely done?

I thought, whoa Dobbin. I did not need my confidence undone.

I asked him how he came into Sumper's circle.

He spilled some volatile oils onto a handkerchief and dabbed at his cartilaginous nose. In the candlelight his nostrils seemed alight with blood.

Why, he demanded, had I not asked Sumper for letters of reference?

I was perhaps naïve but I saw where the road was heading: he was saying that I had made myself the quarry of a gang of criminals. He would rescue me, for a price.

As he spoke, he leaned forward, but looked down in the manner of a hen who spied a likely worm.

Had I not been troubled to learn how Herr Sumper had fled the village years before?

He did not look at me. He sipped his beer fastidiously. He said he had not taken me to be the reckless type.

I assured him I was not.

Just the same, he said, as if excusing me: Herr Sumper was a big man. People were frightened to say a word against him. It was very, very hard to find the truth.

He darted a glance across his shoulder as if he was in danger of being victimized whereas, in fact, his sole purpose was – surely – to have me as his prey.

Was HE not frightened?

Oh no. Fairytale collectors were accustomed to the most dangerous situations. It was these violent types, here, in the inn, who were frightened of Sumper. On the clockmaker's return from England he had been 'opinionated'. He had claimed to be 'better qualified' which astonished those who had not previously imagined that a man would be 'qualified' to be a clockmaker, no more than ride a donkey or void their bowels.

A less brutal man would not have survived, but Herr Sumper was Herr Sumper. He never went to a dance without first stuffing into his long pockets a dozen of the heavy iron axes – *speidel* they are called – used for splitting wood, and so even the notorious quarry men kept out of his way. Sumper's greatest happiness was to dance for twenty-four hours without stopping, or rather to stop only so long as there were pauses between the dances. During these opportunities he drank unceasingly, quart after quart of wine.

In order to know what he had to pay, he tore off a button each time, first off his red waistcoat, and then off his coat, and redeemed them at the end of the evening from the landlord.

As this was the man I had commissioned to save my Percy, I did not wish to hear that the site of the old sawmill was the most 'backward' part of the district. The fairytale collector perhaps sensed this for now he said there could be no more perfect place to perform advanced work in secret. It was already believed that Sumper had used his isolation to hide his secret trade in blasphemous cuckoo clocks.

This did not comfort me at all. I asked him what such a thing would look like.

M. Arnaud could not guess. But it would be, he said, totally consistent with the clockmaker's irreligious nature. As for his technical abilities – whenever Sumper's conversations touched on matters with which Arnaud was well acquainted – metallurgy for instance – he had found Sumper to be in no sense primitive. Indeed the opposite.

Was he as 'advanced' as he boasted?

Arnaud did not answer me.

Instead he told me that Sumper's old father had been as ignorant as any saw miller and was as violent as his son. His chief pleasure consisted in rolling up into balls the tin plates used at dinner at different inns.

On the most notorious occasion, he ordered the younger Sumper not to go dancing at a wedding but to attend to the business of the sawmill instead. I would have noticed, at the mill, the logs had not been floated, but that was only because Sumper had now let the mill to Kropotkinists and they could not agree on anything. Those logs should have been sent floating down the river weeks before my arrival. They would then have constituted rafts one hundred yards long – nine logs wide at the stern, three logs wide at the bow. It was in order to supervise the construction of such a raft that the father had sent Heinrich Sumper home from the wedding.

This was when the son decided to 'step aboard' as the saying was. As far as anyone could gather young Sumper never said goodbye to his father or mother, and rather than guiding the raft to any customary destination, he (according to the police report) rode it down into the Rhine (which was, I soon realized, geographically impossible). He stepped ashore somewhere, with what money no one knew, and somehow made his way to England, which is where he claimed to have received his exalted education.

It was still not forgotten that logs had been stolen and his parents were left the poorer. Perhaps he repaid them with his English gold, but who can say? Later a letter from London was seen at the post office. Naturally this could not be opened by anyone but his parents, and when they both died ten years later the lawyer could not find a letter, only a will which had never been amended.

Thus the unfilial son inherited the sawmill.

During our conversation Arnaud continually ordered whatever dish he liked. He cut white cheese into exceedingly thin slices and I watched him nip them with his small ratcatcher's teeth.

Arnaud said that no one was in a better position than himself to help me. He intimated that he was far more powerful than he might appear.

So, I thought, as he ordered one more small beer, he is a spy for some Baron perhaps. He began to whisper about Frau Helga. Well, let him gossip if he wished, although I told him frankly that the woman was of no importance in my life. But yes, it was Frau Helga's foolish husband, M. Arnaud revealed, who had taken little Carl to witness the 'victory' of the workers in their so-called revolution. Thus he was shot dead before her very eyes and the bullet, before penetrating the husband's heart, severely injured the baby's leg.

Being a member of that cruel race of fairytale

collectors, he was very pleased by this disaster. He pursed his lips. He sliced his cheese. I was so angry that I could not pay attention to the story until the mother and orphan came to Furtwangen where she had an uncle who had once been kind to her. Unfortunately, the fairytale collector said, on the day before her arrival, the uncle dropped dead in the middle of the town square.

Unfortunately? I thought. But is this not *exactly* the type of nastiness valued by your guild? The child is orphaned. The child dies. The child is lost in the forest. The child walks with a limp forever.

Small men are the cruellest. He told me how Helga had been given shelter by the priest, and I thought, good heavens, thank the Lord at least for that, but of course the priest then threw her out.

I thought, you are a miserable little dung beetle, forever collecting the misery of the poor.

Then or soon thereafter I thought, to hell with you. Do not presume that I will pay the bill. I walked out of the inn and of course I went out the wrong door and then had no idea where I was. Lost again, lost always. Great buffoon. The little fellow found me and led me home, his mother was a cat. What will happen when we die? Who will ever tell the truth?

# HENRY & CATHERINE

I was a rich man, Henry Brandling wrote and Catherine read, and therefore attracted the usual pests. And yet my past and present fears and agonies were nothing in comparison to those suffered by this poor German woman.

Catherine understood that Henry was referring to Frau Helga.

She and I, wrote Henry Brandling in 1854, both knew how a child could sing to your soul and twist your veins and fill you with continual dread and trepidation. I had seen her lay her hand upon Carl's shoulder, cup her hand around his golden head. This was something M. Arnaud could not know.

What conceit, thought Catherine Gehrig, in London, 157 years later, off her face with rage and cognac. How truly pathetic, his pompous discrimination: the love for a child is better than the love for an adult. How could it be?

The poor dull blind posh fool had never guessed his reader would be a woman with no children. Please don't tell me that I don't know love, or that the love I know is of a minor kind. I am eviscerated by love.

I threw the book across the room. It flew into the kitchen, its acid paper pages shattering like dead leaves.

Let Matthew see what he has done to me.

After the catastrophe with the book, the only undamaged paper was a receipt in which Sumper was titled *Monsieur* Sumper. It recorded the purchase of a large amount of silver.

It was intolerable that these crooks should rob Henry in this way, but also it was offensive, if understandable, for Henry to go on with this nonsense about children. He did not *quite* say that parental love was superior to other loves, but it was clearly his assumption. Of course I wished him no unhappiness. I pitied him. But it is true, in general, that these child lovers make themselves deaf and blind to the likely conclusion of these relationships which so often end in heroin, suicides, boredom or estrangement. All those awful fights are waiting for them, when all the poor dears wanted was a perfect love.

When I saw men Matthew's age and older, I hated them for being alive. Yet I had never expected we would live forever, the opposite. Each morning I was given Matthew I held him, contained him like a prayer, filled my lungs with him, his leg between my legs so I brushed him – what other word to use? – to be clearer would be vulgar – brushed him ever so gently and he would rest his nose just by my eye, just there, adjacent those intensely complicated factories, the tear glands, I love you, I love you, I love you every morning, every night.

I had seen my father die. When you have spent days in intensive care you do not easily forget how the body works and how it fails. Afterwards you easily imagine the oxygen-rich blood, the colour of the fluids which swim all around you, inside me, inside him. I had seen Matthew's eyes narrow in passion, the beloved face, the tall rough tender body, the hard silkiness of him, I would have drunk him dry.

We both were conceited about our ecstatic pragmatism. We had no souls but we were *in the moment,* like an ocean wave, like animals we would have said, how perfect we were, we thought, glowing with our love. How unfair we had no souls.

Near Beccles, in the summer, with the silver early light playing off the insulation foil, he would want me from behind and then he would cup his hands around my stomach and I would think, he wants me to be pregnant.

He had his own children all safely tucked in boarding schools where he could write them love letters. Sometimes I lost weekends, when he brought them up to the stables to work with him, two precious days excised from my life. I loved him for how he loved them, but sometimes I would think they were spoiled brats. When the mathematical son complained he was bored by Beccles I was indignant, but very, very happy I could have my place again.

Perhaps, I thought, Matthew's love for his sons was a superior love, sometimes. But there is no end to what I thought. For instance, I had dreams there was a woman's body buried underneath the floor of the stables. In my dream I had murdered her and then forgotten.

I should never have thrown Henry Brandling's notebook across the room. No one, not Matthew, particularly not Matthew, would believe me capable of it. No one would believe any conservator in any situation would ever do such a thing. It launched into the air, fluttering, beyond the reach of technical salvation, breaking apart even as it flew. It died in mid-air and when it hit the floor it became like the wings of so many moths and I cried, knowing what I had done, not as a conservator, but as a poor drunk woman in a rage with a decent man.

I found the vodka where I had hidden it from myself. It was probably after midnight, I thought. I wished I had cocaine. I would have liked to half destroy myself with rot and pleasure and as I drank the vodka I thought Herr Brandling has not bothered to explain the copper cables and I may never get to the end of them. But then I thought, Henry you are thick as a brick. Really, what an extraordinary man to come to a sawmill in the Black Forest and to describe COPPER CABLES like tent ropes, going from the roof into BOXES on the earth and not once (not so far) had he asked a soul what these cables were for.

I remember you, my Matty T. I remember making love with you. I remember your grey eyes, slitted at first then opening so wide, and the pink lovely tunnel of your mouth. You had not one single filling. My mouth was filled with black amalgam. I remember your cries pulsing inside my body. I remember you held me on the station at Waterloo while I sobbed and shouted. I remember you made me still and calm. I remember you left me in the taxi and I thought that I would die.

I forget you are dead. I forget Henry Brandling is dead. I sweep up his crumbling ashes in the clever little Oxo pan. I thought it so beautifully designed. What a banal life I have lived, being happy about a dust pan, never knowing that I would use it to sweep up Henry Brandling's bones and ashes and dump them in the bin.

2

Here is all that remains of Frau Helga's history as relayed to Henry Brandling, as arranged on my kitchen table in north Lambeth in April 2010.

Frau Helga had not been working at the inn two days when the priest (said) she could not stay under his roof any longer be(cause) she was a barmaid. But if the priest had any memory he would know he had not behaved exactly as he should. Accidentally she had scratched his face.

The mistress . . . let her sleep in the kitchen of

the inn. The other barmaid was a divorced woman who had run away because her husband . . .

The other barmaid suggested to Frau Helga that they should live together at Sumper's Mill which was abandoned.

The mill . . . wind blew all manner of machinery clanked . . . groaned . . . the other barmaid returned to her husband . . . alone . . . someone dragging furniture around the floor . . . Helga's baby sleeping . . . an iron poker and go down the stairs . . . a man . . . dancing . . . falling down drunk.

She stayed hidden in shadow . . . she would have to kill him . . . throw the body in the river . . .

Give me the poker, the stranger said to her. Then he took the solid iron poker and bent it across his knee like a celery stick. He bent the iron bar and his face was red and he showed his big teeth in the middle of his beard. Do not be afraid he said.

That was all I, Catherine, could retrieve. I fell asleep at the table, awoken by a knocking on the door. I thought, Matthew. It's how he came, not often, sometimes. I was terrified, stock-still and sweaty, mouth dust-dry, throat adhering. The blinds and window were open to the garden so anyone could see.

Then he – whoever – was in the area going through my recycling. I heard bottles clinking and was actually, incredibly, ashamed. I crawled on my knees into my bedroom and left the kitchen lights ablaze.

My sick leave was a horror. In the morning I knew I could not use it. I ate dry toast to cushion the painkillers and, having left the shameful jigsaw on the kitchen table, got myself to the tube where the claustrophobia tried to crawl back in. I thought, I cannot do this job. I thought, I have no choice.

At Security my physical destruction provoked bonhomie. I thought nothing but a shot of vodka is going to make me plausible.

I shared the lift with the tiny sporty lesbian from Ceramics – Heather, I think. She was so bright and filled with life. She had bicycled to work and I could see it took everything to stop her running on the spot.

'Bit rough?' she asked me.

I thought, she has such lovely perfect skin. She has no idea she is going to die.

'Did you fly through the volcano?'

If I had seen a newspaper I might have known there had been a vast eruption in Iceland, that the airlines of the world were grounded, but I did not need to read the *Guardian* to get the joke. She meant I was hungover. I had been slaughtered, legless, trolleyed, slashed, shedded, plastered, polluted, pissed. I thought, I do love my country's relationship with alcohol. How would I ever exist in the United States? I suppose I would have grief counselling instead.

My ID card had no idea of my chemical condition. It opened two high-security doors as if I were completely sane and sober. My own studio, of course, was quite unlocked, unlockable.

I thought I will feel like this forever.

It was just on nine o'clock when I donned my rubber gloves and examined the first of the glass rods which it was absolutely not my job to clean.

There must be a procedures meeting before conservation or restoration could begin.

But I could not bear to talk to anyone.

I laid the glass rod on the bench and considered it awhile. These rods, also mentioned on the invoice to Herr Sumper, would simulate water. Then the duck would place its fake anus on a bed of these rotating rods, eating fish and shitting, or counterfeiting life in whatever way the bullying clockmaker had devised. Somewhere there must be a reflective plate to fit beneath the rods and this would help produce the general effect of water.

Perhaps it would be little Heather's job to deal with the glass rods, but I really did not wish to talk to little Heather. Nor did I wish to dig deeper into the boxes and find God knows, perhaps the embalmed body of Percy Brandling with its jaw broken so it could appear 'at peace'.

Heather should be grateful that I would wish to remove all the grease and oil that had seeped into the hollow centres of the rods. They would be a nightmare to clean, but I would happily do it for her. I would use thin brass rods with cotton-wool buds attached. And if the Swinburne procedures could, in all their Victorian wisdom, just cede me this, my pain might stop intensifying.

Before the glass cleaning began I would have to remove the brass collet at the end of each rod. The collet would fit into some as yet unseen mechanism which would rotate the rods. Successive generations of awful pragmatics had visited the site before me, depositing shellac, plaster of Paris, silicon and each of these inappropriate substances would now require ingenuity, time and patience to remove.

Please let this be mine, I thought.

Please do not be sticklers.

I can do this job in solitude, until I am completely cured, or dead myself.

On this first glass rod someone had used black pitch much as amateurs nowadays use superglue – that is, they had slathered it on the glass then jammed it into the collet and held it while it set. The glass had been damaged by thermal shock. Because of these difficulties, the repaired rods would finally differ slightly from their original length – only a few millimetres' difference is enough to make reinstalling them a tricky job.

I opened my email account. I read: RE PROCEDURE MEETING.

Delete.

I remained on my swivel chair and looked at the glass rod waiting for ten o'clock when I knew the offy would be open and I could buy a flask of vodka.

I was not worried about the drinking or the stolen notebooks, for both of which I could lose my job. Instead I fretted over a misdemeanour – I had decided to start work without a procedures meeting.

That is, I would make no request to the Head of Section. Instead I'd go to Glenn the Building Supervisor who would innocently give me welding rods and cotton tips.

I found Glenn in his lair and while he was 'locating' the welding rods and the cotton tips I went to the offy where I heard that London was the driest capital city in the world. We were to have a desalination plant, it seemed. I expressed amazement. I slipped the bottle in my lovely bag and returned through Security.

By ten past ten I was examining all the dusty glass rods on my workbench. Surely my present dentist had first seen my mouth exactly in this way – the work of fifteen different mediocre technicians over the course of twenty years. I felt the vodka roar down my throat and heat my blood.

I thought, this was how my father felt, each day. This is why they packed me off to boarding school in High Wycombe. When he died we discovered the most ingenious little hiding places for his bottles, carefully crafted little coffins he had constructed when he was allegedly 'fixing the wiring' under the floor, or in the ceiling, or the wall inside a storage cupboard. He was such a fastidious, patient man who did not deserve to be changing watch batteries and straps and I would have done anything to have him take my museum job, to use his unwearied enquiring mind to understand a mechanism. I must have tortured him by living the life he would have wanted for himself.

Sometimes he would go to talks at the Guildhall and drag home the lecturer to dinner – what a sad lonely soul he must have been. It would take so long for me to know that I, his daughter, was the Oedipal son.

The white spirits worked rather well on the pitch, and I was gently separating the brass collet from the first rod when Eric Croft entered.

I looked straight into his bloodshot eyes.

'For Christ's sake, Catherine, please. Go home.'

'Opening my present, like you said.'

Did I slur? He was staring at me rather hard. 'If you want to work, there has to be a bloody procedures meeting. What on earth are you trying to do to me?'

'My bronchitis is much better.'

'Catherine, old love, we both know you cannot do this without a meeting.'

There was another knock and the little lesbian opened the door with her elbow and entered, a coffee cup in each hand. Part of me was touched, the rest of me quite horrified.

'Sorry,' she said, but her eyes were on the glass rods and the solvents on my desk. I was in her territory without approval. She spilled her coffee in her rush to get away.

107

'OK,' I said, and reached to fetch the rod and place it back.

I am not exactly sure what happened next except that Crofty tried to prevent me dealing with the rod and as a result it slipped from my grip and hit the tiled floor vertically. It bounced. I saw it rise six inches and then I caught it in my hand.

We neither of us spoke.

I laid the rod inside the crate and slipped the collet into a plastic pouch and wrote 'Collet #1' with a steady hand.

Eric picked up my handbag and gave it to me.

'Come on,' he said. 'I'm going to take you home.'

I thought, Henry Brandling is in broken pieces. Eric must not see.

## 3

Crofty sprinted up the road to catch the cab and fetched it back, reverse gear whining. 'Kennington Road,' he ordered.

I thought, you nosey parker, but he didn't know the number so that was OK.

'Eric, were you a bit of an athlete?'

'In the service,' he said, and blushed.

'You weren't really a sailor?'

He slapped at his wrist and held out, between thumb and forefinger, a dead mosquito.

'Asian tiger,' he said.

'What?'

'Asian tiger mosquito?'

'I have no idea what you are talking about.'

'I thought you always read the *Guardian*?'

'I can't read anything,' I said which made me think again of Henry Brandling and the fact that I could not possibly let Eric see what I had inside my house. Of course, when we arrived at my door I was completely useless in my own defence.

'Eric. You must wait a moment.'

But he was already picking up my mail.

Amongst all the junk and Waitrose fliers there was a good-sized envelope which I snatched from him.

'Wait,' I said. 'Stay here. Look at the books. Let me tidy up. Please.'

In the kitchen I set to shoving the bits of Brandling's fractured exercise book inside the envelope. Dead dry fragments spun and spiralled to the floor.

'What on earth are you up to in there?'

Naturally he had come to spy on me. Fortunately my Mr Upstairs was practising chip shots in the garden, and Crafty's social antennae were always sensitive.

'That's whatshisface.'

'Indeed.' I removed the cognac bottle from the table and slipped it beneath the sink.

'The Speaker of the House of Commons?'

'Retired,' I said and turned to see that, far from being distracted by the Great Man, Eric Croft had, without permission, opened my handbag and removed my vodka flask and stolen notebooks.

No word was said. No facial expression suggested anything. He gave me the notebooks without comment and I carried them into my bedroom. I returned to discover he had opened all the windows and was settled at my kitchen table, my gutted handbag abandoned on the chair beside him.

'You are very wilful, Catherine.'

'A little mad, sorry.'

'For God's sake, don't hover.' He slid the glass across the table. 'Sit.'

I drank the vodka standing up.

'Poor Cat.'

I wished he would not call me Cat. I said: 'I will not see a grief counsellor if that is what you're thinking.' The vodka had a fierce hard solvent burn.

'Where did you ever hear of such a horrid thing?'

'Never mind.'

'The thing is, you see, we must placate the edifice.'

He meant the Swinburne, the great mechanical beast inside its Georgian cube on Lowndes Square, the wires, the trustees, the rules, the stairs, the secrets, Crowley's Hole where someone hanged themselves, the entire jerry-built mandarin complex of rat runs which is a two-hundred-year-old building in twenty-first-century space. It was a very beautiful, quite astonishing, chaotic, awful thing. I fitted there as I would fit nowhere else on earth.

'I have no choice,' I said. 'Where else could I ever be employable?'

'No,' he said, helping himself to another shot. 'I have made this much harder on you than I intended. This project is upsetting. Life, death, all that sort of thing. Cat, I am very sorry.'

'Please don't call me Cat.'

'Is that not your name?'

'There is only one person called me Cat.'

He lowered his lids. Perhaps he was simply holding his temper but he looked, suddenly, unexpectedly like a dreaming Buddha.

I sat, and received a second glass as my reward for my obedience. 'I'm sorry,' he said.

'It's just unthinkable that this is happening to people every day.'

'It's awful.'

'It's banal I suppose.'

'I will take the bloody thing away. I am a complete fool.'

'No,' I said.

'No?'

'No.'

'Very well,' said Eric.

'Don't say "very well". It sounds like you are managing me.'

'Actually, old love, that is my job.'

'That's what I mean. You're going to send me to a shrink.'

'Jesus, Cat, I am not going to send you to an anything. Where did you get this nonsense from?'

'When my father died they made us have grief

counselling. They would not let us out of the hospital without seeing this cretin from Social Services. They would not give us his clothes even.' I was crying now. I wished I wasn't. 'They tortured him, Eric. They played with him. We had to make them turn off their idiot machines.'

'Cat.'

'Please don't.'

'Catherine,' he said. 'I am sorry. He always called you Cat. To me.'

I immediately felt so sad I could hardly speak. 'Did he?'

'To me, yes.'

I was so determined not to bawl, I suppose I glared at him.

'We are going to have a very small team,' he said, 'we will have a procedures meeting you can tolerate.'

I had begun to snivel, but I did grasp what he was up to – finding a way for me to continue in employment.

'Ceramics are all Margaret's friends. I can't bear it.'

'Hilary isn't.'

'Heather. The little lesbian.'

'She has a perfectly lovely little baby.'

'Spilled her coffee, that one?'

'Will she be acceptable? Catherine, you really must have mercy on me. Please.'

But I wished to punish him. I could not tolerate him being alive.

'We all miss him, old love. Not like you do. But he was my friend for thirty years.'

'Yes, I know. He loved you. I'm sorry.'

'No, no. Forgive me.'

Sorry, sorry, sorry – how British we were. I thought he was fetching a handkerchief from his pocket, but then I saw it was a small glassine bag filled with white powder.

Of course I was an adult. I knew exactly what it was, but it was giving me an unsafe feeling to watch him tap it up and down. 'What's that?'

'Painkiller.' He spilled a small pile onto the table top, slightly yellow and rather crystalline.

I don't know him at all, I thought, not really the tiniest bit.

'That was rather risky wasn't it?' I said.

'Compared to what?' He produced his wallet and found a Barclaycard with which to chop the powder fine. I thought, he means compared to stealing notebooks.

'Jesus, Eric. Stop it.'

But he had no intention of stopping anything. 'You know, Catherine,' he said, and he was once again the dreaming Buddha but busy with his chop, chop, chop. 'You know when himself wanted a little toot, he would never talk to a dealer.' He smiled directly at me. 'No one would ever think of Matthew as a nervous chap, but he was very antsy about drug dealers.'

'You were our drug pimp?'

'Let's say, every time you had a recreational

experience, someone else took care of the low-life aspects.'

He set aside a very small amount of powder, what is called a 'bump' by those who know. I thought, I'll say 'no' of course. He took a ten-pound note from his wallet, rolled it up, and hoovered.

'What about me?'

'Very well then, just a little.'

The former speaker of the House was still chipping so I lowered a blind. Then I applied the ten-pound note and felt the cocaine whoosh itself around my nasal cavities and then that lovely medicinal drip down the back of the throat.

'So,' he said, and he was at it with his Barclaycard again. 'Here is how I propose we deal with the edifice.'

'OK,' I said when he had finished whatever it was he said.

'OK?'

'Thank you Eric. I've been a cow. I'm sorry. Can I have a little more, please Eric?'

He smiled at me, but I must have appeared absolutely wretched with my sunken blackened eyes.

'Do you know why I wanted to meet you in the greasy spoon?'

'The greasy spoon particularly?'

'I had driven the Mini there to give you. Not the easiest thing to do in the circumstances, given it had to be registered first. Did you know when applying to register a rebuilt Mini one must declare whether one's fucking chassis or monocoque body has been replaced or modified in any way? That took my own mind off things. Anyway I had it parked in front of the greasy spoon. I told you, but you refused to see it.'

'You should have said.'

He helped himself to a big fat line and edged another line toward me. 'You saw it.'

'I would have recognized it.'

'He wanted you to have it. Himself.'

It could not possibly be true, but I wanted to believe it just as all stupid people want to believe in what they want.

It was weeks and weeks before I understood Eric had gone up to Beccles and basically stolen our car, but for now I took another line and instructed him to put the remainder well away from me.

'Where is it now, the Mini?'

'I'll bring it round for you.'

'That's awfully sweet, but I could not bear to see it.'

'Later.'

'Yes, later.'

'Everything passes,' he said. 'You will not feel like this forever.'

But I would. I had no doubt.

He was at my cupboards then and I knew he was searching for aluminium foil in order to leave a 'little toot' for me. I snatched my handbag and put it on the floor. He returned to his chair and placed his gift before me. He held my gaze and his eyes were rather moist.

'Catherine, I have to go to an awful meeting with Sir Necktwist, if you know who I mean. We are going to compare our admittance numbers with the bloody Tate. Do you know the Ministry of Arts has to subsidize the Swinburne twenty-three quid for every punter through the door? The Tate need only five, I hate them.'

He gave a funny little smile, all contorted and wrung out and I remembered what he had suffered when his wife ran away. I kissed him on his rough broad cheek.

'I'm OK,' I said. 'I'm sorry I forgot you loved him too.'

He rather crumpled then, poor Eric, not for long. When he left, I immediately went to the bedroom and began to read.

# HENRY

Carl was Sumper's golden shadow, following him up and down the stairs. Sometimes they were both sequestered above the gorge and I would hear, or imagine, amidst the roar of water, fine sharp hammer blows as they pegged away, also small explosions, like stuttering fireworks, gunshot or dry pine catching in the fire. Their door might spring open, slamming rudely against the wall, and next would appear that wheaten-haired child, laughing, hippity hoppity. I confess it hurt my heart. Soon I would observe him from a window, leaping across the fallen stooks, like a lucky hare recovered from the trap, speeding strangely across the harvest stubble, on his way to places I could not pronounce. He was surely an immensely clever little fidget, returning with his oily secrets wrapped in handkerchiefs or rags.

In my German hours I could bear to think of little else but what progress they were making with their secret instruments. Would they not hurry? Could I not push them faster? I was half maddened by the puzzle of their sounds. Was that gunpowder? Was that success? Was that failure?

The manufacture involved all my emotions to an exhausting degree.

If I enquired with any subtlety, Sumper would pretend to misunderstand, or he would use his mobile eyebrows to affect a comical astonishment. Worst of all, he made me fear that he was not following my instructions.

Why, he would ask, would an educated Englishman want a cheap and gaudy circus trick?

'Herr Sumper,' I replied – every time I took the bait – 'you have accepted the commission and my money too. You know time is of the essence.' And so on.

'But a duck you do not need.' Et cetera.

Then: 'I have come all the way to Germany.'

'Who wants to copy Vaucanson? Vaucanson was a fraud. The duck's digestion did not work. Its anus was not connected to its bowel. Do you understand, Herr Brandling? You love your child and now you are spending money to deceive him.'

Late one morning I was called to drink coffee, a most unusual treat so therefore not a situation in which I expected to be mocked.

'Do tell us, Mr Brandling, do all English fathers deceive their sons?'

The offensive fellow winked at Carl who twisted his fingers around each other, squirming in his seat to contain his amusement and thus, poor servile boy, betrayed me. As for his mother, she clearly judged me the agent of my own distress. Forgive them all.

118

I am normally placid – indeed, it is said to be my flaw – yet I am a strong man too. I have a great capacity to suffer. I can eat dirt and carry rocks upon my back, but I could not let Percy suffer through their indolence. What good was a duck if he could not live to see it? Would a father not be better for him than a wind-up toy? In my passion I forgot my situation. I pushed away my milky coffee. In my room, I packed what would fit into my walking sac. I 'borrowed' one of the stout ash sticks kept in a box by the door. I did not say goodbye, but goodbye was what I meant. I must go home.

Soon thereafter I was greeted by the mistress of the inn. It had been my first impression that she was a comic figure but by now I knew this was in no way true. Never mind, it was for one night, then back to England. The old procuress thought me rich and I did not disabuse her. She gave me her best room and said she would dry my clothes by the kitchen fire.

Rage did not make me reasonable. I thought, I will go home tomorrow. I did not yet consider that I had neither funds nor home to return to. I thought, to hell with everything. I will do what I wish.

I rejected the asparagus and ordered veal stew and dumplings. The first glass of yellow wine arrived wrapped in a pearl-white cloud of condensation. I felt a quite ridiculous confidence. It was really not until the fourth glass that the dark cloud settled on me. Cloud? It was a rock to crush my chest. I had no home to go to. I had had my childish outburst and tomorrow I would have to go crawling back inside my cage.

I was in this miserable condition when the door swung open and a damp wind blew across the room. It was the relentless Sumper, of course, his great wet head shining like a river rock. When he sat at my table I thought, thank heavens, he is sucking up.

He sat sideways, his great legs splayed out, surveying the room.

'There are beings superior to this,' he announced (as the landlady, bending and bobbing deferentially, served his stein). 'If there were not superior forms of life to this,' he said, 'I would hang myself.'

I thought, is this an apology? He would not look at me. The stein returned to the table and was replaced immediately while the procuress, again, performed her servile dance. I noticed how studiously the habitues avoided looking at us. They understood Sumper had the power to harm. Of my true nature no one had the least idea, particularly not me.

'Don't be concerned,' he said, still avoiding my eyes, 'not one of them speaks English.' He called, 'Who speaks English?' and none dared answer.

'There,' he said triumphantly. But he had only proved himself a boor.

'Are these truly human?' he cried in that great booming voice. 'Look at them. Tell me your opinion,' he demanded. And finally he turned his chair and I realized there was something shifty in his gaze. Is he frightened he will lose me?

'Come Brandling, what do you think?'

I thought I had put myself in thrall to a most eccentric bully, but I gave him the courtesy of a civil answer, saying that our fellow drinkers looked very human to me, all gathered together in their differences and similarities, the marks of toil on their common people's hands, the sad erosion of life upon their features. I thought to relate to him certain parts of 'The Stigmata of Occupation' wherein the author studies corpses and remarks on the swollen fingers of washerwomen, the particular calluses of metal-workers and coachmen and the similarity of the thumb's expansion in shoemakers and glass-blowers. He also gives instructions for boiling the skin and nail clippings of suspected copper-workers. A 'beautiful blue colour' is a positive sign.

He followed me closely, to an unusual degree.

'So,' said he when I had finished. 'That is your opinion?'

'A little more than opinion.'

'Yes, of course, they have stigmata, as you say.' (Was this the first time he agreed with anything I said?) 'But do they have souls?' he demanded.

'Yes, like all men.'

There, finally, I saw his mind move elsewhere and of course his interest could never be in 'all men', only in himself.

'This is my birthplace, can you imagine? When I understood my mother had carelessly delivered me into such company, can you understand my rage? But you can fathom none of this,' he said. 'You are English.'

I groaned before I knew what I had done.

'You were not born locked up in this dung heap,' he said angrily. 'You do not believe in ghosts and hobgoblins and the sacred heart of Jesus. You have travelled. It does not help to be able to identify the stigmata of their occupations. Even when alive, these creatures you see do not travel. They stay here with their hairless thighs, their depressed chests, their fairy stories. They have Puss in Boots but they have no idea the entire universe is changing. They cannot imagine a magic beyond a bean. They have never seen a simple threshing machine. They have not known the Englishmen I knew, the machines I helped make. You have no idea how insulting it is that you should ask me to make this toy. Of course,' he said quickly, 'you meant no offence, I understand.'

'All men,' I said, 'need money to live.'

'I am not making it for profit,' he said, 'but because you love your son.'

'You also have a son,' I blurted. What made me say it, I have no idea. To stop him? To cancel him? In any case, I knew Carl was not his son.

'Are you blind?' he cried. 'This boy is no one's son. He is what these idiots would call an angel. If they knew the truth they would crucify him. Of

122

course the ignorant father dragged him off in the middle of a riot. He might as well have offered up a Dresden bowl, he had no idea of the treasure. The universe is blessed that the child was not really cracked and broken. Beer,' he called, or words to that effect. 'You do not want a duck,' he declared.

'You accepted my plan.'

'I am instructed to make something far superior.'

'It is I who instructs you.'

Then suddenly his manner was very soft and gentle. He laid his big hand on top of my arm and grasped it. 'Henry,' he said. 'We need each other.'

I have met men like this before, fierce, hard, rude, but capable of this swift seductive kindness. When he said our need was mutual I believed it was the truth. His eyes turned soft as silk inside their bony case. He leaned closer and, with that great hand still holding me, spoke softly. 'What are you doing with your life? To what use is it put? What higher purpose do you serve?'

He would dominate and use me, so he thought. Alas, I must use him. 'Dear Sumper,' I said, 'you must make me the duck or I will make you very sorry.'

He stood suddenly. I thought, what now?

He would leave the inn. I with him.

'You are a sad man,' he said as we came out onto the muddy track. 'You have suffered a loss.'

I thought, be calm, he cannot know that.

I followed him down off the saddle of the road, down into the clear under-forest. I thought, he is a fraud but I was, quite suddenly, hot all over.

As he walked, he belittled the fairytale collector, saying he was a simpleton who bought whatever stories the peasants invented for him in the winter. They were not real fairy stories at all. He however, he told me, had a twenty-four-carat fairy story. He was thinking he might trade it with the fairytale collector for something useful.

I thought, none of this is true. Also, I have not seen a single piece of clockwork, not an axle or a wheel.

He said, a mother had a little boy of seven years who was so attractive and good that no one could look at him without liking him, and he was dearer to her than anything else in the world. He suddenly died, and she could find no consolation . . .

I needed him. I let him talk.

'She wept and wept,' he told me. However, not long after he had been buried, the child began to appear every night at the very places he had sat and played while still alive. When the mother cried, he cried as well, but when morning came he had disappeared. The mother could not stop her weeping, and one night he appeared in the white shirt in which he had been put to rest.

To listen was a torture. Had I not been desperate for his services, I would have stopped his ugly mouth.

'He had the little laurel wreath still on his head. He sat down on the bed at her feet and said, "Oh, mother, please stop crying, or I will not be able to fall asleep in my coffin, because my burial shirt will not dry out from your tears that keep falling on it." This startled the mother, and she stopped crying. The next night the child came once again. He had a small lantern in his hand and said, "See, my shirt is almost dry, and I will be able to rest in my grave." Then the mother surrendered her grief to God and bore it with patience and peace, and the child did not come again, but slept in his little bed beneath the earth.'

He was cruel and vile. I struck him on his big stone forehead, just beside the eye. He staggered. I kicked him in the groin. He doubled, letting out a girly shriek. Then I am afraid I became careless of my life for I knocked him and kicked his great meat carcass until he made no noise. What a lot of him there was, curled up amongst the mat of fir needles like a broken deer.

I was a fool. He had been my only hope. I returned to the inn and went to sleep.

2

My temper was rare and awful, as frightening as a plunging horse that is better shot than fed. It had never helped me, never once. In this case, I was very lucky I had not murdered Sumper.

Next morning I dressed, doing up my buttons

125

with swollen hands, already anticipating the nasty consequence of victory.

The girl brought my breakfast, but I could not eat, knowing only that I had made a mess of everything.

Then Sumper arrived and I was ashamed to see the raw colours of his cheeks, the almost naked bone, the damage I had caused the only person who could save my son.

When I left the inn he followed me wordlessly into the dark fir forest where I smelt my death. I anticipated the type of clearing where such matters are always settled. Low Hall, Furtwangen, it is all the same. Percy, I forsook thee.

We came to open farmland. The sun was reappearing in the western sky. The white charlock, which was obviously as much of a pest in Furtwangen as is its yellow brother in Low Hall, touched the morbid scene with falsely cheerful light.

'Where do we go?' I asked. 'Let us get the business done.'

I had cut his lip and caused his moustache to rise crookedly upon his face. When he rested his hand upon my upper arm, he seemed to leer, but I detected in this single act of gentleness his regret for what he was now required to do.

'Look,' said he, pointing to a man and two women emerging from a small church. He went to speak to them and I noted well the broad shoulders and terrifying neck. I had no rage, and therefore not the least will to attack him from behind. I thought, I must run away, no matter what a coward I seem. But then the young man kissed both women and all the poor creatures began to weep. Really, their pain was almost unbearable. The women were hardly able to hold themselves upright. They made their way into the forest, staggering and howling in the most awful way.

The man turned his eyes upon me and all I saw was dark and dry. Then, with a lingering look of hatred, he raised his bundle to his shoulder and walked down the hill.

'A clockmaker,' Herr Sumper announced as he returned. The young man swung his bundle from his back and slammed it angrily against a tree. 'Poor chap,' he said and his injured face looked particularly ugly in its sentimentality. 'But he fell into the hands of a packer.'

Enough. I had always known that the world was filled with millions and millions of hearts, like gnats and flies, each with its own private grief like this one. But where was my punishment to take place?

I asked, 'What is a packer?' but I was more concerned with sizing up his mighty arms.

'It is the packers,' he said, 'who buy up clocks from the poor families who make them. The makers must accept whatever mean price they are offered.'

I stopped and put my fists up. 'Where are we going, damn you?'

'Damn me?' he grinned at me and slapped my hands aside.

All around me were the signs of good sane Germans who cared for their little plots, carried manure, mould, whatever disgusting thing that was needed. They were industrious. They were humble. They were wilful. They tilled the subsoil, hoed and weeded until they compelled fertility. Why did I have to deal with a maniac? I knew the answer. I was a fool to have forgotten it.

'When I was young,' he said, placing his hand on my shoulder and thereby, while affecting to be companionable, forcing me to walk beside him, 'the packers used to make the round of the cottages and collect the clocks themselves. But now the vermin have grown fat. They compel the clock-makers to come calling on them. They keep them waiting. Of course they are mostly inn-keepers,' he added. 'The longer they are kept waiting, the more beer they drink and that is all subtracted from the price.

'So the young men are forced to go to England. They leave their mother and their wife behind.'

There, at the bottom of the hill, beside a narrow little stream, I was truly sorry for the swollen brute. 'Just like yourself,' I said.

He considered me a moment, as if amused, then turned his attention to the view. 'Here is my wife,' he said.

Amongst the many, many fanciful and quite insane things Herr Sumper would later insist on – his ability to cause lightning storms for instance – this small comment has its own peculiar place, for his 'wife' appeared to be nothing less than the so-called 'dung heap': Furtwangen, with its lanes exceeding narrow and irregular, with its winding streets, its curious old buildings, its wood-carvings, and its profusion of old-fashioned metal-work. The only flaw in the picture was the obtrusively ugly modern structure, rising high and level, and looking gravelly and prosaic.

'What is that building?' I asked him.

At which point, while I was off my guard, he lurched at me.

I struck his throat.

His eyes bugged.

I spat at him.

He took me in a bear hug so tight he crushed my lungs and forced from me a most unmanly squeak, lifting me up high, turning me clockwise, anticlockwise, then upside down, and back again upon the earth.

'Why,' cried he, as he kissed me on both cheeks, 'it is where they make your springs.'

Thus I understood this madman intended – after all that I had said and done – to make the automaton. Then, out of sheer relief, that my sick child would truly live, I slapped his face.

# PROCEDURES MEETING

Room 404 Annexe
3 May 2010

Present: E. Croft (Curator Horology), C. Gehrig (Conservator Horology), H. Williamson (Conservator Ceramics), S. Hall (Line Manager)

The purpose of the meeting was to decide a schedule for identifying, restoring, and reconstructing the automaton presently identified as H234.

It was decided that C. Gehrig would make an inventory of the automaton and present the findings to the Curator and the Ceramics Conservator in the last week of June. As the physical condition of this bequest is rather 'pig in a poke' it was agreed that C. Gehrig and E. Croft (together, perhaps, with Development and Publicity) would meet before the August holidays to see where things stood. C. Gehrig asked if this object was primarily a 'crowd-pleaser'. E. Croft said that 'crowd-pleasers' had never been part of the museum's mission. He added that although the budget for this restoration would be initially limited, he was not pessimistic about the future.

E. Croft then provided for the committee a receipt for weighed silver made out to a 'Monsieur Sumper'.

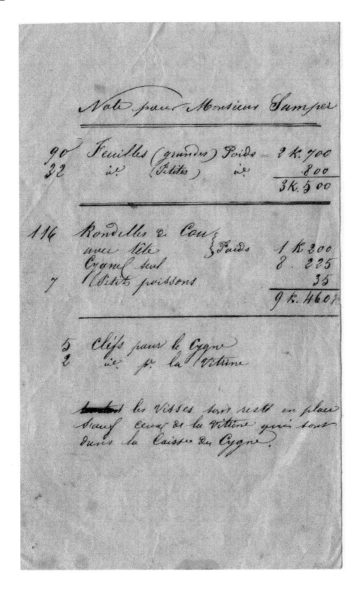

The presence of glass rods and small silver fish gives some indication of the action. However it will require a full assessment to know the value (if any) of the swan both in an historical sense (*c.* 1854) and in terms of whatever use it may be to the Exhibitions Committee. It was clearly 'early days'.

It was the Curator's strong recommendation that the Conservators undertake this work in three stages.

1 : assessment and identification.
2 : restoration of the automaton and the accommodation of the clockwork within a newly produced pedestal or plinth à la Vaucanson. This would enable us to exhibit sometime in 2011 and would attract funds for stage two. The Conservator expressed her general agreement with this strategy.
3 : restoration of the original chassis, which not only presents its own set of puzzles, but requires greater resources than the museum can contemplate at the present time.

The meeting shared the Conservator of Horology's opinion that the assessment and identification could be conducted by a single Conservator in a timely manner.

S. Hall said that an assistant (graduate of both Courtauld and West Dean – young but highly recommended) could be made available almost immediately. E. Croft agreed to assess progress in ten days and discuss what resources might then be required.

Given the age of the automaton and its imperfect storage, C. Gehrig warned that it was likely both spring and arbor were dried out. Removal of springs from the spring barrel would require the manufacture of a wooden jig which would not be inexpensive, particularly as the work must be done offsite, at University College London. E. Croft will speak to the College and attempt to arrange a favourable price estimate. He stressed that although the budget for this restoration would be initially limited, he had great hopes of 'turning on the taps'.

# CATHERINE

The last thing I require is human company, but there she is, my unwanted assistant. She is appallingly young and eager, with long fair hair and dark eyebrows, a slim figure made for jodhpurs and wind-cheaters and a white plain shirt.

'You are Amanda?'

'Yes.'

'You are the Courtauld girl?'

'I suppose so, yes.' The voice is upper-upper but has some wobbly vowels, a weird mélange of Faubourg St Germain and Essex. It makes my teeth ache, the pitch of it.

'Come in,' I tell her carefully, treading around the edges of my hangover.

Piercing voice or no, she is very pretty, with a porcelain complexion and very blue eyes and long lashes. She waits obediently while I turn on my computer but when I realize the museum server is now functioning, all I can think of is how to get to Matthew's emails. This is far more important than the resuscitation of a swan.

'You can hang your umbrella over there.'

I have had an idea about Matthew's password. It will be a secret no one else would ever guess.

After I have tested my idea, I will be extremely nice to her, take her to Fortnum's for tea – she looks like she might enjoy that. For now I am very agitated but I force myself to ask how long has she been with us, what has she done so far.

'Nothing very much I'm afraid. I must say those glass rods look fascinating.'

I really, really do not wish to talk. 'Do you know what they are?' I ask.

'I think so, yes. That is, of course not. Do they rotate to simulate water?'

Has Crofty planted her? Is she someone's daughter? 'You went online?' I suggest.

'What do you mean?'

'You've been researching automata online?'

'No, oh no, I wouldn't do that.' She seems so shocked, I smile. 'They will be jolly hard to clean, won't they? I was thinking how you would manage it. Is there a trick to it?'

'Only to have Ceramics take care of it.'

'Oh.'

'You are disappointed?'

'I like to clean things. I think that's why they sent me.'

So that's how I will get rid of her. She can fetch Hilary from Ceramics. She pays very close attention to the complicated instructions – the normal response to Swinburne directions is to panic, but she listens, alert, her head cocked. I expect her to ask me to repeat. She leaves. A moment later I am attempting to access Matthew's account.

Username: MTINDALL

Password: CATHERINE, and my lovely man opens like a flower. And here it is, everything I want, me to you, you to me, years of them. Dear God in heaven. I love you, Matthew. How sad to have to throw this out.

I have only begun when the two women return and I am forced to quit. My guilt and excitement must be obvious but the Courtauld girl is starring in her own movie. Her colouring is very high and I know that she is, quite reasonably, very pleased with her success.

The glass rods must now be carefully loaded on a long steel trolley, a process that takes them no more than five minutes, but I must wait and wait beyond endurance before, finally, I am left alone.

'Meet you outside the place.' Delete.

'See you there.' Delete.

'I kiss your toes.' Delete.

'I love you. Sorry I was a beast.' Delete.

There are thousands and thousands of them. I should keep them every one, I do not dare. I have no idea of time. I do not even hear the girl return and it is a shock to realize she is by my shoulder.

'You must get an awful lot of email?'

I am aware my eyes are peculiar. 'I don't like to talk very much,' I tell her as I quit again. 'I hope that won't make you feel uncomfortable?'

'No,' she says, but clearly my appearance is unnerving.

'Very well,' I say, 'you might as well unpack the tea chests.'

'By myself?'

I speak without engaging her. 'Do you think you can manage?'

'Oh yes. As long as that's OK.'

'There will be some rather heavy pieces. If you have any doubt about anything, you fetch me.'

'May I ask what it is?'

'A swan apparently.'

She remains, startled, staring at me. She says, 'Do you wish me to begin the inventory,' and I can see the pink of her tongue behind her teeth. The vowels on *inventory* are slightly odd.

'No. Just remove them very carefully. Keep all the newspaper they are wrapped in. Watch out for any documentation at all, even a postage stamp.'

'How will I arrange them? I mean, what is the principle of order?'

I cannot talk. I will not look at her. 'I don't care. Any way you like.'

My colossal lack of curiosity is completely inconceivable. In real life this would never happen, but even in the middle of my own personal rollercoaster ride, I do manage to keep some sort of eye on her. I realize she is ordering the components by size, smallest to largest. You little pickle, I think, you cheeky little thing.

'How is your day?' Delete.

'I hate everyone, not you, my sweet.' Delete.

'I am a genius. Come and see what I have done.'

The girl unpacks and classifies. I slice away my heart. Delete, delete, delete. There may be a faster, less painful way to do this, but I doubt I would use it even if I could. It is a field of electric turbulence, bone-breaking updraughts, emails from his wife. Delete. I never asked him if he had sex with her. I trusted him completely. Just the same I always sniffed his skin. Delete. There are emails to women I do not know. These I cannot help but open, and every time I am ashamed. Delete. I dig deeper and the Courtauld girl digs in the tea chests.

'Now are you up to this?' I ask her.

But I see she is listening to music on some device I cannot even see. On another day this would annoy me.

There are so many emails to his sons. I have to read them. I cannot delete them.

'Did your pills arrive?' he writes.

'You need a warm coat?'

'I'll pick you up at six. Set two alarms.'

'Love Dad.'

'Love.'

'Love always.'

Around noon I abandon Amanda Snyde 'to have a smoke'. When I return I have been crying. I also have a fresh flask of vodka in my perfect bag. My assistant is eating an egg sandwich and bent over what I later learn she calls a Frankenpod, having cobbled it together from abandoned pieces.

'You can eat with the others in the caff if you like.'

'I'm sorry. I'm not very used to being around people.'

'Surely you went to school.'

She removes the single ear bud and I catch sight of a black billowing image on the screen.

'Actually my grandfather tutored me.'

'Had he been a teacher?'

'He was a sort of soldier.'

'You were in London?'

'Actually, in Suffolk.'

I do not ask where in Suffolk. She might say Beccles or Southwold or Aldeburgh or Blythburgh, the litany of love names, private, ours. I would not have our private Suffolk stolen or polluted.

'But then at the Courtauld?'

'Then West Dean. I've become quite civilized, learned to use a key and so on.'

Learn to use a *key?* Well, I am rather strange myself, for I cannot acknowledge the body parts of swan she has laid so carefully upon the bench. I am a highly specialized creature and I could have identified much of this jumble in my sleep. Even whilst reading heart-wrenching emails it is impossible not to see the tarnished silver, some pieces rather like napkin rings. I have noted the reflective backing plates which are made to fit below the glass rods and are a common convention in these automata. Their function is to make the 'water' sparkly. These plates on the bench are in a most unsparkly condition. They really need to be covered with reflective silver leaf which can, of course, be removed in the future. I cannot deny the barrel of a music box, a very familiar object for a horologist. I do not wish to count but of course it has about a thousand pins. This Herr Sumper made, not for Henry Brandling but – this is very clear to me – for himself. Most of the pins are brass, but have sometimes been replaced by steel. I have no curiosity at all, but I cannot help knowing that many of the pins have been moved to new positions.

It is like leaving a child to walk alone on a busy high street, but I am near her, watching her with my peripheral eye. I wonder who her grandfather was or is? When posh people say 'soldier' they mean a field marshal or a spy.

She continues to dig up the bones. I continue to burn my past.

In the midst of this Eric 'pops in' wearing that ridiculous tight striped suit, all waist and wide shoulders. It is too hot for this costume. He stinks of the Ivy – the wine list, not the shepherd's pie.

I secretly watch to see how he will react to the Courtauld girl. He affects to not see or know her and that pretty much proves he has planted her. I wonder if the 'soldier' is a trustee.

Eric rushes around the room like a dog at the airport and then rushes out again.

A moment later I ask the girl, 'Did he say "Toodle pip"?'

She giggles.

'Who says "Toodle pip"?'

'Bertie Wooster, I think.'

'You're too young for Wooster.'

'Stephen Fry is Jeeves,' she says. 'I saw him once, in the pub in Walberswick.'

Walberswick. Delete.

'Why do you think Mr Croft says "Toodle pip"?'

She smiles.

Everyone thinks it is Americans who make themselves up, but it is we English who are the fantasists, not only Crofty either. There is a strange meld in Amanda Snyde's voice when she says: 'I think this is the neck of something.'

Poor Henry Brandling. He never got his duck. When I read the invoice I was rather pleased it was a swan but now, in the studio it has some other creepy quality – a life, a penis, the neck of a goose on Christmas Day. It is spooky, dirty, an unearthly blue-grey. The fine articulation of steel vertebrae could not be achieved anywhere in London in 2010.

She holds it out for me.

'No, put it down.'

For no good reason, I begin to cry.

'Oh dear,' she says, and through my blurry eyes I see the afternoon light catching her pretty face, her hope and hurt. She is too sane and generous for this room.

'Miss Gehrig.' And that is when I see, beneath the hair, she has an ugly plastic hearing aid, and

I recognize her accent as belonging to a class of injury. This is why she uses just one ear bud.

'It's all right,' I say, 'I have lost a family member. That's all it is. It's nothing.'

'Are you all right?'

'Completely. Someone died. That's all. It happens every day.'

'May I ask questions?'

'No, you may not.'

For the rest of the day I have her follow me around with a notebook while I dictate functions and allow her to allocate the numbers.

I make a rough sort of classification of the unpacked components – a beginning anyway, although we have not come to the main engine.

'Wear gloves,' I say.

'Yes,' she says, looking at me suddenly. 'The parts leave a funny feeling on your skin.'

I think, she can see my pain in colour, poor girl, but I suppose she can deal with almost anything.

# CATHERINE & HENRY

Time and time again, in the early hours, I took refuge with Henry Brandling whose slightly mechanical handwriting served to cloak the strangeness of the events it described. His was, in the best and worst sense, an intriguing narrative. That is, one was often confused or frustrated by what had been omitted. The account was filled with violent and disconcerting 'jump cuts'. One would imagine the author had returned to live at the sawmill and it was a shock to stumble into a sentence and realize he was sitting on a chair outside the inn. I imagined a rather Van Gogh sort of chair, but who would ever know?

Then here was Carl, materializing, and not even a whole body but a graze on his arm, or the mud on his boots. Henry clearly loved him, and was jealous of the boy's attachment to Sumper who 'filled the little fellow's head with dangerous rot'. Such was the nature of Carl's 'toys', Henry concluded that the only possible explanation was 'they are made by the dreadful Sumper to tease me'. As a reader I far preferred the other possibility, that the child really was clever, that these were his inventions. He owned (or constructed?) a glass-plate camera and 'wasted time' photographing tourists. No more was said of this, but then, on the line below, Carl appeared without warning, arranging voltaic cells at Brandling's feet.

If voltaic cell meant a battery (and I confirmed it did) then it seemed anachronistic. But of course it wasn't. One did not seek science fiction from Henry Brandling.

Carl, according to Henry's account, laid the batteries on the road outside the inn and produced a dead mouse which he proceeded to connect to cables. The mouse leapt into the air, its eyes bulging 'in astonishment', its teeth bared to bite the unprotected neck.

Then 'the Holy Child' 'scampered' back across drying flax, his 'instruments' inside his 'sac'.

Much more than a century later the reader in Kennington Road drank her vodka icy cold. She looked away from her lonely reflection in the black glass of the kitchen and found the fleeting image of the angelic trickster arriving at the inn with a tiny 'engine'. What did 'engine' even mean in 1854? It is hard to visualize a motor with 'one big wheel and one small' which 'limps and hobbles' and goes 'roaring down the road in a cloud of smoke'.

Of all these 'tricks and notions' Henry's chief concern was that they took precious time away from the manufacture of his duck.

To the grieving horologist, working daily at the

Swinburne Annexe, it was very clear that, if Sumper had been a crook, he was also a highly advanced technician. It was difficult to name more than two of his contemporaries who might have devised and produced work at this sophisticated level. Presented with the obstacle of Sumper's size and personality, Henry was more naturally disposed to accept the Arnaud version in which the clock-maker was a violent brute.

Every morning I knew this was not true.

As for Arnaud himself, my (rather inspired) guess was that he was neither a spy nor a pedlar but an itinerant silversmith whose identity was kept secret from the sponsor – to learn his true occupation would have warned Henry that a great deal more money would be extracted yet.

This was also consistent with the daily evidence in Studio #404 which revealed an exceptionally single-minded and wilful character. Sumper had clearly done whatever Sumper wished, and it was upsetting to read the word 'duck' so often in the customer's manuscript and know that the undead creature had been, and always would be, a majestic swan – 113 solid silver rings fitted in such a way as to make a long swan neck; each of these rings engraved with the pattern of swan feathers; every-thing photographed, measured, weighed, identified.

At my side, the Courtauld girl was immensely diligent, and she was certainly a whiz with Excel, a computer program that had always irritated me.

Yet work went slowly. By myself I might have done eighty-six rings in a day and loaded and identified the JPEGs. Working with an assistant it took over two days.

I often imagined that Herr Sumper had foreseen that Amanda and I would grapple with his puzzle. He was certainly a lot more helpful to us than he had been to Henry Brandling, providing us with assembly instructions by stamping numerical coding on the rings.

'Is this damaged?' asked Amanda Snyde. 'Is this a stress fracture?'

I was pleased she saw things, but although she was fresh and thirsty for knowledge, I was still looking for excuses to send her away – so I could read our emails. In truth, this was the reason our progress was so slow.

For instance, there were 122 silver leaves which would surround the automaton in a fringe or wreath. I had her take one of these leaves to Metals. There was a pretty boy down there, rather of her tribe, clean-cut and pink-cheeked who arrived each day in his father's too-big coat.

She returned to announce the swan had been made in France.

This was twaddle, but I was very pleased as it would require another errand.

'Alas,' I said, 'we happen to know it was made in Germany.'

'How do we know that?' she asked, and of course I was not going to produce Henry's evidence.

'It has Minerva stamped on it,' she insisted. 'Doesn't that mean it was made in France?'

'Did the young man help you?'

'He seems very knowledgeable.'

I smiled at her and caused her to blush. I was pleased she liked the metals boy with his rather posh blue-and-red striped tie. Would a boy kiss a pretty girl with a hearing aid? What a stupid question. She was a beauty.

'Yes,' I said, 'but it was really made in Germany.'

'How do we know?'

'I'll show you,' and I showed her the little mark I had found. Nothing more than an A. In truth it could be anyone's.

'This is the mark of a silversmith named Arnaud,' I said. 'His name is Huguenot, but in fact he worked in Germany.'

I should have been ashamed (even if I would later turn out to be precisely right).

'As for the Minerva, it has been stamped by the French assay office in order for it to be sold in France. There was a Paris International Exhibition in 1870. It is possible the swan was displayed there. So this is the next project for you, Amanda. Are you familiar with the British Museum?'

Of course she was. She was a gem.

It did not yet occur to me that I would miss her, or that I would be actually waiting for her return on the following afternoon. She came in at around three, dressed for her weekend with her Burberry bag and her Liberty scarf. Why do those

Sloaney girls dress like that, in those awful coloured tights?

'You're off for the weekend?' I asked when she had delivered her findings.

'My grandfather.'

'That's nice.'

'I love him. I know that sounds rather odd, but I do,' she rather glared at me. 'Do you have a place in the country?'

I had been deleting JPEGs of the green at Southwold. I did not laugh or even smile, just shook my head.

'I'm sorry about your friend.'

At first I was grateful for her intuition, and then, immediately, certain that she knew far more about me than she should.

# CATHERINE

Since removing the tarpaulin I had lived with what the procedures minutes had inaccurately described as a chassis. It was better understood as a timber hull slathered with pitch. That it had once contained the clockwork engine was obvious, although this insight was of no use in the present exercise – our job was to restore the mechanism and mount it in and on a modern plinth.

It was irritating, therefore, to return to my workroom and find the Courtauld girl studying, not the huge feast of Sumper's wizardry, but this nasty hull which was as attractive as a squashed hedgehog on a country lane.

Three times I had reason to physically draw her away from it, and the fourth time I snapped, 'Get back to bloody work.'

In response she took my hand. 'Go on, Miss Gehrig, admit you are just a little bit intrigued.'

I could have slapped her face. God knows what would have happened had not Eric barged in. As usual, he ignored my assistant. He called me Cat and commanded me to wind up the music box. He then performed a touchingly graceless vaudeville dance to the time of the melody.

'Splendid, splendid,' he said, rubbing his dry square hands together. 'It is the sixteenth wonder of the world.' Then he left.

Then I had Amanda help me remove the main spring and she seemed to forget about the hull. She got oil on her expensive sweater but did not seem to care. I gave her a big lecture about wearing a dustcoat and she listened with barely concealed impatience.

'Isn't it lovely,' she said when I had finished scolding her.

'Yes it is.'

'This is my bloody work, innit?'

The little imp. I had to smile.

The music box spring was extremely old and clearly hand-made. It was highly textured and very different to modern springs. Together we managed to get it to the bench and by then we were both very oily. Her sweater was ruined, but her face was flushed and her eyes were very bright.

This brief moment was the first time I felt alive since Matthew died. Of course I didn't notice until later, when all the warmth had seeped away.

It was already five in the afternoon, but I pretended not to notice and we set to work on the hammer frame and thus became the first people in a century to read the rather alchemical ciphers on the bells. This was a real secret. How delicious it felt. How nice also that I did not need to ask her to set up the lights so we could have a photo-graphic record. She had already proven herself very capable with a camera.

While she was busy I turned my attention to the barrel – although some of the pins had been replaced many were original, meaning some of the music might also be original. I rolled the barrel on carbon paper and thus produced an image which I could scan. Then with two or three clicks I sent the pattern of the pins to a lovely chap at the Museum of Mechanical Music in Utrecht who would, one day soon, play the music on a piano and send me back an MP3 file. I imagined that Herr Sumper would not be at all astonished by these wonders.

When the photography was complete it was almost six o'clock but Amanda stayed while I loaded her images and was, quite rightly, praised. Her work was very crisp and detailed.

'You know that thing,' she said at last. 'The thing you don't like me looking at.'

'Yes, Amanda.' I busied myself on the Mac, rechristening the file numbers of the swan JPEGs.

'I have been looking at it.'

'You have many more worthwhile things to study.'

'You called it a hull.'

'It doesn't matter. It needn't concern you.'

One might reasonably have expected an under-ling to hear this message, but she persisted.

'I tried to work out if it would stay afloat with the weight of the engine.'

I said nothing.

'I am hopeless at physics,' she said passionately. 'Really awful.'

'Well then, that's that.'

'But it would be rather splendid, wouldn't it? If the imitation water of the swan had been contiguous with real water. I'm sorry. I know I am very irritating.'

Yes she was irritating.

'I'm sorry,' she said. 'I cannot stay away from it.'

I made no comment.

'I have done a drawing,' she said, opening up her Moleskine book.

'Amanda,' I said, 'you are no longer at university. Our curiosity is not disinterested. We will not be having seminars. We are employed to do a very particular job.' But of course I looked at her damn drawing. She had shown the long staves and the double skin of timber. She had a lovely hand, extraordinarily confident for one so young, and that also was the general problem with her character.

'Black chalk,' she said. 'I know that's terribly pretentious.'

'Why?'

'I'm not Giorgione.'

I can't say how unusual it is when you find a young conservator with this degree of will. I saw it would now be my job, not only to reconstruct the swan, but to harness all this dangerous energy.

I took the book from her and closed it.

'Do you think you might manage to write a

condition report? Might that occupy your mind productively?'

I was not simply being generous to a beginner. Indeed I never doubted that I would end up writing most of it myself, but if Crafty really had a catalogue in mind, this finely detailed drawing would reveal so much more than the very best photograph.

'Please,' she said, 'could I show you something now?'

Did she not understand the reckless favour I had done her? No, it seemed not, because she was back at the hull again. She was like a blow fly in a temple attracted only to a pile of shit.

'I rather think this might be dry rot.'

And yes, she was correct – here was a spot a few inches below what you might call the ridge beam, or keel. Here a scab of pitch had fallen away and thus exposed an area of grey timber.

'See.' Before I could stop her, she picked at the broken edge of pitch which came free with a lump of flaking wood.

'No!' I was shocked by the ugly noise that had come out of my mouth, torn and ragged like a gull.

'I'm sorry.' I had terrified her.

'Never mind,' I said. 'Do me a favour and forget it.'

'Oh but I do mind. I mind awfully. I've totally screwed up.'

I looked at the poor messy beauty with her pearls and oil and saw how queer we both must look. I began to laugh. She burst into tears.

'I'm sorry, I'm sorry. I've hurt it. I'm sorry. Don't laugh. You mustn't –'

How could I not feel sorry for her? 'Why don't you fetch me that little pen light from my desk.'

'Pen?'

'It's a tiny LED, with blue nail polish on its switch.'

She returned all black and smeary, holding out the light.

Examining the damage, it was clear that she was perfectly correct about the rot. This would be a perfect excuse to get the hull removed from her surveillance.

However, the hole was the size of a 50p coin and the LED had a tight sharp focus and when I played its very bright white light into the cavity I saw something most peculiar.

'Amanda, come here,' I said, which was very stupid of me.

'What did I do?'

'Tell me what you see.'

'Thank you,' she said. 'Thank you so much.' She took the little torch between her thumb and forefinger.

'Oh, Miss Gehrig.'

'Well?'

'It is a cube,' she said at last. 'A one-inch cube. It is cornflower blue. I am good with colour,' she said rather fiercely. 'I'll check the Pantone number but I'm sure it's cornflower blue.'

I did not think, not for a second, of the effect this would have on her. I thought only of Carl's

154

blue block, his clever trick. It took my breath away to find him buried in the hull.

## 2

I deleted, forever, the celestial light through the beech forest behind Walberswick, the heath at Dunwich in full flower, a very tanned Matthew, that lovely English shyness in his smile, one hand in his pocket, his eyes hidden in the shadow of his brow. I deleted his white shirt, his baggy slacks, the surviving elm he leaned against. Dear Matty T. He was one of those physically graceful dishevelled beauties my country does produce so very well. Delete.

I also deleted JPEGs of Bungay and Walberswick and Aldeburgh and Dunwich, the melancholy concrete bomb shelter behind the stables.

Amanda entered, charging at me. I hid my business and I admired her hair clip, velvet-covered, very 1960s.

She, in turn, admired my silk pants. I would have expected her Sloaney aesthetic would have made her blind to such things as are produced in the rue du Pré aux Clercs, so I was rather pleased.

I then took her to the far end of the studio, right up against the wash room, furthest from the damaged hull. It was too late, of course, but I did not know that yet.

Here I had laid out the little silver fish which the swan would 'eat' when it was finally mobile.

The fish would 'swim' along a track. I gave her time to discover something of what she had been given – the tamped punch marks on the tails, for instance. Her Moleskine was produced. Notes were made. I then left her to make a survey of the track, a task she quickly understood. I did not spoil it by telling her that there were only seven fish, although the pin holes indicated that there had been twelve further ornaments. I left this as a gift.

I set to work on the silver rings, removing a century of built-up oil. I had hardly begun when she abandoned her post.

I thought, what now? But she was at her rucksack, pulling out a dustcoat on one sleeve of which a word had been embroidered from cuff to elbow. She saw me looking.

'Boy,' she said, meaning the embroidery was a name. She rolled up her sleeve to hide it.

'Gus,' she said, colouring. I suddenly thought how lovely it had been to be an art student, to be so young. I myself had arrived at Goldsmiths College imagining I might make paintings which would give me peace of mind. I discovered sex instead. Now I mourned my young girl's skin. It was sad and sweet to imagine this little creature sleeping with her face nestled in her young man's neck.

'I have been thinking all night about the cube,' she said.

'Well now you have some fish to think about instead.'

'Miss Gehrig, can I show you something?'

'I would rather you did the fish.'

Instead the wilful little thing extracted a small plain cardboard cube from her rucksack. It might seem a simple matter to construct a cube, but this was very beautifully done, and when she set it before me I saw that it was immaculately clean. She would be a very good conservator when she learned to do what she was told.

'Open it,' she demanded.

'Why?' I asked crossly.

'Please.'

The cube was about three inches. 'Yes, it's empty. Now please go back to your bench. You have a job to do.'

'Yes, open it out, flat.'

Once more I found myself doing as she asked.

'You see,' she said.

'What?'

'When a cube is unfolded,' she insisted, 'it forms a six-part Cross. The Cube is Yahweh concealed. The Cross is Yahweh revealed. Isn't that cool?'

'No,' I said, and gave it back to her. 'You have mystery all about you. You don't need to invent it.'

'Oh don't be angry,' she said. 'It's not invented.'

I raised my eyebrows.

'Please, Miss Gehrig. Isn't it beautiful? I'm not being soppy. I've been reading about cubes. The Cube is "the Soul quarried from God". I'm thinking about our cube of course, and why it might be there.'

'No, Amanda, stop it now. Really. Immediately.

We are not here to invent stories about the hull. We are here to restore this extraordinary object. The real world is beautiful enough. When it is finished it will make your hair stand on end.'

But she would not stop. 'The three-dimensional cube is the Holy Name of Yahweh expressed geometrically. You are religious. I'm sorry.'

'I am not at all religious. You have never met anyone less religious. Now do your bloody work and stop breaking things.'

But I had been too hard. Her eyes were not scary at all. Indeed it seemed that she was going to cry. That is why I really hate working with young females.

'It is not your fault,' I said, 'I'm what you would call a rationalist.'

I took her sleeve and rolled her coat up. 'Go,' I said, 'be clever with the fish.'

Her boy's name was Gus. My boyfriend at the Courtauld had been Marcus. He was generally thought to be a kind of genius. I had not thought of him for years, but now, as I gently removed the built-up oil, I vividly recalled standing under the London plane trees while Marcus, who was terribly large and used his hands in a way I had thought 'expressive', continued to defend the notion that a person could *absolutely* combust spontaneously. I had begun listening to him with what I had imagined was affection, and as we came out into Portman Square that morning I was completely unaware of my own seething irritation.

As I had burst out today, I burst out then. I really did not know I was about to say, 'What twaddle.'

Marcus was tall, but I was only an inch shorter in my flats and thus I was level with his very pretty eyes which now reacted like an oyster, I thought, and I was rather pleased with the cruelty in the simile, of an oyster feeling the squirt of lemon juice.

'Twaddle?' he said, his mouth contracting unattractively. 'For Christ's sake, what sort of word is that?'

Rather a posh word, I thought, and therefore familiar to you, no matter how much you deny it.

'Twaddle,' he squinted, as if trying to look down at me when this was, no matter how he twisted his head, impossible.

'Marcus, how do you imagine that might happen? A person just bursting into flame?'

'What?' He was like a boy in the back row in a subject for which he had no aptitude.

'It is *haystacks* that combust spontaneously.'

'What bullshit, Cat.'

I wondered if Marcus might possibly be thick. It had never occurred to me before, but he was still carrying that ridiculous book of Colin Wilson's. It had been ancient and grotty-looking when he found it, as if a dog had peed on it, and he had brought it to bed, and used a paperweight to hold the pages flat at breakfast.

It was titled *The Occult* and was full of old hippy nonsense, although I had not blamed him too severely at the start. He was not at all thick, very brainy in fact, but just as the garden in Kennington Road was later occupied by a family of foxes, London that year had suffered a second invasion of Colin Wilson, and our group lived inside a false nostalgic fog of marijuana where the most reliable atheists felt compelled to read aloud to you the Book of Ezekiel which was said to describe the distinctive actions of a flying saucer. It was complete tosh, but I lived in this time warp until, all at once, I had had enough of it.

'Marcus you know very well people do not just burst into flames.'

'Don't get uptight.' As this was not the first time he had said these words, there was no reason for him to think that he was crossing any kind of line.

He was a beautiful boy, with dark blue eyes and long lashes. He was tall and perhaps unfashionably broad-shouldered, and had appeared to me to have a not at all uneducated eye, and he was like a creature who should be forever celebrated in marble. Beauty to one side, he had appeared to me the most rational of young men. It was he who had patiently overcome my rather hysterical resistance to my studies of spectrographic analysis.

'Why do people spontaneously combust?' I was smiling, but I was looking him directly in the eyes and I was aware of a dangerously intoxicating buzzing in my ears.

'I don't know.'

'Then why would you believe such rot?'

'Oh for God's sake, Catherine, don't be a bore.'

'But why do you think a person would just burst into flames?'

'Why not?'

Remembering this, years later, I judged myself prim and vain and self-important, but when Marcus Stanwood said 'Why not?' I could not believe I had given my precious body to a man who would say such a thing.

'It's mumbo jumbo. It's ridiculous.'

'It cannot be explained,' he cried. 'Jesus Christ rose from the fucking dead. People catch on fire and we don't know why.'

Then, to my complete astonishment, he turned on his heels, and walked across the square where he was lost in the shadows of the plane trees. I saw then, too late, he was breaking up with me. I hadn't meant him to. It had not been my intention.

It was soon after this that I gave up art school. I went to study horology in West Dean.

Amanda Snyde and I worked in leaden silence until lunch, by which time she had still not figured out that the missing ornaments had probably been reeds. The sun had gone and the studio blinds had lost their luminosity.

At exactly one o'clock she came and stood behind me.

'Please,' she said, and put her hand lightly on my shoulder.

'Of course,' I said. 'I'll eat myself in a moment.'

'No, please. May I have a peek at the blue cube, if I keep my metaphysics to myself?'

'Do you think you really need to?'

'I thought about it all night. How it got there. What it means.'

There really was no reasonable way I could stop her so I slid the LED torch across the desk. I could not have been more clear about how uninterested I was.

'Miss Gehrig.'

'I am working.'

'Miss Gehrig.'

I put the ring down with a sigh. 'Yes, Amanda, what is it now?'

'Someone has been at it,' she said.

'Nonsense,' I said. 'Show me.'

'Look for yourself.'

I took the flashlight from her and peered into a cavity which I already knew was empty of everything save a little borer dust. She was looking at me. I did not wish to look at her, but in that brief moment I found myself the subject of a rather impertinent enquiry.

I fled on the pretext of informing Eric Croft.

3

There would be no discussion of blue cubes metaphorical, spiritual or physical. Indeed there would be little talk at all. I went to work with a pencil and paper, attempting to picture how the parts of the fish mechanism – the tracks on which the fish sat, mounts, levers, cam and rollers – might all work successfully together.

It took me almost two days to realize it was the swan's neck which must directly control the motion of the fish. This connection, as I had previously understood and then discounted, was achieved by a series of small levers. I had assumed that the fish would swim either clockwise or anti-clockwise and I wasted a lot of mental effort deciding which of these it was. But of course the strange Herr Sumper had not been interested in anything this simple, which was why seven of the rollers were double-action rollers. The fish had been designed to swim in two directions. That is, there were two 'teams': four fish would swim clockwise, three anticlock-wise. They would, as Amanda Snyde put it, when I finally allowed her an opportunity to speak, give the appearance of 'sporting about'. So ingenious was this mechanism that when the automaton's neck turned and the head lowered (when the 'swan' appeared to dart at them) the fish would hastily retreat. When she grasped this, my assistant jumped in the air and I dared to like her once again.

Then we had our usual visitor and my assistant took her micrometer away into a corner. Crofty had never quite got the hang of the Blenheim Bouquet Aftershave which was now gleaming from a recent application. This aftershave cost 'twenty-five quid a pop' – it always gave him a rather sharp-toothed sort of glee to tell me this, but this morning he was odd and querulous. I expected this bad mood would evaporate the moment he understood my sketch.

'What's this?' he demanded, referring to the bruise on my forearm.

'What an extraordinary question,' I said. 'What sort of man asks a woman about her bruises?'

'Are you all right?' he insisted, all lemony, right in my face.

I did not like what 'all right' was code for.

'I slipped in the shower, is that sufficient information?'

'How did you slip?'

'I slipped . . . in . . . the . . . shower . . . Eric,' Amanda seemed to be staring at her Frankenpod. Her pretty neck was pale and still.

I had no exact idea how I got my bruise, except I had been completely trolleyed. When I woke next morning I found my shower curtain all pulled down. I had only the vaguest memory of the fall, but it appeared that I had also emptied a vodka bottle and placed three wind-up clocks inside the fridge.

'You should get one of those rubber mats.'

'Quite,' I said.

He was still not paying attention to my drawing.

'Don't you want to see what we've worked out?' I said. 'It's rather splendid.'

'Of course. I'll drop in later in the afternoon. I'm just on my way to the dentist.' At this Amanda Snyde looked sharply up and Eric said, 'Good morning.'

'Hello Mr Croft,' she said, and returned immediately to her work.

'Are you in pain?' I asked Eric.

But his eyes were darting amongst the pieces on the work bench, as if he was trying to memorize them for a parlour game. 'What?' he asked but had no interest in an answer.

I watched as he sniffed around the bench, examining the silver neck rings but not really looking at anything professionally.

'Just popped in. I'll be off.' It was only then, on his way to the door, that he appeared to notice the dry rot although his 'noticing' was completely bogus – the injury to the hull was not even visible from where he stood, and the strange twisting of his neck did not help his pantomime.

'I'll have George look at that next week,' I said.

'Yes, George,' he said, but the cheeky bugger had brought an LED of his own and now he stooped to scowl into the cavity.

My laugh could not have been very pretty, but he did not seem to hear that either and he rose from his inspection looking both grim and guilty. As he left the room he slipped his LED into his trouser pocket.

When there was nothing remaining but his Blenheim Bouquet, I turned my attention to the Courtauld girl who was measuring a piece of track with her micrometer. With her thick fair hair held back by a Bakelite clip, there was nothing to hide the crimson glory of her neck.

I might have asked if her dear grandpa was a friend of Eric Croft's, but there was no longer any need. You little spy, I thought. I was very frosty with her for the remainder of the day. When I left I did not say good night.

My fall in the bath had frightened me immensely but dusk found me as usual at the Kennington Road offy where dear soft-eyed Ahmad already had a bottle of cold Stoly waiting on his counter. Eric could ask, 'Are you all right,' but Ahmad was the only man in London who had any idea of how much I was drinking. At least he did not know I had put the clocks inside the fridge. This was rather frightening. I had grown up with the sound of clocks and they had been a comfort to me, the whole orchestra of movements like the currents of the sea, an all-engulfing natural order. To refrigerate a clock was an extremely violent act, not one I could explain to anyone.

I crossed Kennington Road without being run over. Once inside I opened all the windows and lit lavender candles to destroy the stink. The vodka went in the freezer, then came out a moment later.

I sat on the sofa, a very plain Nelson day bed, a prime example of that rather Quakerish modernism which I have always adored. From there one could look up through the high back window and enjoy the silhouette of chestnut tree, listen to the blackbirds quarrelling about their places, and watch the sky turn to ink, never quite black, always London's suicidal engine burning in the night.

Against the wall beneath the windows was a low Bruno Mathsson bookshelf. On its normally bare surface I appeared – during my adventures of the previous night – to have exhibited a blue wooden block. Why not? It was a very pretty colour. I clearly had fussed a great deal with the lighting, using the same tiny reading light Matthew had bought from the Conran Shop on Marylebone High Street. Now I fiddled with it until the facing surfaces of the memento were completely shadowless.

Then I sipped my vodka.

It glowed, my stolen jewel, deeply evasive, sad and melancholic, a study in blue but also something like a small boy's slippers placed beneath his bed three thousand summer nights ago. Soon, but not immediately, my mind began to drift down Henry Brandling's paths, narrow lines in the meadow where the grass was bent, broken yellow and bruised, fresh tracks that led to little hopping Carl the hare, clever clever Carl now dead as dead could be. Carl calcified and crumbled and the brain that had made and known the cube had vanished, less than a glow worm in the night, not even a dried cicada in a case. At this point, as I drained my glass, I heard the music of my clocks as I had heard them last night. The wind-up orchestra had always meant Clerkenwell, comfort, safety, peace. I had spent my entire life foolishly seduced by ticking clocks, never bothering to hear the horror underneath.

I sought Henry, Henry alive, good-hearted Henry. How essential was his company in this endless night. I read. He wrote.

167

# HENRY

The pages of Sumper's notebook held a disgraceful mess of floating charts and lithographs depicting wheels of one sort or another. From this magpie's nest he withdrew a densely annotated sheet which had suffered a chaos of amendments. He was eager to inform me it was a list of angels. Then, typically, he tucked it back into the nest and would permit no more discussion.

'Then why did you show it to me?'

He jutted his long chin toward the boy who was sitting quietly by the window working a piece of metal with a file.

'His name is there,' he said.

'He is an angel? I rather thought you were against that sort of guff.'

Had there been a seraph in Furtwangen, he would not, surely, have had such dirty nails and long peculiar fingers. Those digits were host to several warts and Carl had been taught that he would cure these 'apostles' by rubbing them with rosemary. My own dear boy smelled of Pears soap all day long, but Carl was not less pleasing – an earthly aroma always preceded his arrival.

He was not an angel. He was possibly a clever boy with a beautifully shaped head. He made the figure of a leaping deer from wire. Allegedly he sold this to the packer. A similar object was supposedly purchased by a Baron with a wasting disease and one had also gone to a beloved English boy with the same dangerous condition. Should Percy have brought me these gifts I would have treasured them, but in Carl's case they were annoyances. His value to me was that he was the engine of the workshop. When he was absent, work slowed. Whenever he ran up the stairs, the tap of the hammer became faster and the whirr of the lathes accelerated.

Percy needed no gift but mine. When Carl presented his cube to me I flinched and would have left the room had not the mother grabbed my hand. My mind was in another country where the floor was wet and the air was filled with sulphur. While Sumper snatched, Frau Helga dragged my thumbnail across the varnished surface. It tripped a trigger. The lid flew open. Out popped an Englishman six inches tall.

With a face of hair, a pair of popping eyes, a top hat upon his large square head, this ridiculous figure was meant to represent myself, a man who had already lost one child to consumption. I didn't require toys. I wanted only to be shown what I was paying for.

'I have a mind to go to the police,' I cried.

Sumper displayed nothing but exasperation, but

Helga's face was as crumpled as her son's. 'Herr Brandling, we have given you a gift.'

'You stole my plans.'

'No, Herr Brandling,' the boy said. His face was pale as death.

'We are following your orders,' said Frau Helga. 'You have paid us.'

I was exceptionally pleased to have made them so afraid. 'Quite so, Frau Helga, except Herr Sumper can provide no proof of anything. He tinkers. He teases. But all I see is my money as it disappears into his purse.'

Sumper pushed his huge face right into mine and pinched my cheek. I slapped his hand away and he laughed or grunted in surprise.

'If you were the Pope,' he hissed. 'If you were the Jesus Christ himself, I would hide my work from you. I have to bring it to a stage where you understand what you are looking at.'

'It is very simple, Herr Sumper – if you cannot prove satisfactory progress.'

Perhaps Sumper made a sign to Helga. If so I did not see it. In any case it was she who now announced: 'You will be shown.'

I followed them, not up the stairs, but out and into the dark cold air of the mill. Here, in a summer workshop previously unknown to me, I was shown a heavy work bench, freshly built above the shadowed stream. In front of the bench were three trestles. Atop the trestles was a barrel-vaulted structure, the hull of a small rowing boat, but too short and beetled to properly serve that purpose.

Around this folly the four of us all gathered.

'What on earth is this?'

Sumper dared to shrug. 'It is as I said, you will not understand.'

'Did my plan ask for a boat?'

'Did I give you one?'

'Then what in God's name is it?'

'You have a pond,' said the ridiculous Sumper. 'This is designed so the water of your pond will wash across the gunnels and then run along this groove so this whole floating structure will be invisible below the water. Here your duck will appear to swim, eating fish which will endeavour to escape their fate.'

Dear God, my boy lay in his bed, his cheeks pale, his blood sucked by vampyres every hour.

'Ducks do not eat fish.'

Sumper sighed and bowed his head and placed his thumb and forefinger so as to support his naked brow. 'Mergansers eat little else. But that is not the point.'

'I do not have a pond,' I cried. I thought, I have a boy, a dear child I cannot lose.

'You have *something*. A pond, a tank. You are an English gentleman. Am I correct?' And now he was smiling like a magician in a circus and I could not admit to the sulphurous cistern in the nursery.

I said, 'Vaucanson's duck ate grain.'

Perhaps he saw my deep distress for when he

spoke his voice was kinder. 'In every respect you have the truth,' he said. 'Only in one way is there an error. Ask me, Herr Brandling, ask me what is the error? I will tell you – I am not Vaucanson,' he laughed, patting my back as if to give me comfort. 'Ask me what is London?'

'I am sure you will tell me.'

'Yes, London is the jewel of heaven,' Herr Sumper said to me, his voice now soft as velvet. 'Of this I had no idea. When I left Furtwangen I did not seek a noble fate. I fled my destiny, which was to become a patricide. Walk with me,' he said, passing me his handkerchief. 'I am not Vaucanson. Thank Jesus we have agreed on that.'

Dear Percy, forgive me.

2

Paradoxically, as a result of our two conflicts, a greater intimacy was established between us, and we developed the habit of walking together in the melancholy dusk. That he had little curiosity about my own life, I truly did not mind. Frankly I preferred that. Also his talk was hardly boring. For instance, it was on one such walk, on the edge of a ravine, that he revealed that he had planned to murder his father, by causing a tree to crash onto his bed. Alas (his word) a pulley jammed and the tree fell on the wrong room. This, he realized now, was the first truly original machine he had devised. It was in this peculiar way that he spoke to me, showing no remorse, but a detached admiration for his own genius.

As it was a genius that I required I dared not judge him.

When he failed to murder his parents – for of course they would both have died if the plan had succeeded – he jumped aboard the raft of logs and danced away. 'I had no clue that I was floating towards another constellation.'

In the gloom a German goat was doddering up a bare and rocky hill. 'Has not my entire life been a wonder?' he said.

He admitted a 'typical peasant prejudice' against the English until he met an English woman in Avignon and followed her to London. And when she showed him what his valley had hidden from him, he could have sent a flood and washed all the Schwarzwald into the sea.

I could hear the plaintive bleat of the goat. I could see no more than the palest chalk mark of the road.

But Sumper, Sumper was in London, already in the future of the world. Miracles surrounded him, he told me so. Did I have any idea what a barometer was? Had I seen a hot-air balloon? No one in Furtwangen had ever seen a balloon, he said. If he had floated over them, they would not have seen him. They were like the savages in New South Wales who did not even see the English ships, because they did not know that such things existed.

173

Had it ever occurred to me, he wished to know, that I too might suffer from this blindness? What if I walked along this road and it was suddenly illuminated by blazing sea horses? Would I be able to see what I judged impossible?

In the distance Frau Helga rang her bell for dinner. This caused Sumper to say he would not make false digestive systems. He was not a cheat. He tried to persuade me to touch his own stomach where he said he had a scar caused by an incision through which he had received direct Instruction.

I pretended to misunderstand him and he was forced to hurry after me toward the ringing bell.

## 3

Fortunately we did not return to the subject of the scar that night, but when the meal was over and Carl and Frau Helga had retired, he produced what I took to be a joint of meat wrapped in a cloth, perhaps a leg of goat, a bone to give a dog.

I was writing. He sat without invitation and threw onto my page a little silver leaf. I admired it with some trepidation, hoping it was nothing to do with me.

'Perhaps this is more pleasing,' he said, slowly unwrapping the large object he had kept resting on his lap. It was not a bone at all, but five gleaming steel sections, articulated at their junctions.

'Neck,' he said. 'For your boy.'

But this was not the neck of any duck. I'm afraid I rather panicked.

'Please, my patron' – he ensnared my hand – 'you must be happy. You must celebrate your good fortune.'

For myself I could have cried.

'Think, Sir,' he purred, 'how unlikely it is that you would wander into a second-rate hotel in Karlsruhe, and end up with this?'

'But this is not a duck.'

I could not shame him. He made a snakelike dance with his arm and hand, extraordinarily sinuous, and deft, moving down to pick up the salt shaker and then, with a fast flick, letting it slip down his sleeve. In the face of his own fraudulence and theft he stood triumphant.

'The neck is too long,' I insisted. 'You must agree.'

First came the deep coarse laughter and then a curious bright-eyed solemnity.

'As in the case of the male member, that is impossible.'

Perhaps I groaned. In any case, I was the victim of my own considerable emotions.

'I am a rough fellow, yes, please examine the fine work that your money has provided. Here is a tolerance of half one-thousandth of an inch. Consider that. See how the parts move within each other, how they turn.'

'What is this thing, Sir?'

'Herr Brandling, this will be the most extraordinary swan.'

'Damn you man, are you not human? No one gives a swan to a child.'

'You will be the first to do so.'

'You cannot make a swan serve as a toy.'

'But I would never make a toy.'

'Swans break bones. They kill, man.'

'Herr Brandling, what you say may be correct but swans also make love to young ladies. This swan will do no such thing. It is made to be a child's enchanter. It will be beautiful and friendly. No one will be hurt. Nothing shall die. Even the fish it eats will rise up from the dead and swim again.'

'A miracle,' I said.

'You are sarcastic?'

No, I was furious. But then, in the middle of my temper, I glimpsed the half-full glass. Sumper was both coarse and conceited, but might not this other creature do exactly what I had expected of the duck? Might not this incite magnetic agitations just as well? Why not?

'The English are always sarcastic,' said Sumper, 'but when you say "miracle" I say yes, yes it is. And as a miracle placed you in Frau Beck's inn in Karlsruhe, so a miracle placed me in Bowling Green Lane in London. No, sit. Please remain. You are angry. You feel powerless, but you are the patron, and you have no idea of what you make possible. Your power is so much greater than you know.

'Henry, I had seven words of English: "I am a very good Swiss clockmaker." This lie had done

176

me no good, and by the time I got to Bowling Green Lane I had only two coins remaining. Do you know the name Thigpen?'

The pater had a fob watch from Thigpen & Thwaite.

'It is someone who is begging for coin. I was a cold and hungry Thigpen, and I stopped at the window of Thigpen & Co. only because it had my name on it, in gold leaf like a tobacconist's. Behind the glass was displayed an instrument unknown to all in Furtwangen. A barometer, in fact.

'Through the door I found a young Englishman with a leather apron. I told him my usual lie about being Swiss. What did he do? Ask me what he did.'

There was no need.

'Why, Herr Brandling, he fetched Herr Thigpen, as Schwarzwalder as you could get and the minute I opened my mouth he decided I was some useless cuckoo man. But,' Sumper said, holding my wrist as if I would escape him, 'but, Herr Brandling, I had been so pleased to hear my native tongue, I begged him let me labour for one week without wages.'

What Thigpen needed was a vise and lathe man in his instruments factory.

Sumper immediately claimed he was that very thing.

Thigpen seems to have been a shrewd old fellow, with keen blue eyes beneath tremendous eyebrows and his grey hair swept back and tied with a ribbon.

177

'You were a Swiss?' he sneered at Sumper. 'Now you are a vise and lathe man?'

He demanded the young man show his hands. These hands had already been judged too big for the English clock trade.

'You like your hands?' Thigpen asked. 'You think you can keep your hands attached?' He frightened Sumper, naturally, for the only lathes he knew were tiny, used by clockmakers.

'Come, Cuckoo,' said Thigpen, 'follow me.'

He led the way through bench-loads of clock-makers, at their prayers like seminarians, and then down beside the outhouse and into another factory which ran all the way to Northampton Road and here, in a long cold workshop with a ceiling made of glass, loomed some immense scientific instrument, like a giant's abacus, like a locomotive engine, as astonishing as an elephant of brass and steel. Sumper claimed that this strange machine would completely change his life, but at the time he could not afford to see it. He was occupied with being a vise and lathe man.

'Herr Brandling, you cannot imagine the hatred toward a stranger.' The English lathe men drew their hands across their throats, meaning either that they would kill Sumper or the machine would do it for them.

Yet when Sumper was introduced to the bench lathe it did not seem so terrifying at first. Thigpen explained that the other tools in his workshop were of great delicacy, requiring accurate adjustment every occasion they were used. In many cases the time employed in adjusting the calibration was longer than the time of production.

I told Sumper I was not a mechanic. I could not understand him.

'The same for me, exactly, Herr Brandling. There was no time to even memorize the names of things.'

Broadly speaking, Thigpen explained to Sumper, it was good economy to keep one machine constantly employed in one kind of work. No fiddle-farting, he said. One lathe, for example, should be kept constantly making cylinders. His men were proud to spend their hours in fiddle-fart, but those days would soon be over on Bowling Green Lane.

'One lathe, one job,' he said.

Sumper was a foreigner and he was doing what the English would not do. He was not scared of them. He said this many times.

If he was to be killed it would be by tedium. Work at that preset lathe required the murder of all intelligence and skill.

Yet even if he was of the lower orders, he soon noticed that there was a higher game being played. As he became more skilled he had time to look around, and then he understood that there were gentlemen, lords and dukes coming and going all day long, members of the Royal Society.

'The Royal Society,' I said. 'I suppose they came to give you Instruction.'

The joke was not well taken and I leapt to make things right. 'And what did you learn in Bowling Green Lane, Herr Sumper?'

'What did I learn, my little one? Only that there were worlds beyond my knowledge and your imagination.' He lifted the swan's steel bones and danced them before my eyes in such a menacing way that I regretted my silly joke. With his long, long arm, like a dancer, he mimicked the motion of the neck and, standing on his chair, all fifteen stone of him, essayed a vast and fearsome raising of the wings.

# CATHERINE

Amanda had clearly told her grandfather I had stolen Carl's blue cube. The grandfather had then told Crofty. I could see them as vividly as I could see Brandling and Sumper in the inn – Amanda, her grandfather, Eric all gathered in some decaying Suffolk sitting room – glass-fronted bookcases and a portion of the ceiling fallen in – the spy reporting, the three of them making decisions that were not theirs to make.

The Courtauld girl must be taught that she reported to me, not her grandfather or Eric Croft.

So I spoke to her, not about the cube of course. I punished her. I forbade all work 'beyond the limits of your job description'. I was a total bitch. I separated her from her beloved silver rings (which she had been cleaning very well) and set her to inputting all the measurements and functions of each numbered part. This was a stupid use of her time as she was clumsy with the micrometer and emitted despairing little cries with every error. This was upsetting for both of us, but I was determined to have her accept who was in charge. I suppose I made a hash of it. I confused her more than anything, especially when I said she could not use her so-called Frankenpod, not even for lunchtime which she spent nibbling on dried fruits and nuts and peering at some stormy image on its screen.

'What is it?' I demanded as we ended our rather sweaty interview. 'A music video?'

'You don't know?'

'I have no other reason to ask you, Amanda.'

'It is the oil spill. It is a webcam of the oil spill.'

Thus: Catherine Gehrig was the last person on the planet to learn that millions of barrels of oil were spewing into the Gulf of Mexico. This catastrophe had apparently occurred on the day before Matthew died.

Amanda was teary. She packed her things, and took her Frankenpod away but I, being a sneak and a hypocrite, had already memorized the URL. When I was home that night, I watched the sickening image for hours on end.

When I entered the studio next morning Amanda was waiting and I saw she now wanted to push our conflict out into the open. But I could no more reveal my personal relationship with the cube than I could confess my horror at the filth spewing into the waters of the gulf, an 'accident' that seemed the end of history itself.

I immediately made myself busy, looking through the Excel charts Amanda had prepared for me.

'These charts are very good,' I said. It was true.

They were perfection. But I still would not forgive her betrayal.

This must have been the moment when I finally understood Amanda was Amanda, and therefore she would not go away. When I had finished with the charts, she compelled me to deal with her.

'I have been so stupid,' she said. 'I am very sorry for talking out of school. I apologize.'

She was so young and her lovely skin so tight and clean. Who would doubt her contrition?

'You love your grandfather,' I said.

'But I do understand what I did wrong, Miss Gehrig. I should not have gossiped with my grandfather.'

'Mr Croft pays visits to your grandfather I suppose.'

And there it was – some curious fear or sense of honour made her step away. 'Oh I don't know anything about Mr Croft. Really.'

'Amanda! Surely he helped get you this job.'

'No!'

She was now red, crimson really. 'No. My grandfather would never do a thing like that. He despises influence-peddlers.'

I didn't believe her, but it was clear she believed herself, and the result was that our conversation calmed us down.

We shared a sandwich at lunch. Afterwards I presented her with the multi-function cam. It would be hers to dismantle, clean, photograph and document. It was a very handsome gift.

In the early afternoon the sun came out and our blinds were suddenly soaked with light.

At five she asked if she could leave for a 'stuffy drinks'. Who could imagine where she went, but her eyes were clearer and brighter and I rubbed her angora shoulder.

'Did you watch that webcam thing last night?' I asked.

'I suppose so.'

'Does everybody watch it? Your friends.'

'Not everyone.'

'It's horrible.'

'Yes,' she said. 'Please can I go, Miss Gehrig?'

When they invented the internal combustion engine, they never envisaged such a horrid injury. It did not occur to anyone that we would not only change the temperature of the air but turn the oceans black as death.

Henry's saw-tooth pen strokes had cut wormholes into time. I had been there. I had witnessed Herr Sumper unwrap the articulated neck. I had glimpsed Carl's exploding toy roaring past the inn, his voltaic mouse, his blue cube, Thigpen's immense scientific instrument the size of an elephant. Through one of these wormholes, as thin as a drinking straw, I had seen all that bright and poisonous invention.

At home, I put water on the stove and lit the gas. I would cook. Dry pasta, sardines, capers, stale bread, olive oil. I would eat, macerate, excrete.

And then the door bell rang – Eric, come to

184

have his cube returned. I fetched a plate and fork for him. 'No, no,' he said.

'I made too much. I can't stop doing it.'

'I've got a dinner engagement,' he said.

Still, I made a place for him. The blue block was wrapped in a handkerchief. I set it beside his plate.

I thought, surely he wants to see the cornflower blue.

'Brought it home for some tests?' he asked.

I smiled.

'Crazy bugger,' he said.

'Yes.'

'Swap you,' he said, also smiling. I liked his crinkled eyes. I imagined him playing poker. Indeed the envelope he now produced was the size of a playing card. Inside I discovered one of those cardboard-mounted Victorian portraits.

'Your man,' he said, making me remember why I liked him – that impish quality. 'This is the man who commissioned your swan.'

He was looking at me strangely. I thought, yes, he *has* actually taken the time to read the notebooks. He had read them at the very start.

'His name was Henry Brandling,' he said.

'Oh, how do you know?'

Again that smile.

He could not have the least idea of how deeply invested I was in Henry. He would have expected me to be curious, but how could he possibly anticipate what it meant to me, to find my author so very tall and handsome, holding a baby in his

185

arms? I was happy, uplifted, to meet him in this way, to understand his nobility and tenderness.

'Percy,' I said.

'Henry,' he corrected. 'Henry Brandling.'

'The child.'

'Oh, I know nothing of the child.'

There was something rather odd about the photograph, and I removed it from its plastic to examine it more closely.

'It was not uncommon,' Eric said.

'You got this from where?'

My visitor laid his hand flat against my back. 'It's rather awful isn't it?'

Only then did I understand – the child in the man's arms was the product of a Victorian mortician's art.

'This is bullshit,' I said.

'Cat, Cat, what on earth is the matter?'

He reached out his hand toward me, and suddenly he appeared not kind or crinkly, not impish at all. I thought, why are you trying to destroy me?

'Cat.'

'Never call me Cat. Not ever.'

'Catherine.'

'Go, go.' I dragged out his coat and threw it at him. He reached for the blue block. I snatched it back.

Hours after he left I discovered the date on the verso and finally realized that this was not Percy but his sister Alice whose name the grieving Henry

Brandling had mentioned in connection with a clock.

2

I began to read the newspapers again. I learned that the Americans have made a robot to teach autistic children. In many respects it is superior to a human being. That is, being a robot, it never becomes emotionally exhausted; it never loses patience; tears and rage do not press its buttons.

The robot is called KayKay. I am not sure why. It does not attempt to hide its wiring and other innards. The report said that children swarmed it when it first appeared at a 'facility' in Austin, Texas. At the end of the first day, a boy with Asperger's syndrome yanked its arms off.

The journalist seemed a little too happy about the arm-yanking, but the company said it was a 'learning curve'. By the next public exposure, which was reported in the *Guardian*, KayKay had its arms repaired. Now, when KayKay cried, the little Aspies did not 'hurt' it any more. If the sobbing continued, they then gave the thing a hug.

Catherine wants KayKay.

KayKay would move on wheels, tracking Catherine throughout the flat, approaching indirectly and never entering 'personal space'. KayKay would say 'Uh huh' (an encouraging sound in American) when Catherine drew near.

When Catherine moved away, KayKay would say 'Aw' (American for disappointment).

Eric Croft must have wearied of my tears and rage, I thought. Who would blame him? Who would not prefer the company of normal people?

I sat at the kitchen table, peering into the wavering field of marks left by Henry Brandling's pen. When I was above it, looking down into the lines, I could see flickering candles, the deep shadows of the 'not here'. The distance was immense but I saw Henry's sad dark eyes watch the other inhabitants of the room at the sawmill in Furtwangen – four or five of them – assembling tiny links of chain.

As yet Henry Brandling had no clue how the chain would serve the swan.

Catherine, on the other hand, had touched the chain, had tightened it, compelled it to move the skeletal neck of the swan on the fourth floor of the Swinburne Annexe.

In the firelight Henry Brandling's eyes were unsettled and afraid. He had lost one child already. How the minutes must be, each one an agony.

Each of the Germans had a small assembly tool, not much more than a support system for a single groove into which the tiny component parts of chain were fitted so the rivet could be slipped into place and hammered home. The boy was fastest but Sumper, with his huge hands, was the most astonishing to behold. He was covertly competing with the child.

188

As so often, Henry could do nothing but watch. He did this with a terrible intensity that bore no relationship to the nature of manufacture being enacted. He crouched on a three-legged stool by the dying fire.

Might Henry Brandling have anticipated Catherine?

He anticipated someone would watch him through the wormhole, that was clear. He wrote for that person. He thought constantly of the moment when that chain would animate a swan that he stubbornly referred to as 'my duck'.

I thought, he is lying, but not to me.

On Kennington Road the car tyres were hissing. The oxidized lines once made by Henry Brandling's pen evoked weeds waving under water. The fairy-tale collector and the silversmith slowly melded together. They were the same person as I had already guessed. If Henry was not lying to me, then to whom was he lying? To God? I returned to Furtwangen and turned the page.

Sumper spat a hissing glob into the fire. 'Listen to me more carefully,' he said to the fairytale collector. 'It is the nature of science,' he said, 'that what is true is always unacceptable to people.'

And of course I, Catherine, agreed with him. Which of us would not?

'I'll tell you a story that is true,' the fairytale collector offered.

The child looked at Sumper imploringly. Even so his little warty fingers 'never paused'. He was like a bird feeding, constantly pecking at a bowl of chain links.

The fairytale collector administered a light tap with a delicate black hammer. 'On the exactly true date of 15 April 1614, a murder was committed in the old part of Salzwedel just off the street leading to St Ann's Convent.'

Carl screwed up his eyes.

The fairytale collector had no mercy. He described how the murderer's hands were cut off and how he was tortured with red-hot pincers and dragged to the place of execution and placed on the wheel upside down. It was 'miraculous' and horrible, according to the fairytale collector, to see how the hand with which he had committed this terrible deed continued to bleed for three days on the wheel.

'Why am I trapped here?' cried Sumper who did not seem to be aware of the child's distress. 'How could this happen to me, forced to listen to this chaff?'

For that he had Catherine's sympathy. He was worthy of a better conversation. She had a better dialogue with him every day at work.

I was there close by him, by the four of them as they assembled the fusee chain, or four fusee chains. I saw them grow at an extraordinary rate, click, clack, tap, so swiftly. There was a long period with no word spoken, and the spiky sentences, brimful of awful anxious feeling, stretched on across the page. Finally it was Sumper who addressed the 'awful little weasel'.

190

'You have heard of Sir Albert Cruickshank.'

Catherine had not.

Sumper left the table. The angelic boy 'quietly compared' the two lengths of chain, his and Sumper's. He whispered to his mother. The mother removed Sumper's chain from her son's celestial hand. She returned the chain to its place in the clockmaker's assembly tool. No sooner had she done so than the clockmaker returned with 'a much-stained' book in his hand. He clipped Carl lightly across the back of the head and both of them burst out laughing.

Catherine read the title: *Mysterium Tremendum*.

'The author is Sir Albert Cruickshank,' Sumper told the fairytale collector. 'He holds the Lucasian Chair of Mathematics at Cambridge. He is a fellow of the Royal Society and the inventor of the Cruickshank Engine.'

The fairytale collector affected to sigh, but the child looked expectantly towards the book, its Latin title inlaid with gold and glowing in the firelight. It was, Henry intuited, a familiar hymn or song.

'M. Arnaud,' said Herr Sumper, '*Mysterium Tremendum* was written at Cambridge University, and do not fret if you have not heard of that institution. It exists beyond your tiny world.

'"I then begged of my guide,"' Sumper read from the volume, '"that he provide a glimpse of those other higher intellectual beings and the modes of their thought and their enjoyments. These are

191

creatures far superior to any idea your human imagination can conceive."

"'I was again in motion,'" (Herr Sumper stood), "'I saw below me lakes and seas on the surface of which I beheld living beings which I cannot properly describe. They had systems for locomotion similar to those of the sea horse. They moved from place to place by six extremely thin membranes, which they used as wings. I saw numerous convolutions of tubes, more analogous to the trunk of the elephant than to anything else, occupying what I supposed to be the upper parts of the body. Here my astonishment became disgust. Such was the peculiar character of the organs.'"

Oh dear, Catherine thought, oh dearie dearie me. It was as if she had opened her front door to a Jehovah's Witness. But the boy was totally at home. His red mouth was open. His hair 'caught the candlelight' as he reached for his mother's hand with his long thin fingers, 'pale, plastic, bendy as the necks of birds'.

'You,' Sumper pointed to Henry Brandling, 'are in the same state as a fly whose microscopic eye has been changed to one similar to a man's.'

The boy cast on Henry Brandling 'a beautiful and pitying smile'. And then he mouthed the words as Sumper read: "'YOU ARE WHOLLY UNABLE TO ASSOCIATE WHAT YOU SEE WITH WHAT YOUR LIFE HAS TAUGHT YOU.'"

Catherine shivered. What to think of this? Had the great mechanic also been a mystic?

Sumper read: "'Those beings who are before you now, who appear to you almost as imperfect as the lowly zoophytes, have a sphere of sensibility and intellect far superior to the inhabitants of this earth.'"

At the time it did not occur to me, not for a moment, that this was really written by a man of science. I had no idea how much Cruickshank owed to Humphry Davy's *Consolations in Travel*. I did not think of the Royal Society but rather C. S. Lewis on an acid trip. And this from Sumper, whose work I trusted and admired all through my working day.

'You have no idea of where you are,' Sumper told Brandling. 'You have no idea of what will happen here. In this very room,' he said, 'you have been anointed as a courier, and you will play your role never knowing what you have done, or imagining you have been the brave agent in a history you will never read.'

Henry reported the 'full furnace heat of madness' and then a fright that 'mak'st my blood cold, and my hair to stare'.

Catherine reread: 'Those beings who are before you now, who appear to you almost as imperfect as the lowly zoophytes, have a sphere of sensibility and intellect far superior to the inhabitants of this earth.'

Catherine wants KayKay. I was spooked.

★　　★　　★

It was not yet nine o'clock but Amanda Snyde
was already at her correct work station, cleaning
the rings as I had asked her to.

That was our 'object' – not a smoking monkey
but a gleaming phallus stripped to the bare metal,
as if flayed.

To the smooth articulated neck we would soon
attach the fusee chains, like nerves rising within
the vertebrae. These dry chains ran over a series
of rollers effecting the operation of the lower neck,
upper neck, nodding of the head, movement of
the fish inside the swan's bill.

There were five chains, of varying thicknesses.
The finest of these had 170 links which meant,
according to Amanda Snyde who had counted
them, an estimated seven hundred pieces riveted
together. It normally required children and mothers
– small hands, young eyes – to perform such delicate work.

We knew that the first of these chains would
operate the lower bill, the preening, the eating of
the fish. The second chain would operate the fish
themselves. The third would make the swan's head
nod. The fourth would arch the neck and the fifth
was linked to the middle of the neck and would,
if we were correct, make the movement very
graceful and lifelike.

Today would be the first of two 'neck days', but
we did not begin assembly until I had my normal

half hour with Matthew's emails, which I referred to simply as 'my housekeeping'. Amanda kept her distance and asked no questions which made me certain she had figured exactly what I was doing.

Now she was recording the structure and dimension of each fusee link, and I was alone with my beloved. What peculiar people we had been, he and I, rationalists but sensualists, always so proud and careful of our bodies, knowing our lives were finite, acting as if we were eternal. How sweetly he had written to me, and so often. We had not denied time as humans are supposed to. Swimming off Dunwich beach, we had been aware of our skin, our hearts, water, wind, the vast complex machine of earth, the pump of rain and evaporation and tide, timeless wind to twist the heath trees. Afterwards it would make me dizzy to be reminded that the blood from the cavernous spaces of the penis is returned by a series of vessels, some of which emerge in considerable numbers and converge on the dorsum of the organ to form the deep dorsal vein. Dear God, I thought, we lived for it but now I may never have sex again. I closed down the computer feeling desolate. I began to work again but I saw oil spilled across the lichen and heather, roe deer, rabbits, nightjars dripping, submarine robots crawling through the murk.

Then I thought, thank God for Amanda. This may not have been consistent of me, but on a good day she could be an extremely comforting assistant, one of those rare creatures who have the tweezers ready before you have to ask. Threading was slow and fiddly but a good assistant makes this like a highly disciplined duet, and if one is slow and careful one can expect, every hour or so, to have formed a new connection within the mechanism and experienced the huge pleasure that comes when one human co-operates with another. Yet as the day wore on, various unhappinesses, pale glistening things like liver flukes began to worm their way back into my mind. How I missed Matthew, with what ache.

At lunch I sent a grovelling email to Eric apologizing for last night's outburst. I waited until the end of the day and when there was no reply I telephoned him.

'Croft.'

I took fright, and hung up. Then, in my agitation, I broke the finest chain and was the recipient of more sympathy than I desired. Amanda touched my wrist.

She said, 'Does it spook you?'

She meant the swan, not Crofty.

'Of course not.'

'It is incorrect to think of the devil as ugly,' she said.

I thought, why do you need to spin these dreams from darkness? Why can you not appreciate the mechanical marvel before your very eyes?

'Amanda dear, we are fixing a machine.'

'Yes but Lucifer is very beautiful.'

Her gaze was too direct.

'It's Lucifer,' she said, 'in Ezekiel. *The workman-ship of your timbrels and pipes was prepared for you on the day you were created.*'

'Well,' I said, 'I think that's it for today.'

'You're in a rush.'

Yes, yes, I really was.

## 4

The entrance to my flat was a high library, much narrower than the thirty-nine inches legally stipulated for London passageways. The shelves were pale soft coachwood which was silky to touch. Every shelf was illuminated by low-temperature lights. On the floor was an old Tabriz rug which looked a lot better than it really was.

It was a jewel box, and I always adjusted the lights so my visitor would get the full effect. By 'my visitor', I mean Matthew. I had rarely admitted anybody else. In the case of Eric, it would be necessary, if one was to be polite, to step outside in order to admit him.

When the door bell rang that night, I opened the door to discover, not Eric, but ghosts and mirrors of my lovely man, his two sons, dark-eyed in the rain.

The older boy wore his trousers as Matthew did – pleated, narrow-waisted. St Vincent de Paul most likely, but super-elegant. This was the mathematician, Angus. He had his father's hair, exactly, the big nose, the full-lipped humorous mouth.

'Come in,' I said, and stepped outside. They backed away like frightened horses.

The young one was the taller, Noah. In photographs he had also been the prettier but now he had a fuzzy beard and his hair was raging, tufted, hacked at with nail scissors I would say.

'Please go in.' My hands were trembling.

'We're sorry,' said Angus. He had hand-painted the buttons on his shirt. In this light they looked like Indian miniatures.

'Well, I refuse to have you standing in the rain.'

Noah looked accusingly at his brother.

'We're sorry,' Angus said, then walked briskly through my library. Noah followed, ducking at the door. He had mud on his boots and I didn't mind. I was looking at his father's long runner's legs.

Noah stroked a coachwood shelf, as if checking on my housekeeping while covertly identifying a rainforest timber. He was the greenie. He was also the classics genius. He had, at the age of fourteen, come home drunk and vomited in his bed. Never having met him, I had lived with him for years and years.

I found them shuffling on my durrie, the sort of pale delicate rug only childless people have. They did not know what to do with their bodies. So I chose the Nelson Case Study day bed and sat on one end. Then Noah sat opposite on a Gustav Axel Berg whose eighty-year-old bentwood torqued beneath his weight.

Finally, Angus chose the other end of the day

bed. Even from that distance the beautiful creature smelled musty and unwashed.

The stolen blue cube was sitting in the middle of the magazine table. Noah clearly followed my gaze. He was his father's son. He picked up the cube.

'May I smoke?' he asked.

'Of course.'

He produced a pouch of tobacco, balanced Carl's toy on one knee.

Poor boys I thought – their dear eyes, great dark pools of hurt, more like each other than like their father – low brows, a terrible silent mental concentration. On what I did not know. But they carried Matthew's beauty, their sinew, bone, the square set of their shoulders, that same lovely nose.

'I'll fetch an ashtray.'

I thought, when I give it to him I'll take the cube away, I don't know why, but by the time I returned he'd tucked it deep between his legs.

'We have never really met,' I said to his brother.

'No, not really.'

'But you are Angus?'

'Yes.'

'I'm the troubled child,' Noah said, and placed Carl's cube back on the table. 'I'm Noah. And you are Catherine Gehrig. I Googled you.'

Silence.

'Can I have a drink?' asked Noah.

I knew Matthew did not wish me to give him alcohol.

'Do you have any beer?'

'Just some red wine, and a little whisky.'

'Whisky,' he said, and held my gaze.

I looked to his older brother. He shook his head. 'I'm the designated driver.'

When I first met his father, Noah had been in trouble for making a joke about a gay camel. He was just a little boy. He had thought it was funny, that a camel might be gay. The school had different opinions.

'Weird, huh?' I called as I poured the whisky in the kitchen. The 'huh' sounding so old, so fake.

'What?'

I fetched a glass of water and delivered this together with the whisky. Angus was standing in front of the framed photograph of the stables.

'It's strange, us three, here all together,' I said as the child drank his whisky straight. 'I'm sorry if this is awful for you.'

'Did you like it there?' Angus asked, gazing at the photograph. He was being an adult, smelling like a teenage boy.

I stood beside him. 'I don't think you did.'

He produced his Frankenpod or Space Onion or whatever. 'Have you ever Googled it? Would you like to see?'

Of course I did not wish to look. 'All right,' I said.

Angus sat on the day bed, with me on his left side. We crouched over the gadget, not quite touching, and there it was, the stables seen from space, the line of cliff, the trees, the grey roof in the shade.

It was nighttime now in Suffolk, but the daylight image was no less disturbing for being captured in the past. The satellite had spied on us during the summer of the drought, the brown grass, the dying tree. I could make out the Norton Commando so the pair of us were there, alive together, unaware.

'We must have been inside,' I said, and then I was embarrassed to imagine what they thought: all that stinky sex. 'Did you feel I stole your father from you?'

'Let's face it,' Noah said. 'You did.'

There was some unspoken current of conversation between them.

'No, it wasn't you,' Angus said, but I must have existed everywhere around them.

Noah left the room and – don't ask me why – I snatched Carl's cube and sat it on the shelf behind me.

When he returned with the whisky bottle, he spoke directly to his older brother. 'We were going to tell the truth. That's what we agreed.'

My heart sank.

Noah's mouth, like his father's, was an instrument of infinite nuance. He was staring at the shelf above my head, and although he was almost certainly amused, I had no idea what he was thinking.

Then Angus removed the framed photograph from the wall. I have never liked people fiddling with my things but I forgot that when I saw how sad and grimy my walls had become.

'This is yours now,' Angus said.

I was so tense I thought he meant my photograph and I was outraged that he should have assumed the power to give me what was mine.

'Do you mean this?'

'The stables, yes. It's yours.'

My heart did leap at that, but of course they were boys and they knew a great deal less than I did. Matthew and I had talked about his will. He had wished to maintain our secrets after death and if I had been hurt by that, it had not been for long.

'You're very sweet. I wish it was.'

Noah picked up the whisky bottle and we all watched while it surrendered the last four drops.

'It is yours.' Noah had that slightly off-putting confidence young public schoolboys bring to the workplace. I wanted to say, I saw your father's will, you brat. He signed it in 2006 and I can promise you that Catherine Gehrig does not even have a walk-on part.

'Dad couldn't leave it to you, of course,' Angus said.

'No, of course not.' He was pushing all my buttons all at once. For thirteen years I had been made invisible by this family even while I was subsumed by them, their maths problems and their vomiting. I didn't mind. I really didn't mind.

'He left it to us.'

'Quite right,' I said, my bitterness a secret, even from myself.

'He could hardly write your name in his will.'

Well, he could, I thought, although I would never have asked him to. 'It would have looked a little odd to your mother.' I smiled as best I could.

'We've talked about it, Noah and I. And as we are the new owners we have decided you shall have it as long as you live.'

There were too many emotions in the room, but the two young men were keeping themselves together, both of them with their big hands upon their knees.

'It's called a peppercorn rent. We have brought the lease for you to sign. You pay one peppercorn a year, that's it.'

'We brought the Mini here, to give to you.'

'Really? Did you do all this on your own?'

'A friend of Dad's. He helped us think about the lease.'

'This would be Mr Croft?'

'He has been very nice to us.'

'He registered the car in whose name?'

Neither of them seemed to know.

'We parked it outside.'

'We washed it, but it rained.'

'You are very sweet, but I can't drive.' This was not really true.

'You could learn,' said Angus. 'It's surprisingly easy.'

'I could teach you,' Noah said. 'I did an advanced driving course, skid pans, everything.'

I could say nothing in response. I was too moved, too sad, too furious. My young protectors somehow saw I was about to cry. They quickly agreed they would keep the Mini somewhere safe for me and that we would meet to talk about the driving lessons. I signed the lease and gave them both a peppercorn and in minutes we were in the library where I was held in a musty smelly sort of rugger hug. Matthew, in their bones.

When they had gone I lay on my bed and thought about the breeze brushing our naked skin in the summer, the storms rocking us in winter, the German Sea gnawing at the bottom of the cliff.

## 5

At the Annexe, at this early hour, I delete you, my darling, my beloved, with your wide soft mouth against my neck. I would rather scrub your bones and place them in the open air, scrub your sternum, labour at your spine, scrub and scrub, with love, each vertebra, as particular as a nose, and lay you in the grass amongst the bluebells. There on your secret triangle of land I would be your most submissive tenant, would lie beside you until rain, wind, storms raced, threaded like shoelaces through our missing eyes.

Such thoughts as these are mine, at the moment Amanda enters from her world where the Gulf of

Mexico has become a lake of oil. Does she have a mythology or cosmology for this?

'Hello,' she says when she has dumped her backpack.

'Hello,' I say. Delete, I think.

Looking up, it is clear to me that she has a new lover. She has baggy indigo trousers and a sleeveless top like silverfish. Inside these loose coverings is a body so young as to make one weep. Her attention is on the swan. Please, please, I need no more fantastical nonsense. Please learn to see what is before you here and now.

She says, 'What I am about to say is none of my business.'

The hair rises on my neck. I delete a letter I have not even read.

'I only want to help.'

I read, archive, spam, delete.

'It is so painful watching you,' she says.

'It is just a swan, Amanda. A machine.'

'Miss Gehrig, this does not have to take weeks. It could be done in minutes. You do not have to torture yourself like this.'

She is offering me a small plastic object which, in my fear and rage, I mistake for a cigarette lighter. It has one of those crude non-words in white type on its side. A part emerges from the black sheath, steel, like lipstick.

'You just create a new folder for your email, archive it, and export the archive to a flash drive.'

'What's a flash drive?'

'This.' She sort of *thrusts* it at me, which I do not like at all.

'I could download it for you. In a second.'

'I'm fine, thank you.' She works for me, she reports to me, but even as I refuse her help she attempts to get around me.

'Amanda, what is it that you imagine I am up to?'

But she will not answer. 'All I'm saying is – you don't have to spend hours and hours like this. It must be hell.'

'Who told you?'

But she is intent on controlling my computer.

'It was Mr Croft who told you?'

Her doll-like eyes are wet with unwanted sympathy. At the same time her irises are very wide, like a creature living in the dark.

'Please, please let me just . . .' And she has slid between me and the machine, typing as she speaks. 'You can take it home and load it on your own computer. Is it a Mac?'

'No. It's a PC. So, obviously it will not work.'

She looks over her shoulder, appraising me as if I am a dangerous beast, holding my eye all the while. Up close, she smells strangely musty. Then I see her fingernails are dirty.

'You know who these emails are from?' I ask her.

'They're loading now.'

'Who told you, Amanda?'

'We both know who told me.' She places the tiny object in my hands. She wraps my fingers around it. Some subtle shift of power has been effected.

'Miss Gehrig, he worries about you.'

'No.'

'All he can think about is that you be looked after.'

'But we can't say who he actually is.'

'No.'

'Although we already have.'

'The swan is terribly important to the museum, you know that. He has a frightful difficulty getting money as you know. He has to go around sucking up and being charming. How awful to have to beg from all those city yobs.'

Thus I am taught to suck eggs by my child assistant. But what really stings is that the sweet, pretty, clever Courtauld girl has forcibly removed Matthew from my cache. She has made me hold him like ashes in a vial.

# HENRY

Sumper and I departed the village with the heavy brass drum strapped between two poles. Such was the weight we were in a hurry to reach our destination, speeding through the fog across the square, down the lanes to the brook, across the footbridge to the fields, stumbling dangerously in furrows at whose furthest extent the sawmill awaited us. Now the leaves had fallen and nature was revealed, like an old man whose beard has been shaved off to show what cruel tricks time had played on him. Dear Pater.

Such was our speed and so uneven was the field that I feared Frau Helga, charging from the flank, would cause a spill. She passed me at a gallop and rounded on Herr Sumper while somehow trotting backwards, bravely waving letters in the air.

'On,' cried Sumper. 'On.'

'No, it is from England.'

'On.'

I thought, Percy! But I was tied to Herr Sumper in every sense, so 'on' I must and 'on' I did, although together we almost ran the woman down.

I thought, it is from Binns. My boy could not

endure the wait. Dead and lonely and I did not kiss his lips. Then we reached the river path, and the Holy Child burst from the bushes with a savage yell. His eyes were bright, his cry too high. He shook a murdered rabbit before his mother's face before setting off ahead, gambolling and hobbling, shaking his keys in his left hand.

We sped onwards. Dear God, I am a mighty fool, please let him live. In the freezing summer workshop above the river, we laid our burden down.

I took the letter and saw my brother's hand.

'What news?' asked Helga.

Carl was also waiting, dripping rabbit blood onto his feet.

Thank God, thank Jesus, I will join you soon.

But no – my brother was set to delay me further. Two months previously, the spider wrote, he had *been appointed my trustee* and now possessed the power to decide, at his own discretion, what sums would be made available to me at whatever intervals he might deem appropriate, the snivelling little wretch.

He claimed our father had 'lost his wits'.

Of course it was not totally impossible that the paternal mind had collapsed at exactly the moment I walked out of the door, but my brother's assertion that our father was no longer 'sensible' was what the pater would have called a 'hoot'. He had never been 'sensible' in any way at all.

Red-nosed Douglas had had him declared *Non compos mentis*. That was Douglas, worse than

Douglas. To quote: 'What you do not sufficiently appreciate, Henry, is I am a man of business, and there is a great deal more to business than railway tracks.'

He was not a man of any type at all, and what was cloaked by all his ghastly bumph was that he had invested in the Bank of Ohio. I ask you: who had lost their wits? It was Doug the Thug who had placed Brandling and Sons in an 'awkward situation'. Now he regretted to advise me, as my trustee – imagine – that I might draw no more funds until the 'panic in America' was sorted out.

Sumper turned his back. I could not see his face, only his shoulder, his green coat, his large white hand which he ran regretfully along the flat of the spring, as if it were his freshcaught trout.

'Bad news, Herr Brandling?'

He took it well, Frau Helga less so. She ran weeping across the bridge to the house and Carl went hotfoot after her, dripping blood across the floor.

'Dig potatoes,' Sumper called.

Then he turned to me, and without particular expression, made the following speech: 'The trouble with the rich is that they rarely have the patience for great things.'

I assumed he was finding fault with me. I apologized, as well I might, but he waved all that away. 'When it is their own business,' he said, 'they know what to do.'

'Who do you mean, Sir?'

'When they abandon their counting house or factory, when they must have a portrait painted, they turn into idiots. What a state they are in. They go to their club where they seek out other idiots for their opinion. "I am having my portrait done," they will say, "and the fellow is using a lot of blue. What do you think? I'm worried about that damned blue."'

So then I saw what he was saying and, for once, I totally agreed. It was *intolerable* that a fool like Douglas should play with life and death.

'They are in charge. It is their only skill. It is exactly the same with your Queen of England, German of course, and completely ignorant of where she is. It was she, Mrs Saxe-Coburg and Gotha, who disgraced England and my own country by cutting off the funding for the most extraordinary machine. That is the reason that I later came to visit Prince Albert at Buckingham Palace.'

'I see,' I said. I thought, he can only talk about himself.

'You do not look at all surprised?'

I did not look surprised because I did not believe him for a second. It was impossible in every way.

That evening I wrote to Percy concerning what I referred to as 'our secret'. I promised that in spite of his uncle and his mother's 'difficulties' I would return as promised and that if he would only eat his grains and be a brave boy with his

211

hydrotherapy, I would soon make him completely well.

If that was a risk, I did not see it. My blood was up and I would keep my word.

## 2

Herr Sumper says he first mistook the Genius, Albert Cruickshank, for a common tramp, and was mightily offended that this beggar was permitted to walk freely through the door from Bowling Green Lane. The visitor's trouser cuffs dragged on the machine-room floor. His grey hair was long and stringy. His jaw was clenched, his mouth set straight. The author of *Mysterium Tremendum* (for it was he) carried beneath his arm a rectangular board which Sumper assumed to be one of those complaining placards which he had seen mad people display outside the English parliament.

The visitor was allowed to wander freely, 'like a Hindoo Cow', between the lathes and presses of that enormous industrial cathedral. Not a drill slowed, not a canvas belt was shifted from its drive, certainly no worker prevented the intruder from approaching, along an aisle of lathes, the place where an altar might be expected in a church. But never was Christian altar built to the scale of that enormous engine. Sumper compared it variously to an elephant, a locomotive, a series of vertical columns of circular discs, all these so contradictory that a chap was left with – what? – a notion of a very large mechanism, yes, but one that was somehow spectral, golden, intricate as clockwork. I knew my clockmaker was in the habit of lying (about Prince Albert most recently) but such were his powers of persuasion that I had no difficulty in picturing how the interlinking parts of steel and brass caught the light, much like, surely, the gold frames on the high walls of my family's home could contain the flame of a single candle set on a table fifteen feet below. I found myself wishing I could have seen the wonder too.

During his first week at Thigpen & Co., despite the demands of his pre-set lathe (which he boasted he had mastered while complaining of its danger), Sumper seems to have been a most effective spy.

The draughting tables had been set to one side of the altar, and here, in the place where the choir stalls would normally be, he had glimpsed the large stooped Thigpen and his senior mechanics poring over plans.

He learned that only the firm's most respected tradesmen served the engine and that there were still ten thousand more individual parts to be produced. Not one of these ten thousand could be commenced until a very detailed drawing had been made, and as each new drawing was examined, great discussions (and some fierce arguments) took place. He was able to make me see this in a rather comic way, as if the engine was an Idol and the men were its demonic votaries.

'They thought they were all great fellows,' Sumper told me, 'but not one of them, not even Thigpen, knew that the machine was at imminent risk of being broken down and sold for scrap.'

Of course he couldn't have known it either. He knew less than anyone and had been astonished to see the tramp shake Herr Thigpen's hand and to realize that the 'placard' was a draughtsman's folio from which drawings were extracted, reverently, one by one.

An Englishman would likely have deduced that the old man was the designer of the machine, and probably rather grand, but Sumper had assumed the tramp was selling stolen goods.

So it is to be a foreigner.

For Sumper in England, the situation seems worse than mine in Germany – the English workers were allegedly angry he had agreed to man the pre-set lathe. He may (or may not) have been physically attacked outside his own boarding house. He may (or may not) have made cat's meat of them as he claimed. He was a boastful bragging man but it would fit his character for him to be bewitched by the sight of the dignitaries who visited the draughting table – 'wigs of ivory', he said, 'coats like jewels'.

His own work was possibly boring, requiring 'less brain than a cuckoo clock'. As a result of that inattention which is the constant companion of tedium, he twice came close to amputation, and it was after the second of these near misses – just when he knew he must find another job – that the factory whistle blew three times. Thank God, he thought, but the day was not over yet.

There were always a great number of trolleys and steel tables trundling across the dark slate floor, and it was one of these that the men, walking in disorderly procession, like cows at milking time, now followed deeper into the factory.

They were preceded by that grey-haired giant, their master. When he had his mechanics gathered about him, old Thigpen removed a dust cloth from the trolley and there revealed a brass and steel device. He spoke. Sumper's translation was that the device was 'the seed of the great idea we serve'. This is consistent with what follows.

Sumper compared the device to an abacus. I wrote this down.

'It was not like an abacus at all,' Sumper told me later. 'You will miss the point if you go on like this.' Tiresome man. He also said that the machine was precise, ingenious, and strange. It was an automaton whose purpose was addition.

Then the 'tramp' spoke. His voice was deep and mellifluous. No Englishman would be surprised to learn he was the third son of the Duke of Cumbria. He said: 'Men, I am to show you an impossibility.'

The fierce little tradesmen were like greyhounds straining on their leash. They pushed insistently toward the heart of the device – two brass wheels engraved with numerals.

Cruickshank asked Mr Thigpen to set the first of these brass wheels so the number 2 was aligned with the V-shaped cleft. He told the men that the value of this wheel would now be added to the value of the second.

The mechanics' bodies were sour with weariness and sweat but they pushed against each other, nosing forward, watching closely as a volunteer turned the crank through one rotation.

And what did they see? Why, that $2 + 0 = 2$.

That was the great idea they served? The tramp was certainly not embarrassed. He called each worker to turn the handle. One after the other. They were employees. They had no choice. One by one they came. They turned the first wheel (2) and added it to the increasing value of the second wheel.

And the great machine performed no better than a schoolboy.

$2 + 2 = 4$
$2 + 4 = 6$
$2 + 6 = 8$
$2 + 8 = 10$

Cruickshank greeted each answer with ridiculous astonishment. The men became sullen and resistant, slower and slower to answer their names. It was an insubordinate dye-maker named 'Spud' Coutts who added the number 2 to the number 102.

The answer was 171.

Someone dared a cat-call. Herr Thigpen scowled.

Cruickshank clapped his hands together and cried, 'Huzza.'

And Sumper smiled with pleasure.

'Only as a child smiles,' he told me, 'with no understanding of anything. Of course the Genius noticed me. I was the largest man in the room, and the only one not scowling at him.'

It is not known what Cruickshank had previously told Thigpen or how Cruickshank expected his demonstration to be understood, but if it was intended to lift morale it was a failure. The owner of the works stormed to his office.

'This,' said Cruickshank, as the master's door was heard to slam. 'This is what we should call a miracle.'

There was uneasy laughter.

'What you have all witnessed', Cruickshank smiled, 'must appear to be a violation of the law of adding two. It must seem unnatural to you, even to your master.'

At the word 'master', by design or accident, Thigpen blew the whistle. A moment later the men were swarming towards the door, leaving a few uncertain fellows hesitating.

'I am not your master,' Cruickshank coaxed, 'but I am the programmer. If you leave now you will never know that I programmed the machine so that after fifty-one additions it would perform the miracle I programmed – after fifty-one additions it would do something discontinuous.'

The word 'miracle' had a violent physical effect on one of the remaining workers. He spat, shook his fist, and headed for the door.

'And for me, Jim, that is not a violation of law. It is a manifestation of higher law, known to me, but not to you, Fred.'

But it was hopeless. He could not hold them.

'You expect two plus 102 to equal 104, but I wrote a new law that 102 plus two would equal 171. As a result,' Cruickshank told his sole remaining listener, 'as a result of a decision *beyond your knowledge*, a certain lever clicked into place. You saw two plus 102 equals 171. In nature this is what we call a miracle and I, who predicted it, would be called a prophet.'

Thus the Genius confirmed that Furtwangen's ideas of God were puny and pathetic, that there were mechanisms beyond human knowledge, that there might be, within our sight but beyond our ken, systems we could never know, worlds we had seen and forgotten. There, in Bowling Green Lane, Sumper recalled thoughts he had had as a child when he wished with all his being that he could know what it was to be the dragonfly in all three stages, as a grub beneath the soil, as an animal living in the water, as an insect flying in the air. Would the dragonfly in its last stage have any memory of its experience of the first? Might he be a dragonfly at last, and if so how would he understand the world? '*Mysterium Tremendum*,' he told me. The awe and wonder of the universe. Not for a moment did he doubt that Cruickshank was a Genius, perhaps even a Superior Being with a completely different nature. Why not? We believe Jesus walked upon the water.

'We are arrogant in our ignorance,' said the arrogant clockmaker, with his alarming eyes glittering in the firelight in Furtwangen. 'If animals possessed senses of a different nature from our own, how would we know? Those creatures, despised by us, might have sources of information we cannot dream exist. They might have a bodily and intellectual existence far higher than our own, why not, why not my Englishman? In London I was twenty-eight years old,' said Sumper, 'and I was drunk with ideas like this, some of which I had carried in secret like pebbles in my pocket since my childhood. So when the Genius met my eye, he saw I wished to serve, and when the fuss was over in the works, he asked me to walk with him to the west side of Soho Square where he made his home.'

## 3

I was Percy's engine, his pulse, his voltaic coil. With the ink of my pen I nourished him, describing the manufacture of an automaton I had never seen. Thus were my days spent. My nights, on the other hand, were quite impossible, for nothing would stop Sumper talking. Carl and his mother escaped to their bed. Then it was the worse for me. I was swallowed, buried. The drifts of snow built up to the deep sills.

Sumper claimed to have been 'born' with the opening of Cruickshank's front door. Here, in Soho Square, he would soon come to 'completely understand' the Cruickshank Engine. He claimed this, glaring at me. He had proof. That is, he had been able to give a 'very practical but not theoretical' report of the invention to Prince Albert.

His huge horse eyes demanded some response. What could one say? It was not only a lie, but completely beyond all possibility. Herr Saxe-Coburg, as the pater had had good reason to know, had a character remote and isolated in the extreme. He could not even see a man like Sumper.

Yes, it might seem unlikely, the clockmaker finally admitted, but it had 'precisely the same degree of probability' as a foreign saw miller's son walking in the company of the Honourable Albert Cruickshank. 'Eh, Henry? Eh.'

There was a *deep order* in the world he entered at the top of Cruickshank's stairs. The worshipper continued, speaking nonsense like a convert to a Baptist sect. Trapped in Germany, I watched him stride up to the tiled stove and around the table, and it soon became clear to me that what he so excitably described as 'deep order' was a True Believer's attempt to give meaning to a mess – children's toys, oriental figurines, turned brass implements, fragments of marble and a huge library of books in front of almost every one of which was placed some curiosity or object, each one of which beckoned one's attention.

In the centre of the old man's solar system there was, allegedly, a large vitrine which housed silver automata, two ladies which Cruickshank frankly confessed he had loved since his childhood. They were both naked, alive and not alive, gleaming silver, thirteen inches high.

Cruickshank set the silver ladies going.

'Extraordinary,' I said.

'You do not understand.'

What I could not grasp, apparently, was that Albert Cruickshank was a Genius. And this Genius knew that Sumper understood him better than anyone ever born. This was all the more remarkable because he was a saw miller with no education.

The silver lady examined young Sumper with her eyeglasses – could she see the huge oafish body with its coarse and musty coverings, the enormous hands clasped across a secret pittering heart? When she had finished she returned to her companion. This second lady was a dancer. On her hand there sat a silver bird. While its mistress wiggled it wagged its tail and flapped its wings.

I told Sumper he was exceedingly fortunate. I said a man could live in London all his life and never see such things.

I don't know why I said this. It was not true.

He became excited. He related how he had followed Cruickshank down a narrow staircase where there was a workshop growing 'like a shelf fungus' against his house.

The sanctus sanctorum was cold, but filled with wonderful lathes and drills and presses and, to one side, a large drawing table where he produced the plans he brought to Bowling Green Lane.

Cruickshank tried to hire him there and then.

But Sumper was unworthy. He was not a vise and lathe man. He had no maths or calculus at all.

'But you laughed,' insisted Cruickshank. 'QED. You are my man.'

'I gave only the impression I had understood. All I did was smile.'

'Indeed.'

But anyone could see, Sumper told me, that a clever man would not have added 2 + 2 without good reason. 2 + 2 was predictable. He had smiled, because he had been waiting to see what the surprise would be. Of course he knew 171 was 'wrong' but also he assumed it must be right. All he knew was: he who makes the programme is the god.

'One hundred per cent correct,' said Cruickshank. 'Here is what I want from you: just shape the wood patterns from which the engine's bronze cams will then be cast.'

'But you don't need *me* for such a thing. It is a skill possessed by every common cuckoo clockmaker.'

'Then have a drink because I have my man.'

Sumper smiled. The Genius offered him a penny for his thoughts.

'I will tell you, Herr Brandling,' said Sumper. 'I will tell you what I could never say to him. I was thinking I had arrived at my soul's true home.'

Who would not envy him?


# 4

All my life, it has been assumed I was a dunderhead who would not understand, for instance, why his wife had moved her room.

Hence Sumper: Henry, you could not understand.

At the same time he was determined to test me out.

'The thing is, Herr Brandling, I had been peacefully asleep in bed.'

Not a squeak from me.

'I'll wager you will not conceive what happened next?'

'Rather not, old chap.'

'I was being murdered.'

Clearly this was not true.

'No, no. A weeping man had fallen on me,' he declared, 'like a monkey from the rafter. He bawled and struck me.'

It had been the middle of the night when the Superior Being, now in his nightgown, had thrown himself at Sumper, howling and striking at the sleeping man's big face. Sumper's first response had been characteristically violent, but his second thought was less expected – he took the old man in his arms and held him until he went to sleep.

Dear Pater, I thought. The horrors of old men in the night.

When dawn came, the employer had departed. Sumper dressed and descended to the breakfast table. And there was Cruickshank, reading from *The Times*, undamaged except for a scratch on his high and hawkish nose.

'I was no doctor,' Sumper said. This did not prevent him diagnosing palsy.

In the months ahead, apparently, he decided that Cruickshank's condition was not attached to Cruickshank but was, in a sense, Cruickshank himself. Cruickshank was the terror. He had moulded his body around the terror's shape, deepened his own eyes, straightened his own mouth, set his jaw like steel.

Further, Sumper concluded, showing an unattractive astonishment at his own intelligence, the very trauma that brought Cruickshank each night flailing and wailing to the room upstairs, this same pain had also formed the Cruickshank Engine. The Engine and the Madness were the same, he said.

'Cruickshank's family – his wife, two girls and a baby boy – had been lost at sea. You see that don't you?'

I'm afraid I yawned. I did not mean to. Against my will I learned that the shipwreck had been solely the result of poor Admiralty charts. The Captain would have sworn on those tables as on a Bible but they led him to the rocks.

Mr Cruickshank was a Genius, he shouted. He sought RATIONAL EXPLANATION for the cause of tragedy and he, Cruickshank himself, had personally examined the Admiralty tables and he had found them RIDDLED WITH HUMAN ERROR. It was unbearable that his family had been dashed and drowned not by fate or God or nature, but BY MISTAKE. Was I listening? These numeric errors haunted poor Cruickshank's mind like angry bees, and for many months, while still in mourning, he had sat at his desk with his pencil in his hand and, slowly, carefully, corrected the errors in all their sickening multitudes. Perhaps he imagined that, as a result of these tedious labours, the dead would soon walk, the fire in the stove would light and the kitchen fill with the smell of Yorkshire pudding.

He notified 'the ministry' of the miscalculations and the ministry printed errata sheets and these were sent out to the navy and the merchant fleet. But then, to Cruickshank's horror, he found human error re-enter the charts as relentlessly as water through a leaking roof – many of the errata slips had been copied incorrectly. In 140 volumes of tables he found around 3,700 errata sheets were as wrong as the errors they supposedly corrected. These astronomical tables were calculated by men with celluloid eyeshades who gloried in such titles as Computer or Chief Computer or Computer's Boy. Their penmanship was such a wonder you might imagine it produced by lathe. Alas, they were simple clerks, with holes in their socks and onion on their breath, being so thoroughly human that they were unsuited to reliably repeating a simple action like addition.

As a result there were noxious errors in transcription, which spread without relent in the ground between the calculation and the printer, and then there were slip-ups in the typesetting, a cloud of them like locusts, and blunders of proofreading as numerous as grains of sand, each microscopic inaccuracy an Isle of Scylla, sufficient to cleave an oaken hull, and no matter how many nights the bereaved man occupied himself with the most menial arithmetic, the mistakes continued.

As a result of this obsession, according to Sumper, Cruickshank became ill. During his illness, or after his illness, certainly as a result of his illness, he began to consider how he would replace the pulp and fibre of the human brain with brass and steel, not some 'gilded folly like Vaucanson's which served only to amuse the rich and mindless'. Cruickshank removed all 'lethal sloppiness' from his machine. Those were his exact words, said Sumper.

Cruickshank had previously kept sketchbooks of birds, and nature scenes, no beetle was too lowly for his interest. That is, his eyes had keenly sought to know and understand the natural world. But now all that bright curiosity turned inwards and his eyes, as often as not, rested on his shoes as he sought to invent a steam-driven automaton which would provide navigation charts without a single error. The engine would accept the numbers that were entered and then it would repeat additions to ten places. The machine would add and add and add, like the most dogged human, but without our species' relentless tendency to error. And the results of these calculations would be kept from the murderous hands of human beings. The machine would produce the correct number and from these numbers it would set the type WITHOUT HUMAN INTERFERENCE and from the type it would make a mould and from the mould it would pour a printing plate which would WITHOUT HUMAN INTERFERENCE print the tables. He planned all this inside the grieving cavern of his mind, with equations going that way, and axles turning, cams moving in and out, levers interrupting and releasing, and calculating to seven orders of difference and thirty decimal places so every number was thirty to thirty-one digits long.

The Grieving Genius, said Sumper, walked the streets of London, all the while devising – completely in his head – a series of shapes that never existed on the earth before, and he saw how this three-dimensional cam would drive against that three-dimensional cam and how they would align on an axle. In comparison to this endeavour Vaucanson's duck should be seen as exactly what it is – a machine to produce fake shit, excuse me.

These shapes CAME TO MY MASTER, Sumper said. He received every part COMPLETELY IN HIS HEAD. He drew the part with astonishing precision. He then taught Thigpen how to see the plan, and how to make the wood pattern and how to cast it in bronze, or turn it on a lathe so that all these elements would finally give the illusion, as they turned, that they were like a molten cord, sinuously rotating on columns like the vertebrae of some creature from a distant star. These parts were made to tolerances of one half-thousandth of an inch and were designed so that it was impossible to make an error. When instructed to make an error the machine would jam.

To do this Cruickshank required twenty-five thousand parts in an assemblage twelve foot high and eight foot deep and weighing many tons. With ten thousand parts he was almost half way there. Who could possibly conceive what order of being this was?

HRH the Queen never once said that she found the notion hard to grasp. But as in knighthoods, battles, invasions, the gold standard and the transportation of assassins, there must be, not only the monarch, but thousands of sucking ignoramuses, said Sumper, men who have rights and territories and opinions, and these astronomers, for instance, astronomers in particular, could not imagine, because no human mind could possibly calculate how much a machine like this might cost. By the time Thigpen had spent thousands of pounds the bureaucrats had decided that they had a white elephant on their hands. No one, certainly not Cruickshank, could tell them when it would be complete.

So, said Sumper, no sooner had I been transported to the REALMS OF GOLD, to that elevated position where I might help change the history of mankind, no sooner had I arrived in Soho Square, but the idiots at the palace declared they would no longer foot the bill.

Germans, cried Sumper. Germans. That's what I could not tolerate. Idiots, cretins, stuck up, stitched up, basically stupid people who could have paid for the Engine by melting down a crown or two.

'You see, Henry? In this case you are exactly equal to Queen Victoria. You worry you are being cheated, no? She was just the same.'

He laughed at me and put his hand upon my shoulder, and in what followed assumed a greater degree of intimacy than was his place to assume. 'I was a young man,' he said, 'but once I had been employed it was clear that I had become, in my happiness, the most unhealthy creature on this earth, a monk. In your own situation you will easily imagine the mad bordello of my dreams, which reflected everything but my actual situation, nightly holding a Genius to my chest. How I wished to still his raging soul, if you will forgive the expression.'

With this gamey brothel talk, Henry Brandling, Christian gentleman, was provided all the reason needed to retire.

# CATHERINE

I t had been tantalizing to stare through a glass darkly, to see or intuit what had taken place in Furtwangen and Low Hall so long ago. Reading in this way did not require that you interrogate the unclear word. In fact you soon learned that what was initially confusing would never be clarified no matter how you stared and swore at it. One learned to live with fuzziness and ambiguity in a way one never would in life.

Yet I was a horologist. I had to know how things fitted together. I could not possibly accept that Cruickshank was a superior being or that animals might have a higher mental life. It was not uninteresting in considering these 'mysteries' to see quite startling similarities between the hulking bony Sumper and the pretty blonde Amanda. They had similar habits of mind, like a pair of academics who will always push the evidence to fit their theory. When Amanda and I first ran the engine and I saw the creepy lifelike movement of the neck – so relentless, calculating, sinuous, cold, silver, phallic – I was not immune to its effect. I was therefore all the more pleased she

231

had never read about Herr Sumper's Superior Beings.

Of course the swan would 'serve', as Sumper had insisted, but I doubt he imagined it serving the museum for that was where it would end its days, at the Lowndes Square entrance, lifting the gold coins from the punters' pockets as if by magnetic force. As to whether this income would ever be enough to replace the funds cut by the Tories, one does not need a calculator to know that was impossible.

The swan will not be Lucifer or a transport system for a secret Christian cross but, rather, one of those installations that children are brought to visit, with which old men in split shoes form strange relationships.

And there will be surprisingly expensive post-cards, and posters and videos and catalogues with a scholarly essay from Mr Croft and a more lowly practical one from myself, and then – why not? – Amanda's most particular drawings. It will be very unusual for a first-year assistant to make a serious contribution to a major catalogue, but no matter what eyebrows are raised, there is no doubt that Amanda Snyde, who could not yet be called a scholar, had been producing astonishingly good drawings every day. God knows how the issue of ownership and copyright would be settled, for although she produced many of her sketches on Swinburne time she did not stop at five o'clock. Nor was there, page by page, any true division between her detailed conservator's recording of silver collars, and more personal work: she produced a very thoughtful drawing of me at work which, if I hadn't been afraid of seeming vain, I would have loved to buy.

My assistant was not at all secretive with her sketchbook and I had, on three occasions, snooped. There were two items, very revealing of her state of mind, which were completely and utterly not my business, except I was her boss.

The most fanciful of these was a very careful three-dimensional architectural rendering of the structure of the morbid hull, that awful tomb in which Carl's cube crossed the Styx. I had forbidden her to fuss with it, so I was annoyed to see she had been drawing it for hours on end. She had rendered the arched beams and the cladding on each side, also carefully indicated the bituminous sealant while, at the same time, not hiding the cavity beneath.

And of course Amanda would not leave things in the simple concrete world. She had drawn, meticulously, with fine cross-hatching, an extraordinary number of fanciful objects secreted within the wooden skins. But why should I be angry? Did I wish to make imagination criminal? The objects made me think of provisions for the afterlife, those pots of grain and fruit one might see inside a pharaoh's tomb, but there was nothing to tell me how they should be interpreted, and in any case she was a very fine assistant.

I was returning the book to the bench when the door swung open and I performed what was, I hoped, a convincing reversal. That is, I affected to pick up what I had not yet set down.

'Amanda,' I said, 'have you talked to Mr Croft about your drawings?'

She placed her lunch bag beside the book. 'Oh no, of course not.' She was colouring, not necessarily with pleasure.

'Could you photocopy a series of them for me? Whatever ones you like best. I'm thinking of the catalogue.'

Her eyes were suspicious but as she flicked through the pages I knew that her vanity would save me yet.

I laid my hand on her wrist to stop her flicking past the drawing of the secret compartments. One could feel her physical resistance.

'Its soul, perhaps?' I asked of the tiny manufactured things. 'What are they, Amanda?'

'Secrets,' she said, and turned two or three pages to a highly erotic, weirdly particular, rather Japanese drawing of the swan.

She raised a cheeky eyebrow, but she was less certain now and slightly pinker.

'I don't like him,' she said.

'You've done a lovely job.'

'He's up to something, don't you think?'

We had reached the stage, you would imagine, when someone could have reasonably suspected she was ill, but I would never like to be that someone.

234

'You think it's strange too, the blue cube?'

'Not strange,' I said, 'but rather touching.' Of course she did not know Carl, so my comment could make no sense to her.

'Miss Gehrig, do you find yourself wondering what else there might possibly be secreted in the hull?'

'Dust,' I said, 'a nail, a brass screw, sawdust.'

She gave her head a little angry shake.

'Don't you even think about it?'

'No.'

'Shouldn't you?'

'No,' I said. 'Now come on. We really have a deadline.'

'Do you know, we could predict the probability of there being more blue cubes. Mathematically.'

'No, Amanda, I don't think so.'

'Did you study maths?'

'Amanda, that's enough.'

'I'm sorry, Miss Gehrig, but if you were a mathematician I do believe you'd answer yes. I'd like you to talk to my friend. He is a sort of mathematical genius. Can I get a pass for him, Miss Gehrig? Please. There can't be any harm.'

I am a socialist. It makes me feel uneasy to judge someone who does not know her place. Amanda did not know her place, but I failed to point this out to her. I signed the application for the pass and left it to her to fill out the rest of it.

The peculiar thing was, when she mentioned

this friend, I immediately thought of Angus. Then, because that was so impossible I did not consider it for another moment. Was my 'not knowing' a little too deliberate? Was I actually hoping it was him? I cannot say, but when Matthew's eldest son appeared in my office wearing those long narrow-waisted pleated trousers I was, although completely shocked, uncertain of any single emotion. Perhaps 'extreme panic' would cover everything.

The young man appeared most uncomfortable, but this was likely produced by the expression on my face, or the very cold way I spoke to Amanda.

'Did you know Angus's father had worked at the Swinburne?' I demanded.

'It wasn't here. It was at Lowndes Square.'

'How do you and Angus know each other?'

'Oh, in Suffolk.'

I was invaded, violated. Suffolk was our place, Matthew's, mine, woven with our life and breath, Southwold, Walberswick, Dunwich, even Norwich, were the secret fabric of the secret life we lived alone. How dare she drag this poor beautiful boy into territory he knew was freighted with his father's life.

No doubt I looked ugly and displeased. Something made them go so very still.

'Where in Suffolk, Amanda?'

But I did not want to hear, no more than you would wish to see the bed where your lover had betrayed your trust.

'Miss Gehrig, I don't think it's fair that you control who we know.'

I laughed or gasped depending on the point of view. But I did not want a row with Angus. I wanted him to like me in the end.

'So, of course, it's you,' I said to him. 'The maths genius.'

'I'll do my best.' He was nervous, fiddling with his hand-painted buttons. I thought, ah, Amanda made the buttons.

'If you show me the thing,' he said.

Clearly she had shown him a drawing for he was looking at the hull as he spoke. 'So,' he said, 'I know there is a given volume divided into regions of a certain size. I know how big the blue cubes are. You are asking me can I mathematically predict the likelihood of there being more blue cubes?'

'Who knows what's there? It might not be blue cubes,' Amanda said. 'It might be totally anachronistic.'

I felt an awful chill.

If Angus was alarmed, he certainly did not show it. In any case, she was pretty enough to turn a young man deaf and blind. 'If the cubes are placed randomly,' he insisted, 'then the probability of finding one will be just the size of the region divided by the size of the object.'

'Not just cubes.' She was now very bossy. 'Who knows where they hid things? If we knew that we would simply drill a hole.'

She nodded at me, as if affirming that she meant it.

'I can't predict the unpredictable,' the boy said.

'You told me you could.'

'Let me give you a parallel to what you're asking – walking along the footpath, you encounter a paper bag. It has a pencil inside. You see another paper bag nearby. What's the likelihood that there's a pencil in it? The answer is, I have no clue. I know that there might be one, but that's all I know.'

'Well,' she said, 'there is certainly more than one. Otherwise it makes no sense.'

'Amanda.'

'Miss Gehrig, of course there are many parts inside. It is central to the issue of the swan.'

'What is the issue of the swan?' I asked, the hair rising on my neck.

'Amanda,' said Angus. He held her hand but she shook it off.

'You lied to me,' she said.

The poor boy had no idea of what was happening. 'So there are objects secreted inside the double skin?' he said.

'You know there are. I told you.'

'Well you just X-ray it,' he said. 'Who needs maths?'

'That's impossible.'

'No, it's not at all impossible,' Angus said. 'Museums have X-rays. If there's something inside you will see it.'

Amanda turned to me, her eyebrows pressing down fiercely on her eyes. 'Is this true?' she demanded. 'Is this another lie?'

It is not mad to be obsessive, I told myself.

'Darlings,' I said, although I would not usually use such a word, 'let me just alert you to the fact that Britain has just had an election. As a result, our budgets are cut to the bone. At the same time, we are involved in a very complicated, very demanding restoration of an automaton. It took a three-hour meeting to approve the replacement of one small fish. There will be no X-rays, none, not ever.'

'Please, Miss Gehrig,' Amanda said, beseechingly, and then – quite suddenly – she understood I would not budge.

It was then she scratched my face.


## 2

My injury would not need stitches, but I was very angry and when I had trouble with ID at Lowndes Square, I went completely nuts.

Up the damn haunted staircase, and all around me were Matthew's molecules, oxygen that had caressed the clean pink lining of his lungs. I saw no one I knew, or perhaps they saw me coming.

A podiatrist once said to me, when people hear you walking they'll think you're angry, and there was surely something *incensed* about my walk, the ink blue of my swirling skirt; and me, as always, too heavy on the heels. Did I have an appointment? No I did not, but there he was, Crofty, in the centre of his rat's nest – books and papers and catalogues and cards and hardly a thing of beauty to contemplate unless it was hidden in that wooden crate with straw stuffing spilling across the rug. It was a very fine-looking office just the same, wide rattling Georgian sashes, marble fireplace, and the courtyard as sweet and silent as a nunnery, deep in chestnut shade.

'What on earth has happened to you?' he said and there was such tenderness and sadness in his mouth that when he held out his arms I thought of Max Beckmann in his dinner suit, lonely, haunted, kind.

'That girl has to go,' I said.

'Dear Jesus,' he said. His tenderness was all-engulfing. I had the sudden sense of a secret life. 'Did she attack you?'

I would not let him touch my face.

'Take a tissue anyway,' he said.

'Get rid of her,' I said.

There was an armchair filled with bubble wrap. He cleared it for me and I sat. He wheeled the chair from behind his desk so we were almost knee to knee.

I said: 'You put people together like you run a bloody stud farm.'

For a second he revealed that slightly dangerous Crofty air, as if he was considering which card to play. He offered tissues once again. I was rather pleased to discover how much blood there was.

'Catherine, what on earth do you mean?'

'You have been an awful meddler.'

I thought, he will make tea now.

'Have I, really?' He folded his arms and I saw the Rolex peek from beneath his cuff like a mark of corporate corruption. 'I'm sorry you think that, Catherine.'

'Amanda is the granddaughter of your friend. Lichfield, yes? Lord.'

'That was the photographer, darling. Gerald is actually a baron.' He stood. 'Hang on a second.'

He disappeared and I thought, now he will make his bloody tea. It will be lapsang souchong and he will ask do I mind not having milk. But when he returned it was with elastoplasts and cotton wool and various dark bottles. He made a mess pouring alcohol onto a swab. He intended to clean me up, but I took charge.

'Might sting.'

Of course it stung. 'In any case,' I said, 'Amanda Snyde is the granddaughter of your friend.'

'Not a friend exactly.'

'A board member then.'

'A collector, darling. Quite a different beast.'

I permitted him to accept the bloody swab. I took a fresh gauze in return.

'But still you engineered it?'

'Catherine, I'm terribly sorry this has happened. Of course it is unpardonable, but it does our cause no harm when collectors feel connected to the museum. And besides, she is exceptional. You saw her transcripts. The Courtauld people raved about her. There was a three-page letter from West Dean. She's clearly brilliant.'

'But perhaps a little unstable?'

'My understanding was that she'd been very good.'

'Can you see my face? Can you see what she did? I do not want her in my studio again.'

'Catherine, let me at least get a nurse to look at that. I will explain. It is not simple to fire someone these days.'

'Oh Eric, dear Eric, what is she? What did you not tell me? Is she bipolar?'

'Do we really need a clinical label for enthusiasm?'

'This is not enthusiasm.'

'Obsession then. My understanding was that she was a hundred per cent functional. Is that not so?'

'No, she's nuts.'

'She's upset about this oil spill, apparently.'

'What!'

'I said she is upset about this BP business.'

'She's upset. That's it.'

'Darling, do you read the newspapers? Do you watch television? There was a big feature in *Slate*. Do you read *Slate?* About the psychological damage caused by the oil spill. Her feelings are normal. She's upset.'

'Well so am I. Does that give me permission to assault you?'

'I am only reporting what I know. There are hundreds of thousands of kids who spend their day watching the nightmare webcam of oil pouring into the gulf. It is an addiction. I understand she has been producing the most terrifying drawings. Really, they'd make you want to top yourself.'

'Drawings of what?' I asked, thinking this was a slip-up.

'Of course something must be done. It's awful. She is clearly not herself. This is gross misconduct.'

'Thank you. So she can be fired.'

'If she is, as you suggest, unwell, we have, legally, what is called duty of care. So there is a procedure which is horribly ugly and time-consuming. We would have to produce two doctors to confirm she can't work responsibly, and then – I don't know – she may get it in her head that we're discriminating against her.'

'For being posh?'

'For being posh if you like. Don't joke about it. She could argue that we were pursuing a course of constructive dismissal.'

The girl got in a fury because I refused to X-ray something, which was not her business or within her field of expertise, and now I was *conspiring* to dismiss her for being posh. Jesus help me, I thought, while Crofty, who was meant to be my friend, explained the procedure, trying to put me off because he didn't want to lose a benefactor.

'Do you have the patience for it, Catherine?

Would you really do that to someone who was unwell?'

There was the slight interrogative tilt of the head. 'Oh,' I said. 'You're thinking about *me*?'

'No, not at all. Not in the slightest.'

'I have been unwell, that is what you mean?'

'Let me make some tea.'

'No, don't run away. Why do you go running around, doing things behind my back?'

'Darling, you haven't always minded so very much before.'

'You're discussing recreational drugs?'

He stood and shut the door and came back looking very serious indeed. I was chastened, as I should have been. 'Sorry. What have I never minded about?'

'Well, I have truthfully always imagined it was my talent, my gift to introduce my friends to each other. Not one I could ever use for my own happiness, I must say.'

I didn't know what to say. I was rather frightened of where this was going.

'You don't remember, of course, who it was who put you to work with Matthew?'

'No!'

'But why are you upset? Would you rather I hadn't?'

'Please, please, don't do this.'

'Oh Cat, you were truly the most gorgeous elegant creature I ever saw, there was nothing about you that was not perfect, really.'

'So you pushed me at a married man.'

He spun on his chair and went to fiddle with his electric kettle. I was not sorry his back was to me.

'He was so miserable, and so sad,' he said. 'That awful woman with her sordid affairs. It was too horrible for such a lovely man.'

'Did you really set me up? Did he know?'

'His life was awful. You knew that of course. Everything about her was cruel. She still is cruel. The younger boy can deal with her very well. He's comparatively safe.'

I was staring out the window at the chestnut tree remembering Noah drinking scotch.

'But the older one . . .'

'Angus.'

'Yes, Angus is put in the awful situation of being the man of the house.'

'And you're going to rescue him.'

'He has to do that himself, of course.'

'But you fixed him up with Amanda.'

'Not really. They have a tennis court in Walberswick.'

'Walberswick? Walberswick. So she's practically my bloody neighbour. Thanks a lot.'

He said nothing until he returned with his lapsang souchong. He had sliced a lemon somehow. 'Catherine, will you please stop this? There is nothing wrong with making people happy.'

'Might she be just a *little* schizophrenic?'

'Have you seen her drawings?'

'Of course I've seen her fucking drawings. She is doing them for *me*.'

'Sorry. Quite right.'

'Although when I asked her that very question, she said *you* had never seen them, and this is really what I don't like about this set-up, Eric. Everyone is running around whispering behind my back. You push the boys at me, you send them to my house, at night, and then you get one of them to sleep with a mad girl who you've arranged to work for me. I feel a total fool.'

Finally he had his own tea and although he now sat opposite, there was a greater separation.

'Catherine, would you like to say that again, so you can hear yourself?'

'You mean I'm "enthusiastic" too? Do you know how horrible it is to have all these strangers know more about my life than I do? This is not kindness. It's the opposite.'

'So I've been cruel to you?'

'Yes.'

There was a long pause while he placed his cup and saucer on his desk and then, very slowly, stood. I thought he was going to wheel the chair back to its usual place but he remained, grasping the wobbly back, looking out the window as he spoke.

'Catherine, I do think I have cut you an awful lot of slack. An incredible amount. But now we really must have the written material back inside the museum.'

'You're joking.'

'Darling, enough is enough. I can't turn a blind eye to what you're doing. I could be dismissed for it, and that would be a very, very simple thing to do. Out the door. Clean out the desk. Police escort, all that sort of thing.'

'You're punishing me. I'm sorry. Please don't punish me. Let me keep the books at home.'

'We've all been a little too enthusiastic. It's time we put our house in order.'

'We're out of control?'

'Just a wee bit.'

'Did you really set me up with Matthew?'

'You saved his life.' The window panes were clearly reflected in the saline nimbus of his eyes.

'He saved my life.'

'You transformed him. You were his life.'

I could not help it any more. I began to blubber. Then I was the one who held out my arms. When I felt his penis hard against me I was shocked, but only for a moment. I thought, poor poor man, and then we both sat on our separate chairs. We found something in the Christie's catalogue and then we became perfect 'no ones', all information deleted from our eyes.

# CATHERINE & HENRY

My darling Matthew, I thought of you when the pizza box arrived. I remembered your very superior lamb chops marinated with garlic ginger chilli, cooked on your hibachi beneath the great surviving elm. Wild lettuce, radicchio, treviso, endive, pea leaves, watercress, I kiss your toes.

I gulped down the cardboard mess and read.

Herr Sumper once more explained to me, wrote Henry Brandling, that M. Arnaud was a far better silversmith than a fairytale collector. Arnaud's great misfortune, said Sumper mockingly, was to have been commissioned to make a vulgar salt cellar for a Baroness Ludwig Something. Now he scurried about the forest like a mouse, fearful that the Baroness would force him to be vulgar once again.

Of course, said Sumper, everyone knows who Arnaud is and where he lives. The Baroness could have him brought to her within a week, but why would she bother?

Sumper and I drank acid wine, wrote Henry.

'The fool spends half of his income on buying

fairy stories,' Sumper said. 'I know he is talked of as an inventor, but there is no money in that sort of thing.'

What sort of thing?

'His washing-machine contraption is ridiculous. For Arnaud to show that thing to me is an offence. I, who have been on friendly terms with men of science and genius, must listen while he explains the washing machine to me, again and again, so I am now doomed to carry the parts in my head until I die. He has no clue of my Mechanical Memory which is equal to much greater tests than this. Thanks to this damned wood nymph, I have washing-machine parts rattling inside my head like nails.'

It had been his personal ambition, Sumper continued without drawing breath, to retain all twenty-five thousand elements of Cruickshank's Engine in his mind. This began on the day when he learned that the incomplete machine was abandoned at 40 Bowling Green Lane which had been visited by bailiffs who had padlocked its doors and pasted notices across its window.

Some of the lathe men thought this was punishment for mocking God. 'But the main culprit', said Sumper, 'was Queen Victoria.'

Cruickshank still had hopes he could bring her back on board and for this reason the Master spent his evenings pasting newspaper reports of shipwrecks into a massive presentation folio.

Sumper talked endlessly, Henry wrote, never

ceasing, on and on, never more so, it seemed, than in a blizzard. The gutted Catherine Gehrig peered down through that frozen script.

Why must I suffer, Henry Brandling had written, long ago. Am I not the patron?

The machine's great enemy was the Queen of England, but not her alone. The Astronomer Royal developed a hatred for the Engine. He did everything possible to poison the minds of the Queen and the Prince Consort.

Confident that he would finally win the day, Cruickshank proceeded with his list of deaths at sea. You would need a heart of stone to not be persuaded by these names, so many children, babes in arms. So Sumper said. So Henry wrote, with what feeling none could know. At the same time, Cruickshank assumed nothing – he petitioned Her Majesty, asking, no matter what her decision on the funding of the Engine, if she would immediately decree that the marooned tons of steel and brass might be granted to him as a boon. This would enable him to sell shares and independently raise capital to ensure the completion of this life-saving machine.

Then, because he could never wait for anyone even if they were a queen, he began immediately to seek investors, dictating many letters seeking capital. These should have been despatched immediately, but many hours were wasted correcting Sumper's English. Yet this imperfection seemed no obstacle to their relationship. Indeed it was in this period he first became 'My German'.

Mr Cruickshank was always kind, said Sumper. From him I learned the English language very well although, to be quite honest, his cook was also a very lively little teacher in more ways than one.

When the butcher would no longer supply the household needs, the Genius had himself engaged by the directors of the Great British Railway Company with the express task of investigating some of the difficulties and dangers of this new mode of travel. He had that company supply him with a second-class carriage and he and Sumper removed all its internal parts. To the framework they then attached a long table, designed in such a way as to be entirely independent in its motions. At one end they fitted a 'monumental' roll of paper which would, if unrolled, have stretched two thousand feet. As this paper was mechanically wound onto the second roller, several inking pens traced curves which measured, separately, force of traction, vertical shake of engine, and other things 'you would not understand'. The pens gave exact indices relating to the safety and comfort of the passengers. The inking pens, for instance, measured the physical forces that might cause a carriage to roll.

The fool, wrote Henry Brandling.

The fool did not know that the pater was a director of that company, and would have been the one personally responsible for Cruickshank's commission. However, wrote Henry, I was very interested to learn how the scoundrels had used the Brandling generosity. By keeping mum about the family connection, I easily learned that the two rascals were transported from one part of the country to another free of charge. Admittedly this was extremely dangerous for it was always necessary to attach their laboratory to a public train and there were various tactics – and these I admit I did not always understand, wrote Henry – which involved disconnecting from the main train and shooting into a siding. Red ball top pocket, Henry thought. In all cases the pocket or siding had been selected well in advance. Indeed it was so well anticipated that Herr Sumper was, in one instance, required to write to a Lady Lovelace that Mr Cruickshank and 'My German' should be arriving at a siding 23A being 3 miles East of the Inn at Minehead and as the topographical map indicated level fields, the pair of them might expect to meet Lady Lovelace's carriage in the middle of the afternoon.

Thus they travelled from estate to estate, being welcomed by the Great and the Good in a surprising array of different circumstances. They particularly enjoyed the company of men of science who they met, by previous arrangement, in inns and cottages and, once, a muddy field.

From these latter conversations, Sumper claimed, he was able to visualize the finished Engine. He memorized it with a tolerance of one-thousandth of an inch, describing the pairs of spinning forms like spiral staircases slipping in and out between each other's treads.

At the same time he characterized his own understanding as being not very much more elevated than that of the grocer's clerks who will one day watch the swan's neck, and glimpse in the movement something so unknowable and unearthly their brainless hair will stand on end.

He was by now completely mad, wrote Henry Brandling, and there was not a natural force to contain or check the growth of his mania. But who did 'he' refer to? Cruickshank? Sumper?

It was certainly Sumper who reported Cruickshank's supposed belief that there would be life on other planets.

I felt I must argue, wrote Henry, even if the battle were unequal.

Cruickshank's view was allegedly also held by Sir Humphrey Lucas and Mr Paul Arnold with whom they had shared a leg of mutton in Henley. 'It would be vain,' the great astronomer is reported to have told Herr Sumper personally, 'to think that there was not, at that very minute, an entire people of a distant race, dying, in a corner of the sky.'

'Surely,' Sumper demanded of Brandling, 'you cannot but agree.'

Henry wrote, I would not agree that men of science could say any such thing. Also, being an Anglican, I could not agree, and Sumper stormed out of the room. I thought, AT LEAST I CAN GO TO BED, but Sumper returned to shout that it would be 'stupid and conceited' to not at least allow the possibility of superior life amongst the stars, but as stupidity and conceit were the most common human diseases he supposed that Anglicans must be infected by them too.

'I have met these Beings,' he said in a voice both loud and deep. 'I have observed them close.'

Henry demanded he swear this on oath.

As Sumper would not do this it was clear to Henry that he had met no such beings at all. He said so.

Sumper replied: 'Do you not know who I am? Do you not know you have been sent to me?'

This outburst was so wild and terrifying that, seeking safe harbour, Henry wrote, I drew him into the subject of Cruickshank's final report to the Gt. Brit. R'way Co. Thus, finally, was calm restored, for Herr Sumper answered me directly and with such pride you would think that he, the servant, had composed the report himself. Seated once again, with his big calf resting on his rounded knee, Sumper recalled the three main recommendations in the most tedious detail but I was, by then, wrote Henry, so emotionally exhausted I did not care to hear them. When I was finally safe at home in Low Hall it would be gratifying to unearth them in old Simpson's cupboard, where I was sure they were safely stored, tied up with a ribbon of whatever colour the pater's chief clerk had judged correct for classification.

When Cruickshank and his German returned to London they found no boon from the Queen or her secretary. Instead, a Colonel Minns of the Brigade of Guards wrote to inform the Genius that Her Majesty had made a gift of the Engine, not to him, but to the nation as a whole. The Admiralty then arrogantly asserted the inventor's responsibility to transport said mechanism to a place so directed by Her Majesty's servants, although they could never be induced to say exactly where that should be.

Mr Cruickshank appeared to have been snookered, wrote Henry Brandling, and if this is true, he continued, it is not impossible that, for as long as I live, there will be eight tons of metals standing in the corner of a manufacturing endeavour situated at 40 Bowling Green Lane.

Of course Henry Brandling could not see me, but he expected to have a reader. I, Catherine Gehrig, was that reader. I had peered between the lines looking for codes and signs, staring into the blur of descending strokes where, in a sea of ambiguity, delusion, wonder, possibility, amongst all the murk and confusion, there was one solid physical piece of evidence that might have been made for me alone: Thigpen's Clerkenwell workshop was around the corner from Gehrig and Son, my childhood home.

# CATHERINE

That night I slept with the window wide open but there was no freshness, only the warm and weary air of this unexpected century. Near morning I had a looping puzzle dream in which Cruickshank's engine reproduced itself and it was my job to match and screw together the golden strands of DNA.

In the morning there was blood on my pillow, but Amanda's scratch was not so very bad. In any case, I had been 'cut a lot of slack', and it would not be either gracious or politic for me to seek her dismissal. I would be an adult. I would no longer expect to be exempt from the rules. I would return my notebooks, although I would insist that their access be restricted. For even Crofty would understand that it would not be helpful for Amanda to enter the realms of *Mysterium Tremendum*. None of us needed creatures from outer space just now.

In the meantime I set all ten books neatly in the middle of the kitchen table. On top of this I placed a single sheet of paper addressed to Eric Croft. Why I did this is still unclear, perhaps some sort of premonition that I was never coming back, although that makes no sense – I was about to do nothing more drastic than visit Bowling Green Lane. I was born around the corner, after all.

Did I believe Thigpen's workshop was still in Bowling Green Lane? I had a very clear picture of the deep high space all the way through to Northampton Road, the steel and brass leviathan gleaming beneath a dirty London sky.

It was very easy to reach on the underground. Lambeth North, Baker Street, Farringdon. Why not? What harm? What could be worse than what I had already discovered, that my childhood home had been turned into an X-rated video store?

As I left the house I discovered a strange car parked with its rusted nose angled steeply down from the footpath to my neighbours' door. Of course the Upstairs were on holiday again, but this particular car, which had once been very upper-upper, was now very down and old and grey and chalky with a running board and corroded mud guards. I imagined I saw a body stretched across the back seat. Dead, I thought. Then the body moved, and that was worse. Then there were two, I was certain, moving like moles inside a blanket.

It would be embarrassing to call the police, so I double-locked my door and hurried away down Kennington Road. I thought, I should have written down the registration number.

Outside Lambeth North station the newspaper placards read: TIDE OF FEAR. There was a colour picture of the Gulf of Mexico, a dense black centre with a rim of rusty red surrounded by a coral blue.

The train pushed a wall of hot air before it. I boarded. The scratch on my face was noted, in that particularly British way which contains not a skerrick of sympathy. I changed to the Central Line. I arrived at Farringdon to discover it was disembowelled – temporary ramps and lanes and hoardings and lots more TIDE OF FEAR.

Outside, Farringdon Road was a construction site. Lorries, mini-vans, motorbikes and newspapers floating like gulls above a garbage dump.

I strode north, holding my breath. I turned right into Bowling Green Lane, past the pub (the Bowler) and now I was inside Henry Brandling's puzzle. I felt my mobile phone vibrating against my hip and there was 40 Bowling Green Lane: FINSBURY BUSINESS CENTRE. Of course it was Clerkenwell not Finsbury but there it stood, built a century after Sumper visited the same address.

Who would have anticipated feeling so let down? I had spent so much time maintaining a rational sense of doubt that I had had no notion of how much I wanted the machine. I wanted Cruickshank and his silver ladies but Thigpen's had been bombed, rebuilt, become decrepit in its turn. This was our inheritance: a vast dull postwar building with depressing offices for rent.

From Bowling Green Lane I called Security

to ask if Amanda had swiped her card this morning.

She had not.

The trains were slow and stinking. It was almost two claustrophobic hours before I reached the Annexe where I discovered a large expensive envelope addressed to me in Amanda's hand.

'Dear Miss Gehrig, I am awfully sorry. I am so ashamed. You are the person I admire most in all the world.'

Inside I found the little portrait she had made of me, excised neatly from its book. My first thought was, she knows I coveted it. My second was, she is inside the building.

I emailed Eric to say I was 'reading at home'.

The tube was more infuriating than before. I did not arrive back at Lambeth North until after noon. The old grey car was gone. Nonetheless I double-locked the door behind me.

I found Henry's notebooks violated, scattered across the kitchen table. Beside them was the cube. It looked quite normal for a moment. Then I saw the sawdust and knew she had attacked that too. There was no electric drill in evidence but my clever assistant (who else could it have been?) had made a quarter-inch hole straight through the middle of Carl's wonder. There had been no need. I could have told her. I could have taught her to weigh it in her hand and know that it was solid oak.

# CATHERINE & HENRY

The young policeman searched for my intruder amongst the shameful fluff beneath my bed. He politely requested 'access' to the garden where he indicated which shrubs should be grubbed or trimmed 'for your own security'. I failed to tell him the garden was not mine.

At my front door he offered a business card and invited me to call him at any hour. He had a sweet young face, shy downcast eyes, and a tiny brass earring which I must surely have imagined. He would not look at me, but pointed to the browning tree directly opposite my flat – he said it was one of thirteen London plane trees bearing the name of an American astronaut, Neil Armstrong in this case, he who had once walked upon the moon.

I thanked him. He gave me another business card. As soon as he had gone, I packed a bag.

That night I moved to a room in a pub near the Annexe. It was such a sad and stupid choice, but the brewery had renovated since my previous stay. There was nothing left to smell or snuffle.

I hung up two light dresses, unpacked my block

of cheddar, my knife, my corkscrew, and a bottle of wine. Ingest, I thought, digest, excrete, repeat.

I unwrapped the notebooks and sat in the unrelenting upright chair. I read. I read so deeply that the shouting in the bar did not annoy me. On the contrary – Frau Helga had told Herr Sumper that the owner of the inn had 'been her friend'.

Henry reported Sumper saying this had never been true. He repeated that the landlady was a procuress, a cheat and a liar. She was also a Catholic, by which Sumper allegedly did not mean to speak badly of that faith but to make it clear that a very particular automaton Frau Helga had recently consigned to the inn-keeper's hands would be highly offensive to almost every man who visited the inn, each of whom, Sumper told Henry, feared the Catholic hell and feasted on those Catholic tortures such as intestines wound out of martyrs' stomachs and gathered onto reels like so much cotton thread.

Frau Helga was a strong woman, according to Sumper. He had reason to know this far better than Henry, 'but even you, your Monkship, have seen her swing that scythe'. She had suffered much in her life, and in most respects, in Sumper's opinion, had shown good judgement. Year after year, summer after summer she had managed to demonstrate good judgement completely without calculation. 'But when you, Herr Brandling, could no longer supply the amounts of money we all depended on, she became so terrified of penury she lost her judgement.

'She stole my greatest treasure from me,' Sumper told Henry. 'Please do not nod your head. I do not mean it was the most highly priced item I owned, only that it was more precious than any object I have ever made. She consigned this to the packer for local sale.'

The possibility that Frau Helga might someday steal this valued automaton had never been completely absent from Sumper's mind, but who could have predicted she would sell it, not to Paris or London where at least it would find its market, but to the cursed woman best known for selling women's bodies and cheating the local clockmakers of their labour?

'Herr Brandling, Henry, I had made that automaton for my master, the Genius. He had, by nature, what I would call a positive personality, but when the Queen ignored his petition, when she then gave his Engine to the English Army, his spirit was destroyed.'

Sumper vowed he would produce a device to lighten the great man's heart. He would make 'the dear old bugger' laugh.

'For materials,' Sumper continued, 'I used only gears and wheels such as are used by English clockmakers, but these I elevated by means of specially contrived axles and bevelled gears. There is no point in explaining it to you. For the general casing of the automaton I used sheet tin which I shaped around wooden forms of my own design. I purchased some red velvet. Three inches square.

I manufactured a small wheel-driven bellows. Then a pipe in which a current of fast air could be twisted, warped, stopped, released in such a way as to produce a simulation of the human laugh. Henry,' he cried, 'your Vaucanson would not have had the wit.'

Henry noted that Sumper's tongue was 'white as boiled tripe'.

Sumper said: 'I made my automaton for the Genius, for him alone. I found him on his settee with his sad eyes engaged with nothing but the skirting board. Then I was able to place – just there – like this – my gift.'

It was, apparently, an eighteen-inch-tall likeness of Jesus Christ. It was made of bright tin, but the face had been painted. Hanging from the shoulders was an exceptional blue silk robe. 'Once I had wound the key, my Jesus shot forward on his little wheels, turning first to left, then right, then pausing. You think you can see it Henry? But can you predict what will happen next? After the fifth such movement a hidden rod prevents the movement of a gear, arresting the whole mechanism in such a way that both of the Christ's arms fly open. It is very funny. Anyone can see – Jesus is about to bless the room. But wait. See – the cloak is thrown wide, a great red heart is revealed and this immediately falls under the influence of short puffs of air. The heart is beating, the big red sacred heart. Henry, I wish you could have seen the figure because it appeared so wondrously *pleased* with its own performance. Its head moved down to see what it had done, and then up to the heavens as if to say, look – is this not a jolly show? And so with his head up and down, and his arms first apart, and then together, with the heart being rhythmically revealed and covered, the Christ began to spin like a top.'

Dear Lord forgive my Judas soul, Henry wrote, for I also smiled.

At this point, Sumper told me, the Genius began to laugh and he knew he could save him and therefore, himself, for he would now do great things in the future of the world.

Next the holy figure began to wobble. Oh dear, what was happening, Jesus lost his balance and fell onto the floor. And the old man naturally imagined the design had failed and so he kneeled to raise it from the dead.

But at that very moment the Jesus began to roll back and forth laughing, and it was for this exact reason, Sumper told me, he had made the Son of Man. When the arms opened wide, the body was lifted, and then the body rolled, and revealed the sacred heart, and then, from his chest came a laugh the old man could not resist.

Herr Sumper was satanic, wrote Henry. I was afraid of his influence. Yet when he turned his wet eyes and slightly wobbly smile upon me, I was reminded, not of the devil, but of my wife's face when first she held our Alice in her arms.

That, Sumper told Henry, was how he brought

the Genius back to life. He had concocted a medicine that, if administered frequently enough, would effect a cure.

Cure, Henry underlined.

Endorphins, thought Catherine.

While Sumper had been busy with his Jesus Christ he had conceived a plan to present his employer's 'Ledger of Drowned Subjects' to Queen Victoria. This was stage two. It began immediately.

'You thought I lied about Prince Albert but my master saw my character. When the old man heard my plan he did not doubt that I was determined that the Queen would know the great purpose of the Engine and see how many of her subjects might be saved.'

The Genius correctly feared for Sumper. He was not reassured to learn that 'my German' had been a visitor to Buckingham Palace on three previous occasions; two of them were moonlit nights. Sumper now revealed to him the vaulting pole he had constructed, ten parts to it, with metal sleeves. He drew him a rough plan of those portions of the palace where he would interview Her Majesty.

'The Genius said, They will deport you from England, at the very least.'

For Sumper, nothing could be worse than to be separated from Cruickshank, but he would not be ruled by fear. He had been 'called'. He hoped his service might be long. But sitting inside 16 Soho Square he accepted that it might also be as brief as a butterfly's existence.

'At that moment,' he said, 'I beheld the reason for my life.'

In my room above the pub I, Catherine Gehrig, surfaced. It was about midnight and there was an argument in the street downstairs.

I could have paid attention to the place I lived in, but I had allowed myself to become a citizen of an imaginary world.

Henry wrote. Sumper spoke. He said, 'I had met great men in England. They were of a sufficient size to comprehend their human smallness, and therefore to serve, in their turn, beings of impossible knowledge and magnitude. They were my examples.'

The German had already mocked my God, Henry wrote, so I asked him coldly who these Superior Beings might be. Instead of answering he described how he wrapped the ledger of drowned souls in oilskin and strapped it to his back before departing Soho Square. Of his farewell that night, he reported no single word. He set off to the palace oblivious of the personal disaster which lay ahead.

About the alleged pole-vault, no more was said. Thank the Lord, wrote Henry who was clearly anxious about what he could believe.

Twenty lines later some evidence had caused the writer to change his mind. It was, in all likelihood, the star-shaped scar on Sumper's abdomen which had earlier repulsed him. Now it appeared to him an honest injury suffered in a hare-brained vault across the palace wall.

If the clockmaker described his pain or injury, Henry made no note of it. But he no longer doubted that 'the liar' had not only gained entry to the palace but had captured Prince Albert, not in a reception room or even a study, but reading in his bed. Impertinent, wrote Henry, adding that the greatest barrier between the populace and the Prince and Queen was the belief of the common people that it was completely and utterly impossible for anyone to gain access to their monarch.

The Prince Consort, having looked up from his book and stared directly at the place where Sumper stood, seems to have seen only what he expected. In this case it would appear to be an over-stuffed red chair.

It actually took 'the most forceful tactic', Henry reported, to get the attention of the Prince. Who could have imagined what it must have felt like to be in Herr Saxe-Coburg and Gotha's shoes? Did he think that a poltergeist had seized his book and wrenched it from his hand? What did he expect might be contained in the oilskin parcel the bleeding phantom presently unwrapped upon his bed?

The ledger of deaths by drowning was apparently such a size that it must be shared between two readers, and what fear did the Prince feel to have the injured stranger lie beside him and demand HRH read aloud the notices pasted on every page?

'He was very cold and formal,' Sumper said, 'until we reached a certain shipwreck where he recognized the name of a drowned passenger. He said it was his little niece. So when he began to weep, I naturally assumed this drowning was the source of his grief. To be frank, I was delighted. It made me hope I would enlist his support for the Engine. However, taking into account what happened next, it seems more likely that the coward was crying because he was afraid.'

This view was based on a brief conversation between the Prince and Queen Victoria who now appeared at the door in her nightgown. Speaking in German she asked Prince Albert to explain his bedfellow, although she used a rougher word.

'As we had been speaking that language,' Sumper told Henry, 'the Prince surely realized I could understand his wife. He answered in French telling her that I was about to murder him, at which news the Queen closed the door and went away.'

An 'astonishingly long time' passed before Sumper heard the palace guard running in lock step. It was a great slamming performance they gave upon the marble floors. It was only then, when he was so roughly handled, that he seems to have accepted that his plan had failed.

Even there, apparently, he found reason for hope. That is, they called the Prince's personal physician for him and when he was sewn together they accommodated him in a room in the palace, where 'apart from the barred windows, the view was good'.

At that time Sumper had no idea of how his

adventure might be read by the nation. Only later did he learn that the Royal Family thought it unwise to reveal that one more German had arrived at Buckingham Palace. There had been two previous assaults on Her Majesty, the first by the disgruntled Irishman who had fired a powder-filled pistol as the Queen's carriage passed along Constitution Hill, and then an insane ex-Army officer who struck her with his cane, crushed her bonnet and (as Henry knew from his mother) bruised her arms and shoulders.

Both of these men were sent to New South Wales, but Sumper was not destined to be transported to a gold mine. At first he was well fed, and the English puddings increased his optimism, but early one morning two soldiers escorted him to a blind carriage and rode with him to a wharf somewhere west of London Bridge. Here he was locked in a brig aboard a German trawler and it was only then, at the moment of his banishment, when he was given back the ledger, that he accepted every-thing was lost.

# CATHERINE

I n the morning I returned all Henry's surviving notebooks to Lowndes Square and Crofty, in taking delivery, bestowed on me the most lovely smile. 'Thank you,' he said. 'Would you like some tea?'

I was so relieved to be forgiven.

'Yes please,' I said. Surely he would permit me to keep the final volume one more day.

I waited, swivelling on my chair, looking out the window at the trees.

'No milk,' he said. 'Do you mind?'

'Perfect,' I said, as he placed a very lovely (uncharacteristically restrained) Clarice Cliff cup and saucer on the desk beside me. 'I had the most awful dusty tea for breakfast.'

Why had I said that? Surely I wasn't going to tell him I had spent the night in a room above a pub? Then it appears I was. Then I had.

'For God's sake, why?'

'I wanted to finish reading.'

'Which pub?' His questioning gaze embarrassed me.

'The Rose and Crown.'

'The Young's place with all the sofas in the bar? Up the road?'

I thought, he can't know that Matthew and I slept there for the first time, but men will tell each other the strangest things, so perhaps he did. I tried to sip my tea but the triangular deco handle, while very beautiful, was difficult to grasp when hot.

'I was trying to get the notebooks finished. Actually, I still have one to go.'

I could see the pity in his eyes. I thought, he will let me keep the book.

'Well, I am not going to lock them up, my love. You can read them whenever you wish, in a lot nicer environment than the Rose and Crown.'

'Actually,' I said, 'I do think it would be wise to put them on restricted.'

'You do, do you?' He laughed, rather indignantly I thought.

'Eric, I put an awful lot of make-up on, but I do think the scratch still shows, don't you?' I did not say, Amanda Snyde has been inside my house, although of course she had.

'You mean I should put them on restricted so your assistant cannot read them too.'

'I'm rather afraid they will set her off again.'

I had misjudged him totally. He was incredulous.

'My darling, of course they cannot be locked up. I couldn't justify that to anyone. You know Miss Snyde is very sorry. There was a mess-up at Boots, apparently. It was not her fault at all. Now she has her pills again, she's fine. She's mortified by what happened.'

I thought, she takes pills for her enthusiasm?

'Eric, please, have you read these notebooks?'

In other circumstances I would have enjoyed that impish smile. Now it scared me.

'Keep reading. It gets better.' So saying he whisked all my notebooks from the room. I followed him, but I knew where he was going anyway. In future I would have to take that same staircase, at the top of which I would find myself at the mercy of the dry and secret little Annie Heller who had never liked me, and now would like me less. I had lost my private right to Henry Brandling. I would have to sign him out and sign him in.

The lapsang souchong was still too hot. The solid triangular handles offered no purchase. The treasure was about to slip between my fingers.


2


Annie Heller was a tiny bad-tempered insect of a thing, not at all a scholar, with no technical expertise, with no legitimate institutional power except – she was the one who arranged for the manuscripts to be scanned. I suspected she was exceptionally nice to Crofty, for when he spoke of the empty Victorian sitting room behind her high librarian's desk, he called it a 'very pleasant place'. Why not? It must have been, for him. Even in winter, even in the silence, he was spared the animus the rest of us could feel, even when we had no visual contact with its source.

Annie was unbelievably, habitually rude. Only at the Swinburne could she have kept her job.

We all tried to suck up, and of course she despised us for it. Knowing this I still smiled at her when I came to talk about the Brandling Catalogue. I told her that her hair looked nice, which was far too big a lie. I asked, please, for a form to withdraw one of the manuscripts Mr Croft had just given her.

As usual she made me wait a long time for an answer. Finally she said she would do that the 'very moment' they had been catalogued.

I asked her when might that be.

'Oh, not long – a day or two.'

When she did look up I knew she was lying. I waited until she was more or less compelled to look at me.

'Might I perhaps read it here, in the reading room?' I asked. It should not have even been a question. I was a senior conservator.

'I'm afraid they are needed for cataloguing.'

'I do not believe that Mr Croft intended I be denied the material,' I said, thus somehow forcing her to return to pecking on her keyboard. Her task could not have been demanding for she was able to speak to me between keystrokes.

'You know as well as I do, Miss Gehrig, Mr Croft would not wish me to go against the rules.'

'Perhaps you could ring him up?'

So then the keyboard was pushed aside. The head came up. The tiny wire spectacles were removed.

'Miss Gehrig, I do know what the Swinburne regulations are without speaking to Mr Croft and, in any case, once the manuscripts have been catalogued they will go to be scanned, and then, if you wish, you can view them on your computer.'

'So it is definitely not possible for me to read one of them now?'

'Miss Gehrig, perhaps I don't appear to be busy?'

'Even if there is an important fund-raising project that will now be delayed?'

'That is correct, yes.'

'Thank you, Miss Heller.'

'You are very welcome, Miss Gehrig. I don't imagine it will be more than a week.'

I descended the stairs as quietly as I dared and travelled back to Olympia in the stinky bus. I was in a vile, vile mood, angry with myself for my own incompetence, angry I had lost Henry, furious with Crofty for not supporting me. When I found Amanda ensconced in my studio it seemed I had lost all the power I had ever had.

'Good morning Amanda,' I said.

'Miss Gehrig, I am so sorry,' she said, but I could not trust her. I would not engage her eyes.

'It's past,' I said. 'The swan is more important than either of us.'

She had been with Angus. He had dressed her.

She wore a crumpled white shirt whose single button was sewn with bright red thread. She looked gorgeous, carrying the rumpled cotton the way only the very beautiful can do. She had a new sort of sexual confidence that made me feel dry and wizened.

By this time we had the mechanism assembled on a steel work bench, and the glass rods were all clean, laid on the bright new back plates, their end caps secured by a modern reversible adhesive. As soon as we wound the clockwork, the rods would slowly spin.

The track was in place and the little fish could be connected as soon as this morning, an operation as ultimately simple as hooking an earring in one's lobe.

We were perhaps a month from the very end, but very close to a dress rehearsal for the nobs. Once the neck was clad with rings, once the beak was properly attached, we would do a run-through and then Crofty could show his benefactors the wonder. Of course he already knew exactly what he had. Even before its restoration he had foreseen the swan's hypnotic, eerie being. I am certain that he had laid a more complicated set of bets than I could ever hope to know.

Would it really draw sufficient crowds to please the ministry? The minutes of the procedures meeting had hinted at this angle, but one could have put it much more bluntly – with this swan the mandarins of Lowndes Square had surrendered to the Tory government. They understood their obligation to be 'more popular'.

In any case my assailant and I laboured day after day. As long as we kept our conversation to the job at hand, I did not fear her physically.

Yet I was unable to forget that savage, ignorant injury to Carl's blue cube, and because of this I continued to stay at the Rose and Crown. This brought its own predictable stresses on both my MasterCard and my wardrobe.

I arrived at work one morning and found Amanda already at her computer. I would not have thought about it if she had not closed it down so quickly. A few minutes later, as luck would have it, Security called to say we had a parcel – the long chain synthetic, Dyneema, which I had ordered to replace the steel cable. I despatched Amanda to pick it up, and the moment she was out of the room I looked at her viewing history.

She had been Googling Furtwangen. She had found this in the notebooks in my flat. How much she had read was beyond the point. I was angry and frightened. My skin went cold and hard as leather.

By the time the spy had returned and placed the parcel on my desk, my world had become quite unreal. I picked up the scalpel with the dot of nail polish. Amanda stood very close, wearing Jo Malone, all in black today, with painted buttons.

Before the inner sheath of packaging was revealed,

I turned to her, very conscious of the scalpel in my hand. She stepped back, exactly as I wished.

'Amanda, I checked your computer history.'

'I've not been looking at the webcam.'

'You were Googling Furtwangen. Why?'

Her face showed that infuriating expression which might be colloquially translated as 'duh'. She said: 'Obviously, I wanted to know where it was.'

I casually rested my hand on the bench, but I did not release my grip on the metal handle. 'Why?'

'I think they made cuckoo clocks there.'

'Why are you interested in cuckoo clocks?'

If she was going to scratch again, it would be now. I was very foolish to hold the scalpel. I wished, now, too late, to put it down, but I was afraid of that as well. Then I saw, with relief, her eyes were tearing.

'Miss Gehrig, I am so sorry.'

I did not dare soften. 'What are you sorry about, Amanda?'

'I know about the notebooks.'

'Which notebooks?'

'Henry Brandling.'

'You mean you have seen them? How could you?'

'I went to Miss Heller. She doesn't leave until seven.'

It was not until the next day that I had my moment with Miss Heller and Eric Croft and I discovered, to my considerable surprise, that this was true. And although this resulted in me being given full access to the reading room, I got no apology from Heller.

'When people are nice to me, Miss Gehrig, I am always very nice to them. When people are rude and officious then I tend to be a stickler.'

I sat ten feet behind her desk, reading Henry Brandling.

# HENRY

Now that the Furtwangen weather is so cold, the old sawmill by the river seems to suffer as much as we who dwell there – slates fracturing, nails wrenching themselves free, the whole cuckoo construction seeming to shiver in the winds which have begun to blow violently between the dark cliffs of the gorge. Frau Helga runs back and forth between her home and the inn (I assume it is the inn) driven by something, not clockwork, but a tight spring certainly, a locked action beyond any possibility of change. She returns to pack her trunk, each time the same, so carefully, folding her threadbare dresses as if they were ball gowns. Then – like a customs agent (that is, in a fury) Sumper unpacks, each time more violently. She runs to the inn. She returns. She weeps.

Herr Sumper has suffered a black eye, the cause and occasion of which are complete mysteries to me.

Frau Helga seems to be still in a financial nego-tiation with the owner of the inn. Is this about the swan? I do not know. I hear her conversation with

279

Sumper very clearly. It is mechanically amplified by the chute leading to the workshop.

'She has always looked out for me,' she says. 'She will get a good price.'

'She is a brothel-keeper,' Sumper says.

I think, does she plan to spend this on the swan?

She shouts at him in German, rapping her fist against a wall, a door, the floor for all I know. It is not impossible that she is lying prostrate at his feet.

'You are free,' I hear him, even while the windows rattle in their sashes. He says, 'Free as a fish in the sea.' He says that she may depart any moment she chooses and he will, as the man of honour she knows him to be, deliver Carl back to Karlsruhe as soon as the swan is made.

Then wailing in German in her fright. The Lord knows what it means.

He says the new draught horse is not for her use. He will pay for her to travel by coach.

M. Arnaud is expected any hour to produce the beak. Will the brothel-keeper pay him? Is he paid already? I imagine him, standing alone in the middle of the forest, cloaked in black, half bird, half man. What child would not be frightened of that beak?

The colossal automaton I so desperately summoned forth is assembled on a heavy cart in the so-called summer workshop in the freezing cold. I cannot pay for it. Sumper and the boy continue working around the inconvenience of the cart wheels.

I will have my swan. I will take him home. The draught horse will be backed up the long low ramp. From here my machine shall be carried out into the light of day, like a saint in a procession.

Sumper continues to call the lithe and buxom Frau Helga 'The idiot woman'.

Again and again, Frau Helga insists she had no choice as 'Herr Brandling failed his obligation'.

No one asks me for a shekel.

Sumper, again and again: she has 'sealed her own fate' by letting the Catholics see his 'private business'.

I now suspect the black eye is related to the automaton. They are wasting Percy's time. Arguments take place in the river workshop and the summer workshop to which I am not privy. The discord continues around the dinner table, through the night, echoing in the gorge, as inescapable as the damp, as relentless as the river. We are all afraid, I warrant.

I think of my English boy every minute. There is not the slightest attempt to shield the German boy from the adult opinions, and sometimes I suspect – because both of them continue, even when most unforgivably abusive, to speak in English – that the scenes are a sort of Punch and Judy enacted to deceive me or to blame me for the damage I have caused them all. But what can I do? My brother bought stocks in the Bank of Ohio.

'He is a child,' Frau Helga says. Of Carl.

He is a strange one – his intent dark eyes flicking from one he loves to one he worships. I cannot be held responsible for the damage done to him.

His mother ladles out the potatoes which she mashes so brutally but which, with the addition of salt and butter, make the most delicious meal I have ever known. She serves furiously – splat! – and her nostrils contract in passion. There is an angry burn like a knife blade along her lower arm.

'I need Carl to finish,' Sumper says. I think, where will the money come from? Blood floods the boy's face. With his bright wide eyes and his wheaten hair he might be a choir boy in our village church.

The thick man's appetite is never gratified, his thirst never slaked. He drinks, he eats, he makes the law. 'When the boy is finished here, he will return to the city of the wheel and do what he is born to do.'

How could I have not understood his strangeness the first day at the inn – the map of Karlsruhe, the Baron with the Drais? Frau Helga says now that his mind is broken and she hates him, but later I hear them thumping in the night, dragging at each other like wild creatures, snorting and panting like the partners of a crime. Dare I admit – I would sell my soul for less.

In the morning I am shaken awake. Sumper has shaved, smooth as rock, and gleaming. His eyes are pebbles in a stream.

What he wishes me to understand, before the day's work begins, is that all this is exactly as Albert Cruickshank had foretold.

He lays his hand against my cheek. Who would not shrink from him? He repeats that Cruickshank had predicted my arrival in Germany and my particular role in Sumper's life. My eyes are stuck with sleep but his are clear, without the tiniest ripple of doubt.

This is one more lie. I have everything recorded exactly, as he told it – he has not seen Cruickshank since he set out for Buckingham Palace on that rainy night. At that time there was no talk of me. How could there be? Then he was deported and finally returned to Furtwangen from which place he despatched the ledger of drowned people to his former master. He received in return the blasphemous automaton with a 'charming note' which indicated Sumper might now need the laughter more than Cruickshank.

If there had been some 'prophecy' I would have noted it, just as I have noted all the other symptoms.

But Sumper, as from the start, is slippery as a Rhine fish. 'I cannot tell you everything that ever occurred.' He opens the shutters, raises the windows to admit the howling wind. 'No, I am not relating what Cruickshank WROTE to me but rather what HE SAID. Please pay attention to what I am telling you. When I left for Buckingham Palace the Genius already saw what my fate would be. I imagined I would save the Engine, but he knew the truth. At the moment, when I shook his hand, he said do not despair, another Englishman will come along. Only later did his words come back to me. I might lose him, but another Englishman would come along.'

I rise and stand with my back to the window to keep the storm at bay. He pushes himself toward me, eyes too close, too insistent.

He says: 'Do you not remember how I sat waiting for you in Frau Beck's inn? You did not know it yet, but I already had your foolish plans.'

'Herr Sumper,' I say, 'this is not sensible. Mr Cruickshank never knew me, nor could he know my circumstances, or the character of my wife, or the sickness of my son, or the artists over-running our home. To speak in his own language, Mr Cruickshank had insufficient data.'

'Henry, you have not the least idea of what that great brain thought. How could you?'

I am two inches taller but when I look into those jet black eyes I am but a snivelling beast. I pray that he will release me soon.

It is clear now that Frau Helga has let the villagers see the laughing Jesus. It is my fault that she sold it, but is the price enough for my own purpose? Certainly I saw Frau Helga counting money in the stable. I saw the fair down on her arms. Once I dreamed I might kiss her. Long ago.

I was at the stream washing, naked, teetering on razor shale which can amputate your toes.

When Sumper touched my shoulder I jumped in fright. My private parts shrivelled like gizzards in a stockpot. He was armoured in his leather apron, a beak in his hand, but I did not know that then.

He said, 'You will have been responsible for something far finer than you could ever conceive.'

'I wanted only a duck.'

'You were not born to have a duck. You were born to bring a Wonder to the world.'

And then he turned away and left me in my nakedness.

That night the mother threw the mashed potatoes across the floor. 'You have no right to steal my son.' There was more of it, all very distressing, particularly to watch the Holy Child wring his hands, his long warty white fingers. In the lamp light his chin looked long, his knees high and these fingers entwining like a nest of baby eels.

'I have not come so far to hurt this boy,' said Sumper. 'He is a Genius.'

'You shall not hurt him,' she said. Yet she surely knew what dangerous situation she had created at the inn where they had presumably witnessed Jesus rolling across the floor and laughing. 'He is just a little boy.'

'He is a Genius,' repeated Sumper. 'Here,' he said, 'read this.' And from the pouch of his apron he produced the ebony beak on the underside of which I saw there was silver script inset in the coal-black wood.

'I cannot read.' She drew back from it. 'You know I cannot.'

So he thrust the object to me.

Those awful eyes were upon me, waiting for me to understand the meaning.

I am a dunce, I thought, a total dunderhead.

'Quite,' I said. 'Exactly.'

# CATHERINE

nnie Heller kicked me out at seven with the final pages still unread. I walked down the narrow Danish stairs, all golden at that time of day. Outside there was a warm wind lifting vagrant pamphlets in the air.

I arrived at the Annexe studio five minutes before lockdown, and there, in what we called the 'Ikea box', the swan's beak was waiting amongst all those odd screws and washers, the mostly leftover pieces from our reassembly. Why I had treated it so offhandedly is a question for a psychiatrist. I had not even assigned it a catalogue number. M. Arnaud's handiwork was exactly as I had last seen it, black as black, on a bed of cotton wool, inside a small cardboard box, with the word BEAK in magic marker on the lid.

Contrary to Henry's account, nothing was written on the beak itself. I found this extremely, even excessively, disturbing, as if I had been lied to by a lover. Then I understood the obvious: Arnaud had inlaid the words in silver which would now be silver oxide, that is, the words would be black on black. I could have taken the mystery to the window. I could have used the UV lamp, but it was lock-up time and I was agitated and frightened of being caught with my secret. So I wrapped the beak in Kleenex and popped it in an envelope and belted out of the building as if I was late for some grand, imaginary event.

It was a very strange evening, far too hot, with a strong dry wind that suggested Buckinghamshire had turned to desert. At Olympia, as at Lowndes Square, there were papers everywhere adrift, the *Evening Standard* wrapping itself with a nasty slap around the lamp post. AMERICA'S MESS NOT OURS. One could easily read it upside down.

There was an odd ammoniacal little pharmacy in a side street where I had already bought deodorant and shampoo. There was no cashier or shop girl, only the grey stooped little pharmacist who had a nasty cold. It was a shambles of cardboard boxes, electric fans and menstrual pads, and it took him a while to locate the cotton buds and methylated spirits.

'No bag,' I said, and tried to grab my purchases. But apparently a receipt must be written. When the old man spiked his yellow carbon copy I thought of my father, changing batteries, then upstairs to have a dram.

Finally I was in the street, and the Rose and Crown was just ahead, occupying its renovated corner with its blue tiles and bright green umbrellas and a surprising clustering of drinkers outside – English skin, sunburned half to death.

I attracted some attention which was a little bit

OK. That is, one did not wish to be sexually invisible just yet. On the other hand there is something very nasty about a braying pack, and it was this sound that followed me up the stairs of the 'Residence'.

I opened the window of my room and set up on the sill – it was quite wide enough to accommodate the meths bottle. I unpacked the cotton buds and laid them on a tissue. I sited the beak beside the buds. The rest was hardly brain surgery. Within three minutes the meths had revealed the silver inlay on the under-beak.

Then I understood why Henry had written 'Dunce'.

Faced with *Illud aspicis non vides* I also was a dunce.

I sat on the slippery synthetic quilt and wondered who I could call on to translate. It was then, staring at those framed pink and pale blue prints one finds only in hotels, I realized that I really had no friends at all.

For years and years I had lived in the lazy conceited happy world of coupledom, something so deliciously contained by private language and its own sweet intolerances of everyone outside. I *knew* a lot of people, of course, and was habitually affectionate with many, but I had locked the door when Matthew died. I was a sudden spinster. My mother and father were dead. My sister would no longer talk to me.

*Illud aspicis non vides.*

In all those years of being a secret mistress, I had fancied myself at home with solitude but I had never once felt this stone weight of loneliness inside my throat. There was now no one to call but he whose kindness I had abused already.

When Crofty answered I heard music, something rather difficult, I thought, by which I meant – beyond my education.

'I'm sorry,' I said when he answered, but of course I was much relieved.

'Hang on.'

The music was turned down. He was slow in returning.

'I interrupted you. I'm sorry.'

'My darling,' he said, 'there is nothing to interrupt.' I remembered that he had once been part of a couple too.

From my open window I could see two men support a very drunk young girl, a poor wobbly creature with silly shoes, plump legs, short skirt. Jesus help her. I could not watch.

'Where are you? Not still at that bloody pub?'

'It's what they call Happy Hour.'

There was a pause. Crofty said, 'Would you like me to come and sit with you?'

It would have been such a great relief. But of course I could not.

'How is your Latin?' I asked.

'Rusty.'

'But probably serviceable?'

'Possibly.'

'What does this mean: *Illud aspicis non vides?*'

'Where is the beak?' he asked and I realized he was slightly squiffy.

'You know where the beak is,' I said. 'And I would be astonished if you had not read it.'

'Do you know, my dear,' he said, and it was clear to me that he was topping up his glass. 'Do you know, I find the notion that mysteries must be solved to be *very* problematic. You know what I mean? Every curator finally learns that the mysteries are the point.'

'Please don't tease me.'

'No, I am serious. Why do we always wish to remove ambiguity?'

I thought, why do you always want to polish silver half to death?

'Without ambiguity you have Agatha Christie, a sort of aesthetic whodunnit. But look at any Rothko. You can look and look but you never get past the vacillations and ambiguities of colour, and form, and surface. This is so much ahead of the "analytical clarities" of your Josef Albers.'

'He is not my Albers.'

'He was Matthew's Albers.'

'He was, yes.'

There was another pause.

'This is my project,' I said. 'You gave it to me.'

'Indeed I did. I hope I was not too meddlesome?'

'Eric, I lost everything I lived for. You gave me this. If it is a mystery, that's fine with me. But you gave it to me.'

'Yes, dear girl, I did.'

'Then why give it to her?' I hadn't meant to say

that, but I had. The swan was mine. Henry was mine.

Eric gave himself a splash. 'What do you mean?' he asked wetly.

'This is mine.'

'Indeed,' he said, 'but what is "it" exactly?'

'The Latin.'

'So you wish to know how it translates?'

'Yes I do.'

'You want to know what it says?'

'Yes.'

'*Illud aspicis non vides*. It means, You cannot see what you can see.'

'Oh shut up,' I cried.

'It means, You cannot see what you can see.'

'No,' I said. 'No it doesn't.'

'Sweet Cat,' he said. 'Call me whenever you wish.' The phone went dead.

The marrow of my bones was filled with hurt, envy, rage that this mad rich girl was stealing everything from me, including Angus, that is, the carrier of that same spiralled mechanism that made my beloved's upper lip, that wry funny taut muscle in the shadow of his famous nose.

You cannot see what you can see, said Sumper. What a load of rubbish.

## 2

When I was awoken it did not occur to me that such an enormous noise might be made by rain.

But rain it was, the most unimaginable torrent cascading off the roof and falling, backlit, like Victoria Falls, deep and blue.

I had told Eric to shut up.

There was a sort of banging on the wall outside. Was it a hurricane? Should I shelter in the bathroom?

I saw the shadow of a ladder, waving, slamming against the wall. I thought they will break the glass and I have no slippers to protect my feet. Then there was a very wide white man in shorts, crawling up against the weight of water, his body flat against my glass. I saw his belly button and the black hair on his skin, as if some creature of the unconscious was breaking through the membrane of a dream. I could hear thunder through the rain. I sat holding my sheets across my breasts.

The water roared. I thought, I am totally alone in some hellish place; of all the people on the earth, Eric Croft has been the kindest, the most forbearing, bending when he had no requirement to bend, giving without expecting thanks.

Shut up, I had said.

The world will end like everything must. I think the ladder fell off the roof. The rain kept pouring. Men were shouting. There was nothing I could do that was not ridiculous.

There were now flashing yellow lights in the streets. Then another ladder. Men in bright blue waterproofs climbed past my window. Who in

London wore blue waterproofs? I did not know the stigmata of disaster.

At two o'clock I was alone at my window, observing the empty flooded street. Next morning I departed, with a light soft bag of clothes on one shoulder and my handbag underneath my arm. My clothes were no longer clean, and if I selected a white linen shirt it was only because I knew I could use hydrogen peroxide to remove the sweat stains once I was at work.

A greater olfactory challenge was presented outside the pub where I found surface water rushing down the road. Basements had been flooded. The drains in the street were bubbling with very nasty-smelling water.

The old pharmacist had his doors open and I caught a glimpse of him, standing on a high and dangerous ladder. He had thrown sodden cardboard boxes into the street and from them rose what was, I suppose, sulphur dioxide, although there was ammonia as on the day before, and I was forcibly reminded of all those rich sulphur compounds that accompany human decay. I thought of the bacteria, fungi, the protozoa, the way our bodies attack themselves when we die. I did not like this idea, not at all. I preferred to think of us as something dry and crumbly, with no relation to the moisture-laden sheen of our decay.

Security inspected my dirty laundry, bastards. Later, in the fume cupboard I removed my shirt, applied the hydrogen peroxide and finished the job with a hairdryer. Done. Fresh, not really.

Amanda had not logged off. Her big Mac screen was filled with spewing spill and a chain of protesting voices. Were they children or adults? Dessgirl, Mankind40, Miss Katz, Ardiva, Clozaril – who would know? To read their comments was to live inside a howl. Was this Amanda's underworld?

Clorazil wrote, Who made the machine that kills the ocean? Whose interest did that serve? Not humans, that's for sure. Ardiva believed that flames were coming out together with the oil. Sheread2 conjectured that there was a volcano involved. Much is not being told to us, she wrote. Mankind40 thought we should just nuke it shut. Below, the lowest circle, the voices of the damned continued. I didn't know it had affected me. I didn't even know that all this saline was washing down my cheeks, but when Amanda's arms came around me, hugging from behind, I began to cry in earnest. There was no point in disguising it.

'Miss Gehrig, I'm so sorry.'

I accepted her clean white handkerchief. I blew my snotty nose and went to my computer to generate the work orders for a busy day.

## 3

Of course the PR people have been 'psyched' about our project all along and I have driven them nuts with my postponements and delays. Yes, they must have the website ready, but they are museum people too, and surely they must know that completion always takes longer than one expects or, to be more honest, longer than Publicity anticipates.

Finally we agree to announce the swan in two stages, one public, one more private. The restoration does not need to be totally complete before we show it to the 'loots and suits' as Eric quaintly calls them.

I have been required to sign off a 'safe date' with the publicity director and the prickly website manager, but when the day arrives it is not safe at all. Later, on the morning of the appointed day, the music box refuses to stop playing when the swan's cycle of performance is at an end.

'Does it matter, darling? Think seriously.'

We have not yet had a full rehearsal, which is cutting it finer than either of us would have ever dreamed.

'We will fix it,' I tell Eric. 'I am only telling you in case.'

'In case what?'

'I will have it done in half an hour.'

Ninety-five minutes later I call back to say it's done. I have made Eric unnecessarily anxious but he does not protest or complain. He asks if I can be finished, not finished-finished, by the end of the day. He will cancel now if I tell him to, but clearly he cannot bear the thought of it.

'Don't cancel.'

'You are certain darling?'

'Yes, really.'

'If you need more time I'll deal with Publicity.'

By half past three everyone can see that my calculation is correct – we have our creature set up on a large grey steel mobile cart, which we can spin around as needs dictate. The mechanism is still exposed. Above this the reflecting plate is in place, the glass rods, the ring of silver foliage, the silver body and the articulated neck on which the silver rings lock neat and tight and gleaming.

At four o'clock the poor darling cannot stay at Lowndes Square any longer, and there he is in his crepe-soled shoes, shaven to the bone, gleaming with Penhaligon's, in that tight pinstripe suit straight out of Beckmann. In fact, the suit gives him a morally ambiguous appearance, and one meets him rather as you meet the men in Beckmann, uncertainly.

'No beak?' He peers into the clockwork, staring hard at the pinned music drum.

'Would you have rather we hid the clockwork?'

'No, no. Far better like this.' But he is clearly tense.

'I could have had Harold build a plywood case. We've still got two hours.'

He stares at me. I imagine he is considering it and am sorry I made the suggestion.

'Where is the beak, Catherine?'

Last week I would have been insulted by this.

Today I smile. 'Don't worry about the beak, look at the movement.'

Amanda is wearing a strange white lab coat for the occasion. With her blonde hair pulled back and a pair of spectacles she gives off a fabulously Teutonic air.

'Miss Snyde,' I say, 'would you wind the mechanism?'

'Yes Miss Gehrig.'

After all our horrors, we are actually having a nice time.

'You do have the beak?' Eric says.

'Wait.' I take his arm. 'Watch.'

Of course he will love it. He is crinkling up his Sing-song eyes already.

I am the conservator, but I grant my assistant the privilege of winding the mechanism for our first proper run-through. When I nod, she releases the pin. As the neck begins its first quite complicated sequence, the Brahms melody accompanies the curious predatory twisting.

'Stop.'

'No,' cries Eric. 'No, no, Catherine, please.'

'Did you see that?' I ask Amanda, although of course the old Sing-song has seen it too.

'In the first sequence, yes.'

We play the first sequence again and there is no doubt there is an irritating shudder in the movement. Before the neck rings were fitted this somehow did not show, but now it destroys an effect which must be creepily sinuous, sensuous.

'We have time,' I say.

'No,' says Eric. 'Leave the bloody thing alone.'

He thinks this is a risk but he is wrong.

The caterers and publicists arrive together. I send Amanda to deal with them. Eric holds my arm. 'Don't punish me like this.'

'You know it's just old museum wax. It will be perfect.'

'You're not going to take the bloody rings off.'

'Yes, I am.'

Eric watches for a moment but then he walks away.

Amanda is perfect, or her meds are perfect. She returns to my side and we remove the rings together, and I am so proud of us, the choreography.

It takes approximately thirty minutes to remove the wax, and it is during this long quiet period I hear Eric in exasperated conversation with the publicist, a strange Colman Getty boy with a towering plume of hair.

When we finish, exactly twenty-eight minutes later, I discover Eric is watching me.

'Now, the beak.'

'Yes,' he says without excitement.

I unhook my thief's bag from its hook behind the door. In clear sight, I produce the beak, remove the Kleenex, and, using the two brass Whitworth screws Amanda places in the dry cup of my hand, attach it to the clean steel nub of the undead.

It is 5.55 p.m. when I go to wash my hands, and

only when I return does Eric divulge the news that Publicity aborted the mission half an hour ago.

The canapés are very nice. One bottle of Veuve is already open so we have no choice but drink to our success.

4

The day did come. The studio was flooded with morning light which, being filtered through the blinds and reflected from the opposite wall, contained the very slightest wash of gold. Our object could not have looked more precious. We hid it beneath a muslin cloth, praying that the light would last.

It was half past eight when the 'loots and suits' began to arrive for the unveiling, and perhaps it was a tribute to the Conservative's sense of business that everyone was assembled when the Minister of Arts, he of the boyish polished face, arrived at exactly 8.45 a.m.

As was usual at the Swinburne, no one introduced anybody properly, so Amanda and I were left alone and unexplained. My assistant had gone Sloaney for the occasion but I did not, not even for a moment, see her as more tame.

Eric was very jolly and extremely charming, sprinkling his learning about like holy water and shifting from individual conversation to his general address without missing a beat. He was rather like the swan himself, the way he paused to watch his prey. They became little girls in their communion dresses, these heartless men with polished Eton cheeks.

Crofty gave me no public credit for my work, and I was disappointed but not at all surprised. When it came time for me to wind the mechanism, this lot would think I was some sort of quiz-show hostess.

Then Crofty turned to the minister and I was rather taken aback to see him relieve the great man of his cup and saucer. Then, gesturing towards the swan he said, 'I rather thought you might like to do the honours, Sir.'

This was not his boon to grant. Only the conservator should touch or 'work' the object.

With the crank in his hand, the minister was left to look useless and confused. Meanwhile Eric, in a great flourish, removed the drop sheet and produced the hum of admiration we so desired.

The swan was Zeus. The border of silver leaves was spectacular in that morning light.

The minister approached with the crank.

I thought, dear God, he does not know where to put it, and then I realized – I was dealing with Crofty and all this had been briefed and planned. The minister was not miffed. He was very pleased. To fit the crank he must give a sort of bob. 'Your Highness,' he joked, and everybody laughed too much. To Crofty he said: 'How many turns?'

'Three,' Eric replied.

It was a number that meant nothing. He made it up.

As the boy from Eton wound the easy mechanism, I could smell the sweet light mineral oil. When he withdrew the crank the glass rods rotated, catching the reflected light. He smiled around the room but why would we look at him? The Brahms had begun, and the suits were all bewitched. Henry, your silver swan was beautiful and pitiless as it turned its head to the left, towards the minister, then to the right towards the man from the *Guardian,* and then it set to preen and clean its back. No one moved or spoke. Every eerie movement was smooth as a living thing, a snake, an eel, a swan of course. We stood in awe and, no matter how many hundred hours we had worked on it, this swan was never, not for a moment, familiar, but uncanny, sinuous, lithe, supple, twisting, winding, graceful. As it twisted to look into one's eyes, its own stayed darkest ebony until, at that point when the sun caught the black wood, they blazed. It had no sense of touch. It had no brain. It was as glorious as God.

The fish were 'sporting'. The swan bent its snakelike neck, then darted, and every single human held its breath.

# HENRY & CATHERINE

Percy, Percy, the final page began.

Percy, it is done, loaded on this cart, what we at home would call a dray. It is a rough and heavy platform. Bolted to it is a cubic structure without a lid, and inside the cube is the boat in which the creature is contained. The entire clockwork mechanism is inside its hull, all fitted neatly, ready for the crank handle, for the blue tiled cistern which, having tortured you so long, will now be your continual source of joy.

But for now it is still in Germany, and all its mechanisms are in its boat and the boat is in its box and all around it is packed hard with soil and rocks and turf, and I would suppose there will be a poor German earthworm that will be accidentally exiled to Low Hall where it will get to know the English earthworms and probably do far better at it than your papa has done in this foreign land where I have been laughed at a good deal. The English worms, I am sure, will be ever so polite and charitable to the stranger.

It is late at night, but the whole village is awake, rattling bells and cracking whips. The fairytale collector told me it was a festival called Fasching. Then he said it was something completely different. The truth is that the clockmaker has offended the villagers by his lack of faith in Jesus Christ. I cannot blame the Christians. We at home would also be offended, although never quite so much, I hope, as to burn effigies and set the forest trees on fire.

There is a Baron, I am told, but in all the uproar I have seen no evidence that he insists on the orderly behaviour of his people. I will not be sorry to leave here, and if it must be tonight, then it will not be too soon. Imagine your papa riding high beside our splendid creature, galloping down the forest road with flares blazing in the darkness, all the taunts and beastliness behind, all your splendid health ahead.

They burn the witch. I saw them too. She was only straw but it was a frightful sight.

Soon in Low Hall you will see this wonder – and your hair will rise and your blood will race. Hail Cygnus. Salt tears and burnished silver. Oh Lord, you will watch the Great Creature as he takes a silver fish and holds up his head and goes through that complex swannish dance of swallowing.

There, I have confessed. It is a swan.

Dear Percy, I did not really want a swan. In spite of what I said, I did not even wish to leave your side. I never wanted more, darling boy, than to make you well.

Dear God, may he still be there and waiting for me. Dear Lord I pray, let him be saved. May I deserve admittance, in your sight.

# CATHERINE

Publicity and Development were very happy. The magnificent swan had its place by the grand front doors of Lowndes Square. It was on the BBC and CNN and television sets and servers and podcasts around the world. Eric took me to dinner at the Ivy where I had never been before. The maître d' made a fuss of Eric and we had a fabulous flinty Chablis and oysters and of course we talked about Matthew, and I cried.

Eric handled all this rather well. He told me that tears produced by emotions are chemically different from those we need for lubrication. So my shameful little tissues, he said, now contained a hormone involved in the feeling of sexual gratification, another hormone that reduced stress; and finally a very powerful natural painkiller.

'What is that one called?' I asked.

'Leucine enkephalin,' he smiled. I wrote it down.

The leucine enkephalin did its job and I laughed to hear how Eric took my darling to his club to learn to swim.

We did not talk about Amanda's 'enthusiasm' and I did not ask if her grandfather had been amongst the loots and suits at the viewing of the swan. I spoke only about the sense of awe that a wind-up machine had induced in men you might have thought beyond all human feeling.

I told my anthropological stories about growing up in Clerkenwell and then being dumped in the not quite posh school in High Wycombe. I said my sorries. He was kind and funny and when we had tottered out onto West Street he got me a cab and kissed me very sweetly, very chastely, on the cheek.

I came through the Kingsway Tunnel and did not cry too much.

I gave the cabbie a ridiculous tip, and as the taxi departed I noticed that awful old car backed down in the neighbours' parking space again. This time, seeing the front of the old ruin I realized it was an Armstrong Siddeley, a grand English dinosaur from 1950. The paints of the period were all toxic toluene nightmares, polluting the air even as they began their life. In 2010 its skin was cracked and chalky, more like dead fish than a dinosaur, a skate, dead shark skin amongst the sand and seaweed.

I was at my door when the hand touched my shoulder. My scream must have echoed all the way to Waterloo.

It was Angus, frail and ghostly.

'All right down there?'

That was the neighbour two doors up. 'Sorry,' I said.

He slammed his window down and Angus

flinched. Then a young woman in dark grey over-alls emerged from the shadow. Of course it was Amanda, her hair stretched back off her face, and looking excited enough to give one pause.

We never think something unusual is happening, even when it is. When they were side by side on my Nelson day bed, I offered them a cup of tea.

'We're good,' said Angus, leaning forward and gazing at me intently. 'How are you?'

Amanda was also studying me. She had her sketchbook on her lap and I thought – in the middle of all this – that we must get those draw-ings back from her because they, the ones she had done at work, were the property of the museum and would be needed for the glossy catalogue. It would be something, really something, and it seemed that we would now really get the money to produce it. Crofty had won his bet. The silver swan had pleased the patron of the British Arts. It would be a 'profit centre'.

It seemed that Angus wished to tell me some-thing, but had lost his nerve.

'Go on,' Amanda told him. I saw little to remind me of the young woman who had actually held my hand at the unveiling.

'What is it, Angus?' I touched the back of his big rough hands, my Matthew's little child.

'Ask her, will she X-ray the swan? Will you?'

'Amanda, you must not continue with this.'

'Please sit down, Miss Gehrig. I am not going to do anything, but what would you be frightened of discovering? What if I was Leeuwenhoek? Would you refuse to look into my microscope? The world would look different to anything you knew.'

'Mandy, there isn't anything inside it,' Angus said. 'You just want there to be.' He touched her shoulder but she shook him violently away.

'OK. What if there are ghosts?' she demanded of me.

'But there aren't.'

'You'd call it mumbo jumbo but what if it was consistent with modern physics, or string theory? You would be like those people who insisted the sun went round the earth.'

'Very well. I stand with them.'

By then she was opening her notebook and I somehow knew she had a 'proof' or cosmology of some sort. I was not exactly anxious, but wary, and very careful. I followed her into the kitchen where she began frantically pulling out loose leaves and laying them down on the table like a hand of patience, careless of the spilled jam and butter which polluted those exquisite lines which crossed the borders between one waxed sheet and the next, continuous, as in a map. I immediately appreciated that the assembled whole was exceptionally beautiful, but I was slow to recognize that what lay on my kitchen table was a close reading of Henry Brandling's notebooks which she had presumably conducted in this kitchen and in Annie Heller's lair. It was, like all close readings, very personal, but the combination of her mature talent and her relentless abstract logic had a quality I shrank from.

What if there are ghosts? I thought.

Amanda could not have been more than twenty-three years old but she had produced a detailed and graceful architecture all driven by her strong desire to find 'deep order' amidst chaos.

It took some minutes to grasp that its visual hub was a plan of the city of Karlsruhe as Sumper had presented it to Henry Brandling – the city of the wheel, but also, as she noted boldly: 'Home of Karl Benz.' She had sketched or traced a formal portrait of Karl Benz, ghostly in grey graphite, and beneath it she had written in a facsimile of Henry's script: 'Karl Benz looks back at the home of his childhood: blue mountains, a valley he wandered through, a valley well familiar to him with green mountains and foaming creeks, fir trees clinging to the cliffs and up above the small Black Forest village.'

She had made little Carl into Karl Benz. 'Born 1844,' she wrote. Good God, I thought – can that be right?

This same earnest girl who had tried to prove the blue cube was a Christian cross had decided that the hull was a kind of wooden horse whose double skin had been produced to smuggle, not only a blue cube, but the 'secrets' of an internal combustion engine, and these 'secrets' she had rendered with such skill and care that it was almost impossible to believe they were not 'true'. I know enough about engines to recognize the cam shaft and the valves and tappets, but there were also devices, and variations on these devices, rendered just as 'truthfully' that resembled manufactured objects with functions one could not imagine.

I thought, she is stark raving mad. I also thought: am I too stupid to see this is a critique of the industrial revolution?

'Amanda, please.' I wished to gather up the pages, to take them straight to Eric.

'No!' She slapped my hand.

'Amanda, these are the parts of an internal combustion engine.'

'Duh.'

'And they are inside a hull constructed in 1854.'

'And do you have a good memory for what you have read, Miss Gehrig?'

'Pretty good.'

'I have an *excellent* memory,' she said, and took my hand and held it. I resisted the urge to pull away. '"You are in the same state as a fly whose microscopic eye has been changed to one similar to a man's. YOU ARE WHOLLY UNABLE TO ASSOCIATE WHAT YOU ARE SEEING WITH WHAT YOUR LIFE HAS TAUGHT YOU."'

I began to speak. She cut me off. '"You have no idea of where you are. You have no idea of what will happen here. In this very room, I promise, you will witness wonders such as have been never known." Do you know what that meant?'

'Amanda.'

'It meant that they will kill us all. That is what the machine is for. It is not the work of humans.'

With this fierce announcement she opened her sketchbook where I was confronted with those familiar sentences that begin on one end of the line and end with their toes on the edge of the abyss.

'This is Henry Brandling?' I asked.

'Of course.'

So clearly she had written it herself. She now carried her forgery to the sitting room where she knelt on the carpet beside me.

'Please,' she said, and held my hand again. I thought, the skin is the largest sensory organ of the body. It contains more than four million receptors. It is our skin that lets us feel the gentle blowing of air, our lover caressing our body. Our skin experiences our reading too, or at least it did in my case: covering me in goose-bumps as I read that eerie facsimile of Henry's hand:

'And the filth shall spew forth from the depths, like black bile, like gall, and the ocean shall be as a mother giving wormwood from her breasts. The truth will be like a razor no tongue dare touch. A multitude of idiots shall flee back and forth on rivers of tar, an awful honking like generations of geese.' (Angus sat heavily. I thought, this is the first time he has really seen beyond her beauty.) 'The cruel famines, the droughts – all will be enigma and injustice. And any who sees the truth

312

will be called mad. Is it you, unlucky woman? Then you will be stoned and thrown into a moat.

'*Mysterium Tremendum*. There were ghosts, fabulous beings, but they were our enemies and we died, not knowing what had happened, all and every one.'

Amanda closed the book and clasped it to her breasts.

'Of course,' she said quietly, 'none of this can possibly be true.'

I felt her despair and confusion like sunspots in my brain. Perhaps I was a blow fly. Perhaps this gorgeous creature was a genius. I will X-ray the damn thing, I thought, why not? Why wouldn't I? No one will dare stop me.

Angus was curled up beside me. Amanda put her head on my lap and her filthy hands around my legs. 'I am so tired,' she said.

And then the three of us are, standing, crouching, united and I am not certain of very much at all, only that our essence is enveloped by the largest sensory organ, a universe itself, our human skin.

I hold Amanda's hand as I once touched Matthew's skin as I now touch his son's wet cheek. Machines cannot feel, it is commonly believed. Souls have no chemistry, and time cannot end. Our skin contains four million receptors. That is all I know. I love you. I hold you. I miss you forever. *Mysterium Tremendum*. I kiss your toes.